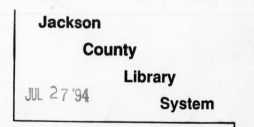

SUMMER of RESCUE

A Novel by
Barbara Nelson

MACMURRAY & BECK
ASPEN, COLORADO
1994

Printed and bound in the United States of America
Library of Congress Catalog Card Number: 93-080393

Publisher's Cataloging in Publication

(Prepared by Quality Books Inc.)

Nelson, Barbara, 1953–
    Summer of rescue / by Barbara Nelson.
    p. cm.
    ISBN 1-878448-58-7

    I. Title.

PS3564.E586S8 1994
                                        813'.54
                                        QBI93-22176

A portion of this novel appeared in the anthology *Clearing Space: Writings from Wordshop*, published in conjunction with the North Dakota Council on the Arts.

MacMurray & Beck Fiction: General Editor, Greg Michalson
Jacket design and illustration by Paulette Livers Lambert

For Scott

I am deeply grateful to my family for their loving and constant support. I also wish to thank those others who helped, inspired, and encouraged my work on this book, including Valerie Miner, Del Kehl, Mike Dillon, P. James Onstad, Jed Mattes, Greg Michalson, Fred Ramey, and especially, Ron Carlson.

Clare has imagined it this way:

Michael.

Falling.

Stretching one arm outward to catch himself as the boat tips.

His hand breaking through air, through water, nothing solid to hold him.

Entering the lake that way: hand, arm, shoulder, head, a cartwheel spin, feet in tennis shoes hitting the boat, then into the water, all of him.

Breaking through.

Falling under.

Surfacing with a cry, his face above water, taking air.

A cry.

Then under. Under again.

His hands: beating against water, beating, beating wings.

His feet: pushing against nothing solid, water, water and no air.

His hair: yellow white, floating in a halo around his head.

His eyes: open, blue as water, blue as sky.

His voice: crying out through water, calling her.

The sound rising to the air, and he falling.

Nothing solid to catch him.

Falling.

Michael.

1

The mantel clock strikes eleven-thirty, half a melody, eight notes stretched long and elastic, and Clare thinks again: the clock is running down. It needs to be wound. This is why Jeanine is taking so long to get home—the minutes are holding back. They could stop and Jeanine would be suspended somewhere—stepping into a car, stepping out of her jeans. Frozen like statue tag in the backyard when she was a child. A younger child, content without lipstick or Jeffrey.

Clare gets up from the piano bench and gathers several loose sheets of handwritten music into a pile. This is the music she's written—her own, original—to accompany the historical play this small town of Mirage, Arizona will put on this summer to commemorate its centennial. She's written eleven pieces of music to fit into strategic spots in the script and lyrics for each that tell the history of the town with poetic brilliance. Her efforts will transform a boring documentary into a stunning extravaganza of song and dance. This, at least, is what she tells herself in the effort to build up the courage to bring her work to the show's director.

Ty Greggory's plan for the music was conceived before

Clare took on the job of being the show's vocal director. He'd obtained permission to use the score from *Oklahoma!* substituting lyrics pertinent to Mirage for the originals. He wrote the opening number himself—"O Mirage!" to the tune of "Oklahoma!"—and his request to Clare was that she transform the highlights of Mirage's history into rhyming lines that fit the melodies from the rest of the *Oklahoma!* soundtrack.

Over the past several months, she'd done it, but all the while she was dissecting those lyrics, ideas were coming for an original score, and she indulged them, too, just dabbling at first, and then with growing heat. She hadn't written anything this extensive since finishing her degree in Music Composition almost twenty years ago. It felt good and then better, and she begged more time from Ty in order to finish.

She didn't tell him or anyone else what she was doing. The dismembered *Oklahoma!* lyrics are still inside the piano bench—she can resort to them if she has to—and just sitting on them day after day, holding them down, has powered her. It's been like sitting on a nest and feeling possibility hatching in herself. This could be the next something to keep her afloat. When Paul's consumed with life at the bank, when Jeanine's immersed in studies, in dancing, in Jeffrey, composing could sustain her. Even if it went no further than her own home, she would be making something beautiful and lasting. Wasn't that what drew her to music in the first place? How could it have taken so long to arrive right back where she started?

She could, of course, be wrong about this.

Her intent was to so dazzle Ty with her original score that he'd forget the other lyrics, but now that it's a Saturday night early in May, less than two months before the centennial events to be held during the July Fourth weekend, and she must absolutely give Ty music of some description no later than Monday morning, her confidence has waned. She could be wrong about all of this. She could be about to make a fool of herself in a very public forum. Compose the music for the town's centennial? Oh sure. Direct the vocals for the commemorative show? Even that's a reach. It was Nate Stover, a choreographer she'd met this past winter, who convinced her to do it. She can't remember now what he said, but it must have been something brilliant. She's not a person who's easily persuaded, let alone by someone she considers impetuous and at least a little foolish.

Clare sits down on the bench again and picks up her pencil. She strikes a chord with her left hand, makes a mark on the staff paper with the pencil. She plays softly so as not to wake Paul. The piano, a seven-foot Steinway grand, occupies a significant part of the room they used to call the living room, but its sound is even more overpowering than its physical presence. It carries throughout the kitchen, dining area, family room, and Clare and Paul's bedroom on the main floor, as well as upstairs to Jeanine's room and the spare bedroom. It can even be heard from the yard, Clare's noticed when she's been out there and Jeanine's been inside practicing.

The piano was a gift to Clare from her father when she and Paul and Jeanine moved to Arizona from Minnesota eleven years ago. It was greatly beyond his means, even secondhand, as he'd bought it. He and a blind piano technician had spent three months reconditioning it. He arranged for it to be transported to Arizona and delivered to their new home without Clare's knowledge. Her first encounter with it was in her living room and it was a shock. "Do you like it here?" Paul asked. He'd handled the arrangements with the movers on the Arizona end. "We can move it to the other side of the room if you don't."

Clare was overwhelmed. Paul told her where the piano had come from and she wept. Paul and the movers pushed it to the other end of the room and she cried some more. Paul sent the movers on their way. He took a soft cloth and rubbed the fingerprints off the piano's shiny black surface and then he took his handkerchief and wiped the tears off Clare's face. She sat down and played part of a Schubert impromptu. It seemed the only thing to do. It was the only thing she could think of to play.

They've been accommodating the piano and its effects ever since. First it was Bach they made room for. Clare would sit at the bench and let her heart have its way with her hands. Fugues and requiems—disciplined, restrained and mournful—filled their home. The sound moved like water through their rooms and their hearts. Clare could see it clouding Paul's eyes. It moved his hands to her shoulders as she played, and then it bent him over her, brought his mouth down to her neck. It washed them inside out. Bach made him sad, Paul said. Please, is there something else?

She changed to Beethoven. She played the *Moonlight*

Sonata because it was familiar and the *Pathétique* because Paul loved it and then she resolved to learn them all, all the sonatas. It was the least she could do, but an enormous task because not only did she feel she should learn them, she wanted to keep them. This meant she had to play them frequently, all the ones she knew, in addition to studying new ones. Maintaining the repertoire became oppressive, and besides, wasn't it a singer she was? Was she forgetting that?

But she kept at it two years, plodding through the thick yellow-covered volumes of music, page by page and opus by opus. She sent cassette tapes to her father in Minnesota. She spoke the name and number of the piece into the recorder and then she sat down and played it. She made mistakes, of course, but she recorded it over again until she got it right. She owed him that much. She put the tapes in the mail in padded envelopes. It was, she was told by that balding therapist she saw twice, compulsive behavior. The thing she had to do to get through her days.

When she came to Paul one hopeless night with the tearful news that there were more Beethoven sonatas than she could ever learn to play, it felt like a huge admission of failure. It seemed like a great kindness when he said with no hint of disappointment, "Well, pick one then. Choose the one you love best and play it a lot."

The *Pathétique*. It was the one Paul loved. It was grave and passionate and its repetitive rhythm comforted her. It was like rocking, swimming, breathing. She played it often and the others not at all. She let them fall from her memory. It seemed important to show she could let them go.

She stopped sending tapes to her father, and she stopped reading his letters. She could let that go, too. She let the *Pathétique* become the one she loved. Daily, steadily, predictably, necessarily. She played it like medicine. Eventually she didn't love it, but only needed it. She was forgetting who she was. She was forgetting her voice. And Paul tired of it, told her: No more. Please, something else.

She decided to teach vocal music, and this demanded more accommodation. People—they would be strangers for a while—would come through their front door, into their home, and fill it up with their voices. Some, they discovered later, would sit in Paul's reading chair in the living room as they waited. One morning Mrs. Daley picked up his *Wall Street Journal*, slipped the rubber band off of it, and read it while she waited. An inside page.

They stopped calling it the living room. It seemed necessary to name the change, but this wasn't an easy thing to do. They couldn't call it Clare's studio because Paul's chair and the desk and the bookcases are there along with the piano and the music stands and the file box of sheet music. All three of them keep books in the bookcases. The desk is more Paul's than anyone else's. It's his center for handling the bill paying and record keeping, as well as any work he brings home from the bank. And in the bottom drawer, though he hasn't brought them out in a long time, there are still a couple of sketchbooks. It's landscapes he draws mostly, and faces of people Clare doesn't recognize. Some of them are women and Clare doesn't know who they are.

But the desk is a family entity in some ways, too. A

place to set the mail and newspaper. Jeanine sometimes uses the laptop computer that flips up from a false drawer and the grocery list is kept in the top drawer, as are Clare's address book and the family calendar of appointments. The calendar of lesson times and lists of music borrowed and fees owed, however, are kept in a green folder on top of the file box.

There are boundaries in this shared room, but there is overlap, too. It is a comfort to Clare that the metronome sometimes sits on the desk and every now and then a receipt or one of Jeanine's school papers turns up in the piano bench. They couldn't call it Clare's studio or Paul's office or Jeanine's study area. When the students started coming, one of them had spontaneously called it the Singing Room, and this name had stuck, despite its failure to say everything. They just began calling it that—the Singing Room—and understood there were things left unsaid.

Clare agreed not to give lessons past six in the evening and Paul agreed to clear the top of the desk when he finished working. They couldn't very well have Mrs. Daley reading the bank's credit risk reports. The mix in the Singing Room has become comfortable, a point of convergence for the mix in the house itself.

What they loved about this house when they bought it was that it is Arizonan and Midwestern all at once. There is terrazzo tile throughout the kitchen, dining area, and family room, and a swimming pool in the backyard, but it also has a second story, which is rare in Arizona, and which the Minnesota houses both Clare and Paul grew up in had. It also has a coat closet in the foyer, which is just plain odd in Arizona. Though Paul has removed the rod and they use it to store skis and golf clubs and the baby cradle Clare's father made for them before Michael was born, they still call it the coat closet, and when Paul's parents visit, his father invariably goes to that door at least once during his stay, looking for his jacket.

After five years of full-time motherhood, Michael's accident, their move to Arizona, Bach and Beethoven, teaching was the something that filled spaces. Clare began to love how the piano and her students' voices sounded in her house. She loved putting dinner into the oven between the four-thirty and five o'clock lessons and then smelling it cooking as she finished her work. Sometimes she'd put a last load of laundry into the dryer before her first student arrived and she'd hear it buzz at the end of its cycle while teaching. Jeanine would come in between the three-thirty and four o'clock lessons and tell her about her day at school and Clare could listen to her. She could listen completely for three minutes every half hour and make it possible for Jeanine to respect the importance of uninterrupted lessons in between.

Once, a young woman came to the door to report she had just sideswiped the car Clare's student had left parked at the curb and Jeanine kept her waiting until the lesson was finished. But another time Jeanine scalded herself microwaving cocoa and Clare was glad her studio was so close to home. She's been teaching in her home for seven years, and now that Jeanine is fifteen, now that cars and a boyfriend have been added to the mix, it feels more important than ever to Clare to keep it all right here under her roof. It feels solid and complete and safe inside this house, inside this Singing Room.

Clare goes over to the fireplace and opens the glass door on the front of the mantel clock. The door's like a toy—child-size. She takes the key from the mantel. The key is giant, too large beside the miniature door. She pokes it into each of the three holes on the face of the clock, thinks as she often does: Paul, Jeanine, herself. She twists the key as far as it will go.

Then she goes to the couch, picks up the newspaper and looks again at the picture of a police officer bending to pick up a pair of small, high-top sneakers from the road. The shoes stand upright, side by side, neater than they were ever likely to be in a small boy's closet. Until a few minutes before this photograph was snapped, there was a small boy. The story gives his name: Michael. A common name. There are Michaels everywhere, but this Michael is gone. He's been tumbled from his mother's care. The car door fell open, he passed through and under the wheels of the car, leaving his shoes at unprecedented attention. An accident. His mother, no doubt, knows all of this, is full of knowing it, tells herself: an accident. But still she'll look for him in every room of her house, every fold of her soul she'll search. Her name, the story says, is Faith. A less common name. An uncommon thing. She'll need that name, all of it.

Mothers have lost children before, for the best reasons, and even through neglect. Clare certainly knows this. Faith is not the first or the last, but she is the one losing right now. For Clare, now, there are these abandoned shoes, this uncommon boy—this Michael—and the steady tick of the clock. He's gone longer and longer every second. Be strong, Faith. Where is Jeanine?

2

Clare sits down in Paul's chair in the Singing Room. If she can't be in bed next to him, this is the next best place to be. It's a large, overstuffed chair covered with a wool fabric that feels warm and comforting against her bare arms and legs. She can smell Paul here and his reading glasses are on the end table next to the chair. There's a matching ottoman on which Clare rests her feet. She can see into the foyer from here, to the front door. The staircase to upstairs opens into the room just to her left.

The bookcases against the adjacent wall are edged with Mexican tile. She tilts her head to one side and reads spines. They are her books, Paul's, and Jeanine's. Some are old and have been each of theirs, at different times, in different places, shared like air and this house. Clare doesn't remember the stories of all of these books. Some she only remembers being places. Zipped into the inside pocket of a suitcase for their move to Arizona: *You Can Heal Your Life*. Piled on top of curling Minnesota leaves: *A Little Book on the Human Shadow*. In her father's raised hand and he asking, "What's making you cry?" *20,000 Leagues Under the Sea*. She was twelve. They had a talk then about fear and preparedness and the things we can't control. Drowning and the sky falling. She was convinced she would meet Chicken Little someday and it seemed urgent to decide in advance — would she follow her to the king? If she were walking along and the sky began falling, or if she were 20,000 leagues under the sea and her air was cut off, what would she do?

"If I knew a nuclear bomb had been launched somewhere and the world would be destroyed," Jeanine once said, "I'd run right to the blast and throw myself in. I'd rather do that than survive." She could have been twelve, maybe she was, when she said this, but more impetuous than Clare at that age. This was a girl who'd been stung by a bee on her twelfth birthday. Yes, she said this about the bomb sometime after that. The bee hadn't come along and stung her. She came to it, though by accident. She stepped on it. Had her middle toe poked like a finger on a spindle. She shrieked and swore: Goddammit. Paul laughed. Clare went for ice. She'd started menstruating later that month, barely twelve, and that stung Clare. There's so little time for childhood anymore. Just a mad dash toward cursing and bleeding and the point of the blast.

The Island of the Blue Dolphins. A young girl alone on an isolated island, left to survive by her wits, her people gone in a boat. Water everywhere. Clare, at ten, wanted the girl to learn the language of the dolphins—how they sing to each other—and she wanted to know it herself, too, that language, those songs. When she recalls the story now, she remembers it that way: the girl and the dolphins singing underwater. For a minute, she's forgotten that this part was her own invention.

Later, after she'd begun to perceive the communications of sex, she'd wanted to know that language in just the same way. Sex was a whispered song, known, it seemed then, by only a few. Not at all like now. Jeanine, now, seems to know all of it. She gives the appearance of always having known and if she's had questions, it's not been Clare she's asked. When Clare's tried to talk to her about sex—it's a necessary thing, isn't it?—Jeanine uses words like *of course* and *naturally*, calls her Mother instead of Mom, and wears that serious sort of smile adults give children who are learning something only temporarily hard, something that in a week will be easy.

But when Clare was young, sex still had secrets and she wanted to be one of the knowers. She studied. Paperback romances and the magazines she found in neighbors' houses while babysitting. And she watched. She began to perceive her father as a knower, though her mother, she thought, was not, and it was from him she felt compelled, at fourteen, to hide the stimulus of her fantasies—the record jacket of her *Romeo and Juliet* soundtrack. On it, Romeo and Juliet were naked, though Juliet had her long hair to cover her and Romeo had Juliet. But more thrilling than their bodies were their faces. Romeo's was eager, wanting something—apparently Juliet—painfully much. Juliet's was radiant. There was laughter and play in her eyes and, on the record, in her voice. It was the wanting Clare wanted. For a man to want her like Romeo wanted Juliet. And the smile. She wanted a smile like Juliet's: shining and knowing. There was joy in that smile, even in the thought of it. A man like Shakespeare couldn't be wrong about a thing like that. There was joy and hope in this mystery called sex.

Once, before these books or *Romeo and Juliet*, Clare's mother came into the kitchen in the middle of a Sunday afternoon and took off all her clothes. She came in while Clare and her father were sitting at the table, eating watermelon. Clare's brother Sam wasn't at home. She undressed methodically and in silence, and then she raised her arms up over her head and said, "Can you see now who I am?"

Clare was too young then to know about the sex song, but she knew later these words and these actions were part of it. When her mother began removing her underwear, her father stood up and so did Clare. He tried to stop her from seeing by pressing her face against his stomach. He'd been mowing earlier and smelled of cut grass and sweat. When her mother had said this, her father took a breath that pressed his stomach hard against Clare's cheek, then he abruptly turned away and walked out of the house, the backdoor slamming behind him.

The air was thick and gagging in the kitchen. Her mother's shoulders crumpled forward and she lowered her hands to cover her face. She shook and sobbed. To console her was an unimaginable task. Clare did what her father had done — ran out the backdoor. She sat for a long time on a manhole cover in the alley, waiting for a knock from a Chinaman who had traveled through the middle of the earth. She thought of her mother as she'd never seen her — naked, her face white and wet, a flush on her chest, her auburn hair mussed and her eyes burning — and she wished she'd drunk her orange juice that morning instead of crying for apple.

Her father came back, came for her on the manhole cover, and when they went into the house, her mother was wearing clothes and bravery. She was brave after that, so brave Clare had to think hard to remember her with her eyes soft, her voice like a song. Her father was solid, and if her parents gave up on joy, they at least persevered. Fifty years. They would mark that anniversary this summer, and Clare and Paul and Jeanine would go to Minnesota for the occasion, their first trip home in nine years. In fifty years there's a lot to celebrate and a lot to mourn. Nine years is a long time to stay away from home.

At midnight, the melody is complete and strong on the clock. It is still striking when Jeanine comes in through the front door. Her hair and clothes are wet, dripping. The clothes cling to the body that Clare is still startled to meet up with in this house. It's a young woman's body, lithe and firm and lovely. It's her own body, twenty-five years ago, and it's the body her mother bared in that kitchen so long ago. The same narrow hips and delicately muscled arms and legs. The same soft, rounded breasts, high on her chest, the size and shape of a man's cupped hand. Her eyes are Paul's: deep blue and full of life. Her hair is Clare's: dark and wavy and, tonight, untamed.

She carries one of her shoes, kicks the other one off and tosses them into the corner. "We ran through the Brandts' sprinklers," she says, breathless, a small, private smile on her lips. The smile hardly changes when she directs it to Clare. *By next week*, it says, *it'll be easy*. But it's a lie. False assurances. It has never been easy for mothers to see daughters grow up. It never will be. There are new secrets and Clare is still not a knower. Next week will always be a week away.

You're late, you're wet, she's thinking, but Jeanine speaks first. "Good night," she says, with the same voice she spoke her first words with. She rolls her hip to one side as she turns to go upstairs and Clare is stung again. She knows this girl and she knows this move. This is her daughter Jeanine. It's a movement a girl learns from a lover.

3

Paul instinctively takes her into his arms when Clare gets into bed. This is how they go to sleep at night and how they wake up in the morning, though they separate mysteriously sometime in between. Maybe the secret of a happy marriage is that simple: go to sleep in each other's arms; wake up this way, too, but let each other go in between. At times, Clare has awakened during the night alone — sometimes very alone, from a dream — and Paul was not around her. But if she comes near him as he sleeps — like just now, coming to bed after he's sleeping — he takes her in, holds her, without even waking up. It has always been a comfort to her that he does this. It seems his heart would be most bare in sleep. But lately she's wondered. If someone else came to his bed while he slept, would he just naturally open his arms to her, too? With this thought came uncertainty. What had seemed a sweet vulnerability could really be danger.

She has this thought tonight — there's so much of that mood in her already — and when Paul pulls her close, she wraps herself tightly to him and whispers, "It's me, Paul."

He laughs softly into her hair. "I know that, Sylvia. You think I can't tell?" he murmurs, so tender.

Clare kicks her legs wildly then, until the covers are a heap at the foot of the bed. Paul is laughing now and trying to press his mouth to her neck despite the rolling motion under them. The bed is a waterbed. He laughs like a boy at things she hardly dares smile at. She envies his easy faith in life and that laugh. She sees more colors in the world than he does, and some of her visions turn him pale and rob him of all his words but her name: *Clare, oh Clare.* Some of the ways he has said her name have broken her heart. Sometimes it sucks the wind right out of her— *Clare*—and sometimes it's like the first breath at the surface after a deep, deep dive.

He lies on top of her, holds her rocking between his warmth and the cooler water. He gives a rhythm to the water's motion, his hands pressing and rising, pedaling. The water churns in her ears. It takes precision to kiss while he does this, but that's the game. The rocking and his mouth soothe her. There and gone. There and gone. Always back again, that mouth. A sweet familiarity. Her legs open to him naturally, like parting waves behind a boat.

☙

"Jeanine was late tonight," Clare says before they sleep. "I think she lied to me."

"Well," Paul says, "it's what happens." So facile. How could he have thought this fast? Really heard her, even? "She's growing up." He has a way of saying what Clare would be least likely to say, and of making it sound as if it's the only true thing that could be said.

"She might be sleeping with Jeffrey."

This, at least, makes him think. "Why do you say that?"

She looks like it. She moves like it. She came home all wet with one shoe off. These things seem silly now, looking for words. "Just a feeling I have." This is worse. Paul frowns, so she says more. "She looks like it. She moves like it. She came home all wet."

Paul turns his head on the pillow. "Did you ask her?"

"Just ask her? Of course not. No."

"Oh," Paul says simply.

She wants it all back now. It sounds unlikely, spoken aloud. Unlikely and unlucky, like inviting it. "It's probably nothing, Paul. My own worries looking to happen." She puts an arm across his chest, ready to sleep.

"Maybe you should talk to her. These things happen."

It's what he said when she told him about Nate: *These things happen. He'll get over it.* That—after she'd said, *Nate wants me to be his lover.* She'd said it aloud—to Paul—to make sure it wouldn't happen. She didn't want the complications, though in some ways, she did want Nate. *He'll get over it.* He was that sure she'd said no. It's the noes we talk about. The yeses go untold. Probably she should talk to Jeanine.

❧

During the night, Clare wakes up. The clock is chiming a quarter to something. Paul has slipped away from her, sleeping on his side. Clare thinks of touching him, but

21

doesn't. She makes a plan: she'll lie awake for fifteen minutes, waiting to hear the hour. Fifteen minutes borrowed from the night. She thinks of the newspaper photo, the sneakers in the road standing stiffly upright, like bronzed baby shoes.

People don't bronze their children's shoes anymore. There are no golden baby shoes — not Michael's, not Jeanine's — on the shelves in the Singing Room, but Clare's have sat for forty years on the shelf in her parents' home, laces solidified into permanent bows. Clare used to wonder at those shoes, at how they could be hers, how she could ever have been that small.

What must her mother think when she sees those shoes? It must be the thought Clare has seen in her eyes as they've stood on driveways and in airports, the thought she has heard in her voice as they've talked on the phone about trips to Minnesota that never materialized: our children aren't ours forever. Her father's thoughts she thinks would scare her more: they never were ours. Not really. They are visitors in our homes and when they grow up, or even while they're small, they leave us.

There's a sound in the hall. In the dim rectangle of the doorway, Clare sees Jeanine pass, in her nightgown, her dark hair flattened against her head from sleep or wetness. Clare sits up in bed, heart quickening. She wants to go to the doorway, see where Jeanine goes. Instead she strains for the sound of a door opening. She hears the clock instead—the whole melody and three chimes. Long enough to cover the sound of a door being opened.

Clare waits. Jeanine comes back and pauses at her parents' open door, looking in. Clare pretends to sleep. When she opens her eyes again, Jeanine is gone.

Clare waits and can't sleep. The clock rings quarter past. She gets out of bed and walks out to the foyer, checks to be sure the door is locked. She flips on the porch light and spreads two slats of the blinds to look outside. An orange Bird of Paradise blossom dips disconnected and luminous into the thorned arms of the ocotillo. She moves from the window, turns out the light, goes into the kitchen. She takes the scissors from a kitchen drawer and cuts the picture of the sneakers and the police officer out of the newspaper. She cuts wide enough to take the caption with the names: Michael, Faith. Then she walks upstairs to Jeanine's bedroom. The door is half closed, and inside, Jeanine lies with her eyes shut. Clare tiptoes back downstairs to her bedroom, puts the clipping under a sweater in the drawer where she keeps her father's monthly letters, and gets into bed. She touches Paul's back. He turns and opens his arms. He holds her.

4

When Jeanine comes into the kitchen the next morning—Sunday—she looks like an angel. Her nightgown is full and white. She's brushed the waves back into her hair. Her face has color, from yesterday's sunshine or some inner source. Her chin is slightly uplifted, as if a hand has come under it and tipped it upward. And she is generous. Not defensive. Not surly. She's a daughter with a secret her parents can't touch. It gives her a patient tolerance for her father's questions.

"Why were you late last night?" Paul asks. He closes the newspaper he has spread out over the table, but he does it like a stage direction, as if he's been pretending distraction and now will give the attention that's been full all along. He's sitting in sunlight, in his blue terry bathrobe. The sun catches the gray in his hair, makes it silver, and gives him a kind of aura. But rather than holy, Paul looks startled—his hair uncombed and his face unshaven—as if he's seen a vision or heard a voice in the night and leaped suddenly out of bed. Clare can see something's settled on him, let him know: this is not sex-generally-speaking. What happens, growing up. This is Jeanine and a young man he's met only once, Jeffrey, probably too old for her and too young for sense. Overnight, Paul's acquired an urgency and Clare's glad to see it. She watches from across the kitchen, where she puts scrambled eggs, now cold, into the microwave for Jeanine.

"Don't bother, Mom," Jeanine says, stalling a moment, putting her attention, unsolicited, on her mother, and not on her father's question. She pulls open the refrigerator and, with a dancer's lunge, takes out a carton of cottage cheese. She moves to the cupboard for a plate, then to the counter where she spoons a tiny mound onto the plate. She is nearly waltzing and her mouth looks thirty instead of fifteen. She looks at her parents as if they're ninety, bedridden, mindless.

"Was I late?" she says then. Calm. Cool. "Sorry if you worried." She pours pancake syrup over the cottage cheese and, standing there at the counter, starts to eat, one or two curds at a time. This restraint, at least, is reassuring.

"You were late by an hour," Paul says. "You'll have to make it up next weekend. Ten o'clock."

Too soon to the consequence, Clare thinks. Closing the case before the questions are answered. That's Paul. Cut to the action. A remedy before the problem's clear.

"All right, Daddy," Jeanine says. Indulgently.

Her tone lets Paul know she's finessed an escape. He gets up quickly, pulls his hand through his hair, an ineffective effort to restore order. "Let's have Jeffrey to dinner," he says.

"Why?" Jeanine asks, spoon freezing in mid-stroke.

"I want to meet him."

"You did."

"Now I want to know him," Paul says. There's authority between his words. Clare imagines she can see it bounce against Jeanine's ears, turning her mouth narrow.

Jeanine sets her plate in the sink, then turns back to her father. She shrugs from shoulder to hip, and strikes a pose that pains Clare. "All right, Daddy." The *right* is sharper this time, as are her eyes. She turns to leave the room.

"How'd you get wet last night?" Clare asks suddenly.

Jeanine stops, looks from one parent to the other. "I told you. We ran through the Brandts' sprinklers." Les and Sally Brandt live on the corner.

Her chin's raised a fraction too high and Clare thinks of a bath, with soap and four hands. Does every young girl have one eventually? Clare once hid a bath like that from her own mother with Comet and Lysol spray. She and Paul had lain there in her parents' Roman tub on a Saturday afternoon while her father fished and her mother bought groceries, risking discovery for the sake of discovery. The down payment is enormous on these pleasures. Just imagine—thinking they could guess about a thing like the length of a checkout line or the likelihood of conception. Reckless, yes, but his hands. She'd felt them—what? thousands of times?—since and still she remembered how they felt that day. Probably a certain amount of recklessness is necessary, a certain amount is sweet, sweet and worth it, but they'd realized the need for care, too. Clare decided after the bath that Comet was more telling than a bathtub ring, so while Paul dressed she refilled the tub with soapy water and drained it again. She couldn't remember whether she'd dried her hair. The thing you think your mother is looking for is never it.

"What were their sprinklers doing on at midnight?" Clare asks.

Jeanine stares a moment. "I don't know, Mom, but I'll call them right away and ask."

A little normalcy at last.

Suspicion and accusation aren't always the wrong thing. Sometimes they're what's needed to shake out the truth. But suppose there was no bath. Jeanine's clothes were wet, after all. Why would she bathe in her clothes? Someone got silly in the wake of pulling off an escapade and threw them in the water. No more unreasonable than midnight sprinklers.

Or maybe Paul was closer to the mark—sticking to the facts. Twelve o'clock. Eleven o'clock. It's hard to argue with the clock. The only known offense is an hour of lateness. It's a moment when even reason seems unreasonable. Clare has no thoughts sure enough to speak aloud.

Jeanine slips out of the kitchen.

"I need a shower," Paul announces.

Outside, sunlight becomes glare on the surface of the swimming pool.

5

Sunday evening, Clare's parents phone. They extend their yearly invitation to Jeanine to come and spend part of the summer with them at the lake. Summer is fast approaching — it's time to be making these kinds of arrangements. Clare's mother reviews the usual plan: Jeanine could fly into Minneapolis; they'd pick her up there, drive to the cabin. "She's welcome to stay as long as she'd like."

When Clare's father retired from the Postal Service twelve years ago, her mother left her job in housekeeping at the Restful Pines nursing care facility and they have lived at the cabin year around since. Winterizing it gave her father something to do in that first restless year of retirement. Most of their friends go south to Florida or Arizona in the winter, and besides, they just didn't have the energy to keep up two places anymore. They sold the two-story house in town, income which a year later financed Clare's piano, she is sure.

Her father loves to fish and seems always to be working on this improvement or that one in the cabin when they phone. Her mother has made enough card-playing friends that there's a table of bridge once or twice a week and, to hear her talk, she's let her long-time hobby of clipping coupons and pursuing refund offers grow into something close to an obsession. They claim also to have taken up cross-country skiing, though it is hard for Clare to imagine her parents harmoniously involved in a joint activity like that. She imagines them arguing about what wax to use, what trails to take, whether the ice is solid enough on the lake to cross.

When Clare was a child the cabin belonged to her grandmother, and she and her parents and her brother Sam would visit weekends and eat cookies filled with dates. It was the braided rug and the purple bedroom Clare most loved. The rug was in the living room, a circle of changing colors spiraling from edge to center. It was a maze for Clare to walk, smaller and smaller, faster and faster. The center was a magic place, getting there dizzying. She walked her fear away on that spiral while her father fished on the lake at night. Darkness and water. He could drown. This had happened to Mr. Morgan across the lake. The sirens had come screaming in the middle of the night, and a day later he was a story in the newspaper. Clare walked and walked. This was the rule: you could not cross this rug. If you did, you were inviting tragedy. The only way was to walk in its pattern, from edge to center and out again. A saving movement.

In the purple bedroom was a dressing table with a three-panel mirror, like one in the fitting room of a clothing store. There were bottles of perfume on the table — lots of them — and it was easy to sneak some because most of them had atomizers that took just a tiny squeeze. It was hardly like stealing at all — two fingers, one squeeze. There was a box of dusting powder, too, with a clear plastic top and a pure white powder puff that always sat exactly in its place — too clean to ever have been used, too dangerous to touch. It was only there to look pretty and to tempt her. In the center of the table was a stuffed kitten with a black velvety coat, pink felt nose, and green marble eyes. If the powder had ever been used there would be white flecks on the kitten's fur and there weren't any.

Clare loved that bedroom until she was old enough to realize that Frank slept in the purple bed, too. Frank was her grandmother's second husband and completely bald. He had no hair, but full dark eyebrows that made him look evil or, if he lowered them, threatening. The bedroom began to embarrass Clare about the same time their engagement picture did. It sat in a silver frame on the dressing table next to the black kitten. The way her grandmother laid her hand on Frank's leg, the way she tossed back her head as the camera snapped, and those eyebrows of Frank's. Clare set the photo down on its face when she sat at the dressing table. There was a copy of it in the family album, too, which Clare flipped past quickly from the time she was eight. Later, she studied the picture for clues about the things people did, sleeping together. By then, Frank had given her five silver dollars — one each Christmas — and he and her grandmother had sunk into a safe, patterned marriage defined by a careful rhythm of exchanged animosity. The movements of his eyebrows had become predictable and his bald head was a joke run under the teeth of a giant comb when he wanted to make the grandchildren laugh.

Clare's father painted the purple bedroom blue after Frank died, and then papered it with pastel stripes after his mother-in-law died and they inherited the cabin. They took up the rug and laid down wall-to-wall carpeting. Now it's their home. They pick up their mail at the same bend in the road where Clare used to pretend to meet the Big Bad Wolf, though the road is paved now and the last time Clare was there, nine years ago, the varied set of mailboxes and posts had been replaced by a neat, compartmented metal box with small, numbered doors, each with a keyhole. Clare supposes there have been other changes in that time. No doubt there have been. She'll see later this summer.

In the nine years since she's been home, Clare's parents have planned and canceled three trips to visit them in Arizona. Her father refused to fly and her mother refused to drive and this became another of those impasses that could not be resolved and so could only be steered around.

Every summer, her parents have this ceremony of inviting Jeanine to the cabin. Though Clare once loved that place and the thought that Jeanine is almost too old to be a child there is a regretful one that dries her mouth for a moment, this is a request Clare can't say yes to. She's never been able to tell her parents directly that the thought of Jeanine going to the lake is unbearable. It would seem they'd know this, sense this, but it's not something they can talk about. Instead, Clare offers an excuse. Every year, the invitation. Every year, an excuse.

This year, Clare tells her mother: "I just don't feel comfortable about her traveling alone." Clare knows her mother is thinking it but won't say it: you and Paul come, too. Her mother knows they're planning to come later in the summer, for the anniversary. She knows the plan is fragile and could be knocked over easily by too much insistence.

"We'll all be coming later for the anniversary, Mom. The centennial will be over by then — maybe we could stay for a good long visit." This raises Paul's eyebrows an inch on his forehead. He sits next to her on the couch, hearing half a conversation, but one predictable enough that he can fill in the blanks. Jeanine sits, surprisingly unsolicitous, across the room, watching TV.

Clare's mother is careful, measured. She chooses words to make them feel welcome but not pressured. Clare's father is silent on the extension. Clare tells them they plan to leave July Fourth, the day after the centennial show. They'll be there in time for fireworks. She fields small talk for another minute, then puts Jeanine on. Clare wants her to talk forever, listening is shoring up her heart so. Long distance to Grandma takes years off her voice. She is sweet. She is pliant. She's no more than ten years old.

❦

"You know," Paul says later. "Going to the lake might be just the plan for Jeanine." There's a forced lightness in his voice.

Clare, undressing for bed, feels a shiver. Paul's words surprise her. This is something he doesn't challenge. He knows how she feels about Jeanine going to the lake.

"Why?" she says, engaging his eyes in the lamplight.

"It would get her out of town for a while." He shrugs, something he never does accidentally. "At fifteen, even half a summer is long enough to forget a boyfriend."

Even half—his concession to her.

"She has her dance lessons," Clare says, walking to the dresser. She sets her watch there, then turns back to Paul. "And her voice lessons. She wants to try for a part in the centennial show." Clare realizes she's offering more excuses. Paul isn't discouraged. "She doesn't want to go anyway," Clare says finally, sorry already she's said it.

"Of course she does. She always does. She begs every year, Clare."

"Not this year. Didn't you see her? She doesn't want to go."

"Why not?" Paul says, like a boy. A younger boy would have stamped his foot.

Clare pulls her nightgown over her head. "Because," she says, "she wants to be here. This is where Jeffrey is."

Paul takes this in. "Well then," he says, "that's just my point. That's just why she should go."

He follows her into the bathroom and watches as she washes her face. "Clare, kids now are . . . older than we were."

"Heaven help us," Clare says into the washcloth.

"Older younger, I mean. Things happen. Have you talked to her?"

"Since last night? No." She speaks to his image in the mirror. "Paul, there are boys in Minnesota, too. There are boys at the lake. And they're only wearing swim trunks there."

"Don't . . . trifle. I know how this is with you, but just promise me you'll think it over." He takes her arm, makes her turn to him. "Some dangers outweigh others, Clare." His eyes are full of what he doesn't say.

Clare sees this, puts her hands on his shoulders, and kisses him lightly next to his left ear. "I know that," she whispers. She looks at him and gives a little push to his shoulders as she takes her hands away. "Do you think I don't know that?" she says, her voice more strident than she intended. She pushes past him and out the door.

6

Monday morning after Paul leaves for the bank and Jeanine for school, Clare is at the piano with both sets of music. She's made a cassette recording of the *Oklahoma!* music, with the Mirage lyrics sung by a couple of her students. She wishes now she'd made a tape of her music, too. How can she hope to impress Ty Greggory with notes and words on paper? And if she was reluctant to let a couple of students hear her music, to sing it, how could she bear the whole town hearing it?

She took on the job of vocal director hesitantly. Nate Stover recommended her to the centennial committee while the two of them were working together on a production of *Carousel* this past winter. The community college, where Nate teaches dance, put it on. He did the choreography. Clare directed the vocal music, a favor to Jeanine's voice teacher, who was the more obvious choice for the job, but who had just had a baby in November.

It was sweet knowledge—that Nate thought enough of her work to recommend her. *Carousel* was her first turn at directing and she felt shaky all through it. She told herself working on the centennial show would be challenging, it would be good experience, maybe it would be the something. She told herself it would take a lot of time and she warned herself that Nate's interest in working with her again could be personal. There were people more qualified for the job than she was. Maureen Connolly, Jeanine's voice teacher and instructor of music at the college, for instance. The baby would be six months old by the time they started rehearsing.

Then she told herself that Nate had kissed her after the last night of *Carousel* because of post-performance euphoria. The things he'd said came from the same source, or they came from the uneven keel he was on with his girlfriend, Susanna. What possible interest could a thirty-year-old, single, very good-looking dancer who was built like one, recently separated from his long-time live-in girlfriend, but who had kissed her, seriously kissed her, have in a forty-year-old, married, happily married everyone even herself would say, still nice even youthful looking singer, a fraud actually since she never sang publicly anymore and only taught it and even that she did in the secure comfort of her own home? What possible interest?

Clare takes both sets of music and the tape, puts them into her bag and goes out to her car. She backs out of the driveway and heads toward the community college where she'll give Ty Greggory one or another set of music at his office in the Department of Theatre. She wishes as she drives that there were some way to get Ty's reaction to her music without having to own it. Isn't there some way to do this anonymously? Leave it unsigned in his box. Let him find it and be impressed. He'd call her and say, "Clare, the most incredible thing just happened. I went to my box and there was the most perfect score for the show you'd ever want to see. I have no idea where it came from, but let's just grab it. Let's just take it and use it. It's so good."

The directorship was the job Nate wanted, and when the centennial committee gave it to Ty, Nate was a little nasty about it. Ty, he told Clare, should have been cast as the show's narrator, an old-timer who is presumably telling the story from his personal recollections. Clare preferred it this way. Ty as director, Nate as choreographer. She had become convinced in the course of *Carousel* that Nate was no more confident of himself on stage than she was; he was only better at pretending he was. In fact, he was forcefully insistent on giving that appearance and would be a little hard to take as a director. As a co-worker she could find this need to disguise his insecurity kind of sweet, endearing, attractive in a boyish sort of way. But as a boss, he'd be a pure pain in the neck.

At a red light, Clare pulls alongside a panel truck. "Sunrise Carpentry" it says on its side. At first, Clare reads it "Surprise Carpentry," and this amuses her. Surprise Carpentry. "Oh, right. As though we'd call for that," she could imagine Paul saying. "Hey, I've had a foundation poured and here's a bunch of 2x4s. Surprise me."

After that, they could call for Surprise Plumbing. Surprise Masonry. Surprise Electric (she thinks she already knows these guys—they were at the house last week). It makes her want to run an ad in the Yellow Pages just to talk to the people who'd call a place with a name like that. Something about them would be delightful.

The carpenter catches her smiling. He takes the cigarette from his mouth and risks half a smile. His eyes narrow into what her mother used to call bedroom eyes. Clare wonders how much longer strange men on the street will look at her this way. Maybe not long. Maybe this carpenter will be the very last.

The thing that makes last chances so terribly poignant is that you rarely get to recognize them as that while there's still time to take hold of them. Losing them is what identifies what they were. Clare winks. The carpenter looks away and then back. The eyes again. The light's turning green as he smacks a kiss into the air. Surprise!

Clare takes a right at the intersection of Main and Cholla and heads toward the outskirts of Mirage, where the college is located. Along the way, she circles once through Roadrunner Park, stalling for time, and then when she's driven the mile and a half that brings her to the turn-in at the college, she goes on past. She hasn't decided yet which set of music Ty Greggory gets.

In two minutes, she is driving through desert toward Phoenix on what Jeanine used to call the roller coaster road because of its gentle hills. At their peaks, the town can be seen in the rearview mirror and ahead, ragged mountains stretch upward from the horizon, magnificent until compared to the expanse of blue that is the sky.

In the dips, with vision limited to short-range, you notice those things closer to the ground: spindly ocotillo, furry cholla, and the cacti—hundreds—preening like dancers before the sky. They're in bloom now. Surprising, delicate blossoms sprouting along with the prickles out of those swollen, corrugated limbs. Are those stories true,

Clare wonders. That each arm takes one hundred years to grow? That the age of the cactus is counted in centuries? All those years, stored with the water. Or is that true either? That cacti store water inside them? Is it water or age or just what is it that swells them up like that? All those years. All those dancers, stop-motioned in the desert.

Clare turns the air conditioning to high and pushes a cassette into the player. She sings soprano to Billy Joel's tenor: *You can get what you want or you can just get old.*

Sometimes there's a lake on the highway, a watery mirage she can never catch, made by layers of heat and cool. It's there today. Her voice fills the car, pushes at its hinges. She turns up the bass. She thinks she feels it vibrating against the highway. She is sweating, despite the air conditioning. *Only the good die young.* Her voice is straining under the effort it takes to sing and hold back tears at the same time. She can't do this. It's the wrong time. She pulls off the highway and turns her car around. She heads back to where she's supposed to be.

7

The offices for the theater faculty are in the Arts Center at the community college. Clare parks in the lot at the side of the building and comes in through a short hallway with student artwork displayed on the walls. It is final exam week and Clare sees only one other person, a woman in bicycle pants and sandals that slap her heels as she walks. The woman carries a cardboard box like those cakes come in from a bakery. Somewhere close by, someone is playing "Heart and Soul" on a piano with a key that doesn't sound. Clare plays through the song in her mind and it's the high C that doesn't strike.

At the theater department, Clare locates Ty Greggory's office. His door is open a few inches. She can see his desk, his elbows in a pressed white shirt leaning on it, and a pair of feet, one swinging nervously, on the other side of the desk. She hears the words *incomplete* and *requirement* and the foot swings some more.

This is her chance. She can go to his mailbox in the department and leave her original music. She won't have to see him. She can leave it and go.

At the department, a secretary asks if she can help Clare, and the unexpected prospect of having to hand her music to another person rather than sliding it directly into Ty's box jangles her. The necessity of responding presses on her, and then she does, by handing the cassette tape and two typed copies of the altered *Oklahoma!* lyrics to the secretary. She turns and leaves then, her heart pounding and face burning with more humiliation than fear. She hates being reminded of what a coward she is.

On her way out, Clare again sees the woman with the slapping sandals, this time without her box, and then, in the hallway gallery, she sees Nate. He's dressed in gray cut-off sweats and a faded T-shirt identifying him as a participant in a 10-K run held in Dayton, Ohio, in 1984. He's wearing his Reeboks without laces or socks and he hasn't shaved today.

He smiles and tells her "Hi," and then she's standing in a hallway between a metal sculpture giraffe and a man who makes her heart race, telling herself, No. No, that's not it. It's that spineless little maneuver she's just pulled outside Ty Greggory's office that's got her off balance. That's it. That's all.

She's seen Nate just once since *Carousel*, at an organizational meeting for the centennial show a few weeks ago. He was his old self, friendly and energetic. The kissing backstage hadn't changed the way he treated her at all, which was exactly the effect Clare wanted it to have: none. It attested to how bizarre it was in the first place. It meant nothing.

It's nice to see him.

"Hey, come on," he says, touching her arm. He lifts a paper sack up to her face and shakes it. "Donuts."

She hesitates. "I've got students coming in less than an hour, Nate." It's nice to say his name. It would be nice to hear him say hers.

He opens the bag and looks in. "Custard-filled. Chocolate. Sugar raised. They were a dozen for two bucks. I pigged out. Come on. Save me, Clare." He puts a hand across his stomach.

She smiles and tells him okay. Okay, one donut, but then he's on his own.

She walks with him to a room on the lower level that's mirrors on three walls. There's an orange mat at one end of the room where two leggy young women in leotards are performing some kind of stretches that appear humanly impossible to Clare. A bronze-colored bar runs along the mirrors at hip height.

The room is a deluxe version of the little ballet studio Mrs. Bonet had in her back bedroom at the lake when Clare was a girl. On Saturdays of the weekends her family was at the lake, Clare would climb the hill to the Bonets' cabin with her ballet slippers in a pink drawstring bag and take a lesson with five other girls from along their stretch of shoreline. Mrs. Bonet was French and spoke with a heavy accent. She wore her hair in a long braid that swung as she danced. For three years, Clare wanted a braid like that and it seemed the way to get it was to learn to dance. She moved obediently through the positions as Mrs. Bonet called them out, imagining she could feel her hair growing, and checking every now and then in the mirror to see.

Two ceiling fans whir over Clare and Nate's heads, one whining ominously. Books, bags, and pieces of clothing are scattered around the edges of the room, and near the door where they came in are a complicated stereo system playing, she thinks, Liszt, and a pile of stackable chairs, carelessly stacked. Nate untangles two of these and sets them out for Clare and himself.

They sit, and Nate opens the donut bag and offers it to Clare. She takes what's on top, a sugar raised. Nate digs through the rest and finally takes out a chocolate-covered one, slightly flattened. The girls with the pretzel bodies look over at them and the blond one gives Nate a smile that makes Clare flush. Nate calls hello with his mouth full and then asks Clare what she's doing at the college.

Good question. What possible interest . . .

"I brought Ty Greggory the lyrics for the show," she says.

"Those *Oklahoma!* lyrics?"

"Yeah. Changed, of course." There are no napkins and she needs one. She feels weird in this dance hall on this temporary chair with two beautiful young women watching her, and now her hands are sticky, too. Nate's solving the same problem by licking his fingers. Clare flushes again and then she laughs, just nervousness.

"I hated that idea," Nate says. He's fishing through the sack again and brings out another donut, glazed. "Really," he says, looking at her now. "What a dumb idea."

Clare suspects he still has it in for Ty. Should she tell him she thought so, too? "Well, at least the melodies will be familiar to people," she says. Nate rattles the bag in front of her and she puts up her hand. "No thanks."

"Familiar?" Nate says and laughs derisively. He wipes

his hand across his lips. "Worn out is more like it. The choreography I've come up with so far is awful."

The two dancers gather up some of the clothes and books from the floor and as they leave Clare has the opportunity to observe that, at least among this small sample of female dancers, it is customary to wear the body-hugging spandex suits sans underwear.

"Time for me to go," she announces when they're gone. The stereo has stopped playing and the ceiling fan sounds more dangerous than ever.

"How come you don't sing anymore?" Nate asks, standing up.

She's caught off guard. He's so disarming sometimes. "I love your mouth. It's beautiful," he said to her after a rehearsal of *Carousel* in January. "I wish you'd let me kiss it." Clare remembers a rush of blood into her legs and the self-conscious awareness that this (beautiful?) mouth of hers was standing open. Closing it was a deliberate effort. Only the very small feeling of safety she drew from the touch of her upper lip against the lower allowed her the composure to turn away from him. Those words — despite her realization that Nate was at least one part reckless, immature, and foolish — drove the first wedge into her heart. It was an unexpected pleasure and so long as she stopped with thoughts — no words, no actions — it was safe. Privately sweet. "I sing," she tells Nate.

"Oh? Where?" He's putting their chairs back onto the wobbly stack.

"In my studio." She's never called it that. "With my students. And that's not all."

"No?"

"I sing on the highway." She says this and then hears it. It makes her laugh.

He got his kiss—stole it really—behind the heavy red curtain of the Arts Center stage after the last performance of *Carousel*. He pressed himself to her and kissed her long and hard and then he told her, "I want the rest of you, too." She'd stared. That close, he didn't look like himself. It was odd and exciting to feel him against her, so unfamiliar. "I'm too old for you," she whispered. She could hear feet on the stage and she could hear her own heart. This, she thought, is the kind of thing that happens on the other side of the curtain, in make-believe, not here, not in my life. Then he kissed her again and it was unquestionably real. Something true, something to be reckoned with. Something, all right. She skipped the cast party that night, went home to Paul, told him: Nate wants me to be his lover. And Paul said that amazing thing: *He'll get over it. These things happen.*

"In my car. I put in a tape and sing along or I sing a cappella, just myself." It feels like a secret and she can't imagine why she's told him this.

He brings his hand to her face and brushes a finger over her lips. "Sugar," he says.

8

Clare has three midday lessons today, two women who come over their noon hours and Mrs. Daley. The rest are school children who come between three-thirty and six o'clock. It occurs to Clare today that Mrs. Daley is lobbying for a part in the centennial show. She's a middle-aged woman, older than Clare, who began lessons about six months ago. Her therapist, she told Clare, recommended either this or aerobics "for her mental health," so she chose singing, "for obvious reasons." Mrs. Daley is fifty or sixty pounds overweight. Though not particularly talented, she is pleasant enough when she stays off the subject of her husband.

Today she wants to know about auditions for the show. She asks the date, though Clare remembers her asking this last week. She asks Clare if the piece she's just sung would be a good selection for the audition. And she leaves Clare a chocolate bar along with her check.

It makes Clare wonder if many of her students plan to audition for the show. She imagines herself having to choose between them. She imagines having to choose between one of her students and a friend. One of her students and Jeanine.

She sits down at the piano with the music she didn't leave with Ty Greggory. She plays a few bars and then she sings the number for the Building City Hall scene. She thinks how she could go back to the college right now and take Ty Greggory to that piano with the broken high C and play this music for him, sing the lyrics. Or she and Jeanine could make a recording tonight and she could take it to him in the morning. Or she could mail the music to him with a note explaining her uncertainty about it. She thinks, as she goes back out to her car after the three noon-hour lessons, that she could do any of these things. And then when she comes to the intersection of Main and Cholla, she turns left instead of right and heads toward downtown Mirage.

Clare is already inside the quiet cool of the Mirage Public Library when she remembers she's tried this approach with Jeanine before, without success. The realization is deflating, since a book seems such an easy way to talk to your child about sex. Facts: accessible by call number. Books are wonderful things to have around at awkward moments. They are tangible. You can hold them in your lap. If the pinch of embarrassment gets too great, you can create a diversion by turning a page, closing the cover.

What's Happening to Me? The book Clare brought home for Jeanine when she was ten and things were beginning to happen. The cover was illustrated with cartoon characters—obvious in their male- or femaleness. The text was intended to connect with young adolescents, but instead slid down that merciless precipice that leads to the final resting place of the uncool cool.

"This is sick," Jeanine diagnosed. She made value judgments with great ease in those days. This was the time in her life when she would hold her nose whenever she walked into the Singing Room because she'd seen Clare use White-Out correction fluid there. White-Out was bad to sniff. Addictive, like glue. Drugs. Jeanine was saying no before it was the patriotic thing to do. Just say no. These pronouncements were easy.

And public. Once, Paul lost her in the supermarket. He'd abandoned his basket in the produce aisle and recruited a woman with twins in one cart and groceries in another to help him search before Jeanine turned up near the cigarette counter, cautioning customers that smoking, too, was a Bad Thing. "You'll cough your fool head off," she said, borrowing from the current TV commercial. Paul took mostly embarrassment from this incident, but there was a measure of comfort in it for Clare. A fanatic, after the distilling process of adolescence, may emerge with a survivor's portion of decency intact. Excess at ten seemed a good idea.

At fifteen, Jeanine is much more difficult to read. She no longer spouts her beliefs in the supermarket. At best, she may sing them in a song. At any rate, Clare listens to her singing for clues. In the shower this morning it was, "I Think We're Alone Now." Tiffany sings it these days, but someone else sang it to Clare and Paul's generation, with bass guitar thump-thumping a heartbeat in the background. As a sophomore, that thumping was enough to make Clare fall in love with the bass player in the school stage band and dream about running through the alley with him, tumbling to the ground, and saying (breathlessly of course), "I think we're alone now." It brought a rush, that bass. She still likes the bass turned high on her car stereo and a tenor sax played just so could still bring her to tears or a fevered pitch of desire, one as easily as the other, though it was impossible to predict which way she would go.

Clare leaves the library, walks out into heat, and feels sweat moving down her neck before she reaches the car. The temperature on the bank sign across the plaza is 106. She thinks for a moment she'll stop in and say hello to Paul, but then the sign flashes the time: 2:34. The door handle of the Honda is hot. She opens it quickly and gets in. She lowers the windows as she pulls out of the library lot.

A book is the wrong thing anyway. It isn't facts Jeanine needs this time. They did that already. Now, Clare thinks, rolling up the windows and turning on the air conditioning, they are dealing in things more miraculous: a young man, a young woman, a song familiar and unknown, a dance as ancient and new as daybreak.

☙

During Frankie Lawson's lesson, Clare hears Jeanine come in the backdoor and through the kitchen. She goes to the window near the piano and looks out as Jeffrey is pulling out of the driveway. Jeanine used to ride her bicycle to school, but lately she's been riding with Jeffrey, who's a year older — a junior — and has his own car.

A car. That makes Paul squirm, too. He knows about cars. Within a desperate, teenage context, cars, in darkness, are as good as bedrooms. Paul's old Mustang convertible had even had the accoutrements of a bedroom: he carried two pillows and a blanket in the backseat. Heads against armrests were decidedly unromantic and the blanket assuaged Clare's fear of passersby with flashlights. Of course, they put the top up on the car when they used it as a bedroom — an act that became so specifically connected to lovemaking as to be arousing. That was about the only time, in summer, that the top was up. Otherwise, Paul kept it down because that also was arousing. The rush of wind into their faces, through their hair. And the sight of each other with hair swept back, face and neck bare.

All of this up and down with the top got to be fairly labor-intense, with the downness inducing the upness as it did. Paul finally suggested they just leave it down. He reminded Clare of the blanket and pointed out that, with the top down, they'd be better able to see approaching flashlights while they were still at a distance. Clare couldn't bring herself to do this, though they did try the one time. There was something so wide open to the sky about it. All those stars. They made her want to cross her legs and fold her hands.

The funny thing is, now that they are old married folks and have a yard with a six-foot wall, it is Clare who wants to make love under the stars and Paul who puts on the google-eyes that mean he's hearing crazy stuff. She imagines them on the chaise lounge, she underneath him, where she could see the stars and his eyes. Or maybe, maybe, in the pool, where their legs would stretch, elongated, below them until they brought them tight around each other. And then she'd have to trust that Paul would hold her, that he'd keep her face lifted toward the air it breathed.

Was it unrealistic to think Jeanine and Jeffrey didn't feel the wind and see the stars, too? Was the best she could do now merely to tell Jeanine how to be safe? What was that even — safety?

Clare's father had tried to do this once for her. "I don't know what your mother's told you," he said to the back of her head. She was sitting at the kitchen table, bent over her algebra, when he came and laid his hand on her shoulder. "But I know you're seeing a lot of that Nichols boy, and whatever else, be sure you play it safe." Thinking of it now, it seemed more like something a father would say to a son than a daughter. Maybe it was a replay of what he'd said to her older brother, Sam. What struck her at the time was that it must have been hard for him to say these words to her — he wasn't one to talk about matters so intimate. But still, he'd opted to do that hard thing instead of another that must have seemed even harder: talk to her mother about talking to her. *I don't know what your mother's told you.*

He said something to the Nichols boy, too, who was only Paul, of course. The day he noticed the pillows and the blanket in the Mustang's backseat. "You have a blanket, I see."

"In case of a blizzard," Paul said. No hesitation whatsoever, in July. Probably it was a prepared response, as ready on his lips as her own "Eighteen," should that person with the flashlight ever come asking, How old are you? A bold lie from a fine young man. Her father himself had called him that, though it was before the discovery of the blanket.

"And pillows, too, I see."

"Traction," Paul said, with only slightly less ease. "Icy roads. Just put one under each rear wheel."

"Well," her father had said, nodding slowly. "I see. Well, it's best to be prepared. I like to see a young man recognizing the dangers out there."

His meaning dawned on Clare a year or so later, of all times, during her high school graduation ceremony. The class valedictorian was speaking of challenges and all of a sudden, it came clear to her, with a rush of heat to her cheeks.

Clare tries to imagine Paul being this veiled in speaking to Jeffrey. (Would he even speak to him?) She tries to guess whether Jeffrey is capable of misleading them the way Paul tried to do to her father. She tries to think of a way of discussing all this with Jeanine. And she tries to give Frankie at least a semblance of her attention. She doesn't give him quite enough, she discovers when he's gone, because there on the desk is his orthodontic appliance. He tends to forget to put it back in his mouth unless she reminds him.

9

The idea, the icebreaker for this talk with Jeanine, strikes her while she's waiting in the Honda at the high school the next afternoon. She picks up Jeanine on Tuesdays and drives her to Maureen Connolly's studio at the college for her voice lesson.

Clare opens the glove compartment and rummages until she finds what she wants: Tiffany. She's complained to Jeanine numerous times about stuffing the glove compartment with her tapes, but now she's glad to see it. She puts the cassette in the player, rewinds, and finds the song Jeanine was singing yesterday morning.

What is it about this nasal voice that Jeanine admires? Or is it something else she loves? The beat? The words? The bass? Clare ejects the tape, in ready position.

She notices the needle on the temperature gauge creeping toward H and turns off the air conditioning. This is something Paul has warned her about each spring since moving to Arizona— a car left idling will overheat.

Clare opens the windows, shuts off the motor. The heat immediately gathers in the car. The first summer they were here, she left a plastic cassette box on the dash one day while the car was parked outdoors. When she returned, it had melted into a warped, arthritic shape that couldn't be pried open. That was the end of that Eagles tape, the one with "New Kid in Town," which didn't seem to bode real well for their adjustment to their new environment.

As a child, Clare once left a shoebox full of crayons sitting out on the picnic table at the lake cabin. She'd left them there in the morning, in shade, but by evening they'd been melted into a grotesque wax sculpture by the afternoon sun. Clare, at six, hadn't considered that the sun would move during the course of the day. She knew about crayons being wax and about the sun melting wax — her father had read her the story of Icarus, after all — but what happened was still a surprise. She thought she'd been careful, and then, something new.

Jeanine comes down the sloped sidewalk toward the car finally, walking beside Jeffrey. Their mouths are moving and smiling, though the words don't travel as far as Clare. Jeffrey takes Jeanine's hand just as she moves away from him. Their joined arms extend, suspended for a moment, then fall back, broken apart. Jeffrey's hand moves to his pocket, Jeanine's to a strand of hair blowing across her face.

"How can you stand it?" Jeanine says, sliding into the car. She's shaking the hand she touched to the hot door handle. "Is something wrong with the air conditioning? It's so hot."

"Hi. No — just trying to keep the car from overheating."

"What about the passengers?" She drops her load of books on the seat between them.

"Once, in Minnesota, you put your mouth on the door

handle and it was so cold you stuck to it."

Jeanine gives her a horrified look. "That's gross," she says, lifting her damp hair off her forehead. "That's so gross."

"Your dad squeezed warm water from a washcloth onto your lips until they let go."

Jeanine makes a sound of disgust deep in her throat and pulls her lips inward, protecting them maybe, or feeling for scars.

This isn't the mood Clare meant to set at all. She starts the car and pushes in the cassette. "*Children behave . . .*" Tiffany drones.

"Did I tell you this song was popular when Daddy and I were young?"

"Really? Who sang it?"

"I forget. Actually, I didn't know your dad yet then. I was younger — about your age." Too young to know a husband.

"Mmn. You wouldn't believe what happened to Stephanie's hair, Mom. She let Diane give her a perm."

"The bass was real heavy in the older version of this song."

"She did it from a box—a home perm. It's so awful."

"I thought it was sexy." Clare reaches over and turns the dial toward treble.

"Noooo. It's disgusting."

Clare looks at Jeanine, startled. "What?"

"Her hair. Stephanie's."

"I meant the bass."

"It's disgusting?"

"No — sexy."

Jeanine considers her mother a moment. Her mouth twists in a way Clare doesn't like. Condescending, sort of. Older, much older. "Kind of nostalgic today, aren't you, Mom?"

"Not at all," Clare says. She shifts a little in her seat. "I'm merely pointing out that things don't change that much from one generation to the next. Like songs."

"Like sex."

Oh — that blunt. Clare lets the meager traffic take all her attention for a moment.

"If you're worried about Jeffrey and me, don't be. We're not going to do it until we're older. Seventeen, at least. For Jeffrey, anyway. He's older, you know."

"I know." Clare hopes she hasn't said the *know* too emphatically. "Or if we do, we'll be safe," Jeanine adds.

Clare can't help shooting her a disapproving look. "Oh? Just what do you know about safe?" This reproachful voice has got to go, Clare thinks. Not what's needed.

"You know — STDs, AIDS, babies."

Clare is truly offended by this lump categorization. "Really, now? Where did you learn these things, if I may ask?" It could have been Clare's own mother speaking.

"I've got a book."

Ha! Clare thinks. "What does this book say about love and commitment and responsibility?"

"Mom, you're positively on the rag today. Is something wrong?" Her voice is sincere, and so young.

Clare watches her for as long as driving will allow. "I *am* worried about you and Jeffrey. You've seemed . . .

close. I just don't want you to get hurt."

"I won't," Jeanine says, easy as pie. She even throws her arms out in a shrug, palms upward.

In that pose, she looks exposed, vulnerable in some intangible way, and Clare has the sudden urge to pull over and tuck Jeanine's arms back close to her body, to fold those white, white palms between her own. Jeanine drops her arms, but the pulse of danger stays with Clare. Her own hands are moist with anxious sweat. "Well, if you need any . . . advice, you can come to me."

"Thanks, Mom."

"Something else. Let's have Jeffrey to dinner."

"I know. Dad already said it, remember?"

≈

Clare delivers Jeanine to Maureen's studio. Even though vocal music is Clare's area of expertise, Jeanine takes her lessons from someone else. There are times when a parent isn't the best one to teach a child something. This is how Clare feels about voice. It's also how she felt when her own mother tried to teach her about sex, which she can remember happening just once.

Clare pulls out of the lot and heads for the supermarket. There's just time. They need milk.

Clare was fourteen when she left a note in her pocket on laundry day. That was Monday and Thursday, absolutely, in her mother's house.

"What does this mean?" her mother asked. She tossed the note onto Clare's open algebra book. There must have been something about algebra that drove her parents to worry for her safety.

It was the note a boy from the Catholic high school had given to her friend Cynthia. Clare was keeping it so Cynthia's mother wouldn't find it in the laundry and hit the roof.

"A piece of what, exactly?" her mother demanded.

"It's not mine, Mom. Someone gave it to me."

"Well, I can see that. Who is this boy? Is this the Brad Cynthia's mother said she wouldn't trust as far as she could throw him?"

"That'd be the one."

"Do you realize what he's talking about?"

"Yeah."

"I don't want you getting mixed up with older boys. It's trouble from the word Go."

"I won't," Clare had said.

She meant it, too. What her mother didn't know was that she'd already decided: she was going to stay a virgin until her wedding night, when there'd be some sort of dramatic moment with sighing and fragile lace dropping to the floor. She really, really meant it.

For three years. And then Paul Nichols, the long-distance runner and tenor saxophonist, showed up in her study hall the second semester of her junior year. It started with a Bic pen and then chocolate Easter eggs and at the spring dance he kissed her better than any boy Clare had yet kissed, which wasn't a lot. She'd been recruited that year to play the xylophone in the band, and from her post at the back of the band room she could check out the saxophone section as often as she wanted to, undetected. In fact, what she remembers most about playing the xylophone is Paul settling his instrument against his body and then running his tongue over the reed.

When Clare comes back for Jeanine, she's not outside waiting. Clare walks up to the building with a check for the month of May. Outside the open studio door, she can hear Jeanine's voice. It has a clarity which right then strikes Clare as something her own has lost.

Maureen waves her in. At the piano, she is dabbing White-Out onto the sheet music. She blows against it, writes something in with black ink. "Try it this way this week, then you can decide how you want to sing it for the audition."

"Okay," Jeanine says. She holds up the music, sings through the altered line. "Yeah, that's good," she says.

"Is there no respect for the composer anymore?" Clare teases.

"Just dynamics, Mom. No harm in that."

Clare inquires about Maureen's baby and Maureen asks about the show and when she and Jeanine get into the car, Clare is still holding the check and has to send Jeanine back in with it.

❧

At home, Clare brings in the mail. The phone bill. A flier picturing a missing child, asking Have You Seen Me? The May letter from her father. She sets everything but the letter on the desk. The letter she takes to her bedroom. She opens a drawer of her dresser, lifts a sweater and lays the letter, unopened, on the pile of others like it. The newspaper clipping of the shoes belonging to the boy named Michael, the boy run over in the street by his own mother, is there, too. The sight of those shoes grabs her heart. Clare folds the clipping in two so she won't have to see them when she puts the June letter away. Then she puts the sweater back in place and closes the drawer.

There are students between four and six and then at six o'clock, Paul's home. He carries his briefcase into the bedroom. Clare knows he'll be out in a minute with his swim trunks on. In the morning he leaves in a white shirt, smelling of aftershave. In a minute he'll have the chlorinated smell of the pool on him. But right now, he's warm and still a little moist, though she knows without looking that at this minute he's wiping the perspiration from his chest with the white shirt he's just taken off. He comes out. This is the moment. She kisses him.

"How was today?" he asks. It's what he always says.

"Today was good." This is what she usually says, too, though once in a while she says something ridiculous. Today was a rhinoceros. Today was mauve. Today was a hundred feet deep. Paul notices when the day wasn't good, no matter what she says it was. He's a good husband when it comes to these things, and most other times, too. There are many reasons to love him. She kisses him again.

After this, Clare has meatloaf to tend to and Paul goes out to the pool. Jeanine's gone to a beauty parlor with Stephanie to inquire about a perm reversal. It's an urgent need that Clare's agreed to hold dinner for. Stephanie will die if she has to go to school tomorrow looking like she did when she went to school today.

Clare sees Paul go to the diving board. She comes to the window in the family room to watch. It's one of her favorite and most frightening things. Paul stands stiffly straight, arms close to his sides, toes curled over the end of the board. He looks up into the sky — he always does this — what does it have to do with diving? A moment's meditation. Then he throws his arms out and up, springs, and this is the amazing part: in the air his body bends like a fish. He tucks his head between his extended arms. He enters the water, straight as he was on the board: arms; head; his lean, tamed body; his legs. His feet, uncurled, follow the line and go in with a little blip that's hardly a splash at all. To Clare, the secret of a dive like this seems to be control. Diving is something she's never learned to do well.

She watches a moment longer just because she must. He comes to the surface and opens his mouth. In three strokes, he's at the steps. He stands, pushes his wet hair off his forehead.

❦

After dinner, Ty Greggory phones to tell Clare the *Oklahoma!* lyrics look great. He tells her they're better than he'd hoped, that they're lucky to have her with the show. Clare sees it's impossible now to ask him to consider the other music. She's done so well with what she didn't want to do that now what she wanted to do is out of reach. He's going on about running an ad in the newspaper announcing auditions, about rehearsal schedules, the rest, and it's all making her sad and heavy inside. She says only what she has to say: thank you very much.

"Who was that?" Paul asks when she comes into the family room.

She sits on the couch next to him. He turns the TV down with the remote. "Ty Greggory. He likes the lyrics."

"Good. That's good."

She showed the lyrics to Paul the night she and her students made the recording. He looked them over, too fast to have read them, and told her they were good. He poked his head into the Singing Room once while they were recording and gave them the thumbs up. She hasn't told him about the other music. She knows if she did he'd do the same thing. He'd tell her: go for it. Do it, Clare. Show them to him. It's how Paul operates. He wants to be in control. It's how he finessed a transfer when they saw the need to start new somewhere away from their hometown. It's how he got to be a senior credit officer at Mirage CitiBank in less than five years. He's solid, a man who can be counted on. He knows his heart and follows it. It's hard for him to empathize with someone who isn't sure what she wants. And he has no tolerance for someone who knows but lacks the courage to go after it.

If she were to tell Paul about the music she's written, he would encourage her wholeheartedly and he would immediately have expectations of her. If she told him, she would have to follow through. She'd have to do it and she'd have to be good.

10

Saturday morning, as Clare's finishing a lesson postponed from earlier in the week, Paul comes home with a sack of grouting compound and a toilet seat. Home repairs? These were things Paul did rarely, usually just before his parents were coming for a visit. That was always in winter. Not even family visit Arizonans in the summertime.

Clare sends her student on her way. "What's this about?" she asks Paul.

"Just a little fixing up. Some grouting around the tub and that toilet seat is holding on by one hinge." He's got on the baseball cap he wears for skiing.

"What is this — a beat-the-heat maneuver? You're doing winter chores and wearing your ski cap."

"Hmm?" He has the cap on backwards and is snapping gum. For a minute, he looks eighteen. He goes directly to the main floor bathroom where he drops his load with a clunk Clare can hear from the kitchen.

"Who's coming to visit?" she calls after him.

No answer. She goes to the bathroom doorway. "Is someone coming to visit?"

"Not that I know of. Why?"

"It usually takes that to get you in this mood."

"No it doesn't." He's reading the box the toilet seat is packed in.

"Sure it does. Your father, usually. You rush around fixing up just like a little boy before inspection."

He squints and snaps the gum. "That's silly."

"Yes, but it's true."

He lies down on his back under the toilet and begins working at something with a screwdriver.

"I can't stand the thought of Jeanine going to the lake without us, Paul."

He looks up at her from the floor.

"It's enough to be going at all. I just don't want to send her ahead."

"I just thought it might give her some perspective. On Jeffrey, I mean."

"I know."

Paul slides out from under the toilet and sits up. "That's why I hate this. I never have the right tools." He gets up and wipes his hands on his shorts. "I'll have to go see Les." He grimaces at the next thought. "He'll ask me again about the band."

Les and Sally Brandt have both been involved with centennial committees. Sally and two other women are compiling a commemorative booklet of people's old stories about the early days of Mirage. And photos. Lots of photos. Les is in charge of the Encore band for the centennial parade. He's been recruiting former musicians to bring out their instruments and march in the parade and he's short in the saxophone section. He asks Paul every time he sees him and he's the sort of guy it's hard to say no to. Les's garage is the neighborhood's tool lending library.

"I'd like to see you play that saxophone again, Paul."

Paul lays his hand on Clare's bottom and kisses her mouth as he passes her in the doorway. His T-shirt is navy blue and a map of sweat—dark blotches where he's pressed against the floor. "Don't worry," he says. "I'll get this Jeffrey dude checked out when he comes for dinner next weekend. Is it next weekend?"

"Yeah. Saturday," she calls after him.

She smiles. So that's who's coming.

Jeanine comes into the bathroom, still struggling with morning, still in her nightgown, still yawning. "Get dressed. The day's going by," Clare tells her airily. Jeanine trips over the sack of grouting compound and scowls.

That night, Jeanine begs Paul to lift the sentence he imposed last weekend. "Ten o'clock is absolutely juvenile," she says in her carefully modulated adult voice. Clare hasn't heard her use that word before. She wonders if she learned it from Jeffrey. *Movies are so juvenile, Jeanine. Let's only tell your parents that. Let's go park in my car instead.*

"Your curfew is eleven, which is nothing short of just right," Paul tells her. "You're due at ten tonight because you were an hour late last weekend, which was nothing short of your own fault."

She doesn't like that. "Fine," she says through tight, narrow lips. "FINE." In case they hadn't heard. "I might as well not go at all." The adult voice has been tossed to the wind. "There'll hardly be time to get home after the movie."

What more did she want to do?

Jeanine goes to stand out front so that when Jeffrey comes he doesn't even come up to the door. Jeanine hops in the car and throws her head back against the headrest, a dramatic show of relief. Jeffrey leans across and kisses her, longer, Clare thinks at the window, than was necessary to express his sympathy for her tragic plight.

Then they're off and Clare is picking up the newspaper. She finds the movie listings. The show Jeanine said they were going to see is rated R. Clare tries to remember—wasn't this the movie Sally Brandt told them about? She and Paul were at the Brandts' a couple weeks ago for hamburgers. Sally showed them all those pictures she had collected for the centennial book and then they talked about this movie where a woman fakes an orgasm. In a restaurant. Loudly. Les made some remark that had turned Sally sullen for a while. Is that the movie Jeanine and Jeffrey went to see?

Clare checks out the picture in the newspaper ad. It's obvious the movie is rated R for sex, not violence. Not that violence is any better. Either way, what ought to be happening is that these theaters ought to be enforcing these ratings better. Fifteen-, sixteen-year-old kids shouldn't be getting into R movies. She tells Paul so as she fills the sink to wash the dinner dishes.

He's in the family room, clicking through the TV channels with the remote, but he hardly responds.

"They should check IDs," Clare goes on, "like bars. You just can't tell how old kids are by looking at them."

Paul laughs. "Can you hear yourself? You sound like your mother. Wouldn't you rather have them in the theater than out doing it themselves?"

"Don't be so stupid," Clare says. Her voice grates a little. She clatters the pans she's washing.

Paul laughs again, as if he knows something she doesn't know and isn't telling. It seems a large offense. Clare wads the wet washcloth into a ball and tosses it over the kitchen counter into the family room and beans Paul on the back of the head. Its main effect is surprise and a little splat of water. Paul flinches, then reaches over the back of the couch to see what hit him. He stands up on the couch, leaps over the back, and grabs the washcloth.

Clare sees him coming and runs into the Singing Room. She keeps going, through the foyer, back into the family room, through the dining area and kitchen, the Singing Room. It's that circle she runs, with Paul in pursuit. She gets in two revolutions before he brings her down — in the Singing Room, luckily, where there's carpet — flat on her back and kneels over her, pinning her arms to her sides with his knees. He squeezes the washcloth and dribbles warm water into her face. Clare gives his rear a thump with her knee but he holds fast. She closes her eyes and mouth and feels the water trickle down her neck like sweat.

"Chinese torture treatment," Paul says. She turns her head to the side, then laughs when he tries to fill her ear.

He throws the washcloth aside then and brings his mouth to her face. He lets her arms loose and she locks them around his neck. He rolls off of her. She tightens her hold and, in one somersaulting motion, goes from under him to beside him to on top of him. They make one more complete roll before they stop under the piano with Clare on top.

"Paul, that's that movie where the woman fakes an orgasm in a restaurant."

"What?"

"The movie Jeanine and Jeffrey went to see."

"In a restaurant?"

"Pretend."

"Let's us go."

"Stop it."

"How did she do it?"

"I haven't seen the movie."

"They went to that?"

"Yes."

"I think we'd better go and supervise."

"You're awful."

"You love me awful," he says, kissing her. "You love me awful best of all."

꙳

Jeanine arrives home just as the mantel clock is striking ten o'clock. Not a minute earlier, which seems to Clare rather deliberate. She tells her parents she liked the movie. Paul sends Clare a look. That Jeffrey will come to dinner next Saturday night. She's dry and goes upstairs with no fancy moves.

11

Jeffrey brings carnations and a knotted stomach to dinner. Clare can tell it's knotted by how it makes the rest of him move with jerky suddenness. The flowers are a kind gesture and this dinner, it strikes Clare as she puts them in water, perhaps isn't. It couldn't be healthy to force down food under circumstances like this.

Paul is almost as frazzled as Jeffrey. He has the over-talkative, over-witty syndrome he gets from trying too hard in situations that really do matter. Clare wants to tell him to relax: when Jeffrey lifts the toilet seat to pee, you'll be seen as a conscientious homeowner, a caring father, and a formidable force to be reckoned with. But *relax* is exactly the wrong word for Paul when he needs to do it. Say *relax* and he shifts a gear higher out of pure self-consciousness.

It's amazing how this matters to these two. Clare didn't think this old dance went on anymore. The father and the boyfriend, circling guardedly around the same precious girl. That fathers still cared to impress their daughters' boyfriends, to assess their merits and scare them just a little bit. Or that a young man gave a rip what his girl's father thought of him. That he'd want to bring flowers and eat dinner with manners and anxiety. Clare wants to hug them both for their sentiments and their nervous wrenching.

Jeanine is in the tolerant, generous mode tonight, with an added element of domesticity that looks as new and surprising to Clare as the sight of Paul making repairs in summer. How can they hope to get better acquainted tonight when no one is being himself?

Jeanine started in this afternoon, concocting a creme de menthe dessert with a loving patience Clare could only remember having as a newlywed, when she wanted to impress Paul with her culinary skills. She couldn't remember ever cooking for him before they were married. There were different risks to love in those days—safer ones, maybe. You could fall in love with a girl who couldn't cook and never know it until after the ceremony. People now needed more knowledge of each other or maybe more faith. Now someone you love could give you a deadly disease. Or this could happen to your child. A rare thing — faith — but maybe that's the thing the strained wit, the careful manners, the tender cooking are reaching for. What a task. Clare feels herself hardly more than an observer, and an awed one at that.

Through dinner—roast beef and mashed potatoes, which, admittedly, is Clare's safest menu—Paul tortures Jeffrey with standard what-does-your-father-do type questions. Jeffrey sits stiffly, exemplifying excellent posture and unease. His nearly blond hair is wavy around the hairline, where it's become moist, and curly in the back, where it hangs longer, the way boys do it now—quite long, below his collar. He doesn't let his eyes stay too long on anything, and hardly allows them to fall on Jeanine at all.

Clare thinks Paul's merciless with his questions.

"He has an auto body repair business," Jeffrey says to Paul's inquiry about his father. "Collision America."

"Oh, I know the place," Paul says. "Near downtown. By the fire station?"

"That's the place. I'm learning how to do window tinting. Polyglycoat. I'm going to work there this summer doing that."

Paul nods. "That's what I ought to have done to the Jeep and the Honda. Keeps out a lot of the heat, doesn't it?"

"The Poly cuts out twenty percent more than regular films. Saves your upholstery too. The sun's really hard on that. And it gives you some privacy."

Privacy? Clare offers Jeffrey more mashed potatoes and he takes some.

"And you deliver pizza?" Paul asks.

Jeffrey grins a little sheepishly. "Well, that's just a job."

"Are you interested in the auto repair business?" Paul asks and Clare kicks him under the table. Paul gives her a puzzled look. "What?" he says.

She tries to convey her message facially. Jeanine rolls her eyes at both of them and Jeffrey goes for thirds on the potatoes.

"I guess I'll find that out this summer," Jeffrey says. "My brothers both work for Dad. That might be enough family in the shop. I'm the youngest."

"Jeffrey wants to learn to fly," Jeanine adds and Jeffrey looks embarrassed.

"Well, maybe," he says.

"Air Force?" Paul says.

"I don't know," Jeffrey says.

"Jeffrey's in the honors math program this year," Jeanine says.

Now Jeffrey really squirms and Clare wonders if Jeanine is being kicked under the table. She tries to think of a way to rescue him. "Do you play Pictionary, Jeffrey?" Clare asks.

Paul's forehead grows lines. Jeanine looks confused.

"Sure," Jeffrey says. He dabs his mouth with the corner of his napkin. Clare's put out the cloth ones tonight and he seems cautious about using it, as if he's afraid of getting it dirty. "Not well, maybe," he adds, "but I've played it before. It's fun."

"Let's play," Jeanine says. She stands and begins clearing the table. "Let's play a round and then have dessert."

Paul won't want to do this. He hates this game, though he's better at sketching than anyone else in the family. Clare thinks it's having to draw under a time constraint that annoys him. One night last winter, when his parents were visiting, he sat outside with *The Brothers Karamazov* in his lap while the rest of them played. Later, in bed, Clare sang the Party Pooper song to him and eventually got him to admit he was faking it on the Dostoyevsky.

"Sounds good to me," Paul says. He gets up and helps Jeanine with the clearing, something else he never does. Jeffrey follows his lead. Clare takes note: good guys are good sports and they do dishes.

The men stand the women. Clare and Jeanine have

been teammates before, but Paul and Jeffrey go through the false starts of learning how the other thinks. Jeffrey draws in stick figures and simple shapes and Paul lets the timer run out while attempting something too complicated. But eventually Jeffrey gets Paul to say *deodorant* with a drawing of a little cartoon man with wavy lines coming out from under his arms. Then Jeffrey says *stop* within seconds after Paul strokes out an octagon shape and Paul is on his feet, slapping Jeffrey's back.

Jeanine pushes her drawing pad over to Clare as Paul carries on his congratulations. She's written, *Why's Daddy so weird tonight?*

Some kind of man thing, Clare writes.

Paul is chanting a little cheer for the male team. Jeffrey looks across the table at Jeanine, embarrassed again, looking for a hint. Jeanine rolls her eyes, then covers them. Paul is shaking the die in two hands, high over his head, to one side and then the other. He resembles a Spanish dancer with a pair of castanets. Jeanine squirms. So does Jeffrey. Clare even feels one coming on. Paul tosses the die across the board and then sits down, suddenly self-aware.

It's quiet for an awkward moment and then Jeffrey says, "Olé!" They laugh eagerly, laugh the embarrassment out of the air, and Clare wants to hug Jeffrey. It's just what was needed.

Paul grins—the truest thing he's done all evening.

The men win this round. Jeanine serves her dessert, which Jeffrey insists he loves. Clare knows by the size of his bites and the number of times he says, "Jeanine, this is great," that he hates it. He eats the whole piece.

When Jeffrey excuses himself to use the bathroom, both Clare and Paul are surprised to see him go out into the Singing Room, round the banister and start upstairs. Paul, Clare supposes, is wondering why Jeffrey didn't use the main floor bath, the one with the new toilet seat, but what Clare wants to know is this: why does Jeffrey go so automatically upstairs, to the bathroom next to Jeanine's bedroom?

They play another round of Pictionary. Pencil drawings are fragile things to build trust with, but we do the best we can with what we have. By the time round two comes to an end, Paul and Jeffrey plainly have something they'll be able to remember the next time they meet, though they lose the game to the women.

"I see you have a car," Paul says as they walk Jeffrey out the door. They're all out on the driveway and so is the car.

"Yeah," Jeffrey says. "There it is."

"Nice car," Paul says. Jeffrey's car is a Datsun from back in the days when there was such a thing.

"Thanks," Jeffrey says. "I polyglycoated it myself."

"My first car was a '65 Mustang convertible. Of course, I lived in Minnesota then—pretty short convertible season. Now I'm here and no convertible."

"Too bad," Jeffrey says. "About the convertible, I mean. And the weather."

"Yeah, it was a lot of winter. A lot of winter driving. They have these survival kits up there now that you can carry in your car. Just a little square box that fits under the seat. If you're trapped in a blizzard, you can open it and there's matches and a candle, a little pan to melt snow."

Clare's amused to hear Paul going on like this.

"A silver crinkly blanket," he continues. "Some space-age material. Very thin, but warm. But back then we didn't have anything like that. I just carried a blanket. A regular blanket. Wool." Paul's hands ride his pockets, deliberately nonchalant. Clare wonders if he'll look into Jeffrey's backseat next, checking for pillows and blankets.

"Did you get trapped in many blizzards?" Jeffrey asks. A native Arizonan. He's already said so and here's proof. He has the wide-eyed respect for inclement weather that those immersed in it only pretend at in front of their children.

When the tornado sirens would go off when she was a girl, which was a few times every summer, Clare's father would rush the family into the basement with blankets, a flashlight, a thermos of water, and a transistor radio with batteries. Clare and Sam and their mother would sit on the hard linoleum floor under the staircase, next to the furnace, until the storm passed.

Her father would go upstairs and stand watch. Once when Sam and her mother were out of town for a Boy Scout event and Clare was put into the basement alone, she crept upstairs and found her father out on the street, along with many of the neighbors, leaning into the still, vacant air, watching the sky writhe. The sirens were wailing. She was afraid and went out to him and touched his leg. He bent over and picked her up, held her against his chest, and stretched his arm out in the direction you walked to get to Elephant Park. "There it is, Clare," he said. "Look." There in the sky, dangling from a black swirling cloud mass, was the elephant's trunk.

It felt like a privilege to see it. Her father's face was serious and watchful, and he kept his arms tight around her. They watched as the trunk disappeared back up into the cloud and kept watching until the ominous stillness broke and the wind and rain started. The young elm trees on the boulevard bent toward the ground like they'd have to break. The funnel didn't appear again.

Clare heard that warning siren dozens of times more before she left Minnesota. Once — it was when she was pregnant with Michael and she and Paul lived in that apartment house near their old high school — she saw another funnel and this time it looked like a huge penis hanging from the sky. But until that summer at the lake when Michael drowned, a tornado had never actually touched down anywhere near her.

"No, I was never trapped in a blizzard," Paul says.

"Well, you would have been safe just in case," Jeffrey says.

"Yes." Paul lifts his chin with a certain conviction.

"Thanks for dinner, Mr. and Mrs. Nichols." Jeffrey puts out his hand to Paul. Paul shakes it and smiles. Jeffrey does the same to Clare. Then Jeanine. Jeanine just looks at his hand a minute, then takes it, shakes it, solemnly, like in a ceremony. Then Jeffrey puts his hand quickly into his pocket. Jeanine's goes to her hair, fusses with a stray piece.

Jeffrey opens the car door. "Thanks again. It was real fun."

"Thanks for the flowers," Clare says.

"Bye, then," Jeffrey says. "It was great food."

"Bye," they say.

He gets into the car, leans out around the open door. "Great dessert, Jeanine."

"Bye," they say again.

Jeffrey steps back out of the car, digs into each of his pockets, the left side twice. "Did I leave my keys in there?" he says then.

Jeanine goes to check. Paul hangs an arm over the open car door and tells Jeffrey about winter driving and traction on ice and salt damage. Jeffrey stands on the other side of the door, listening.

Clare watches their mouths, speaking and smiling, and then the sky, huge and weatherless. All those stars. Stars and stars and stars. A breeze rattles through the palm trees.

12

The planning for Clare's parents' fiftieth wedding anniversary has been a challenge via long distance. Clare's brother Sam also lives quite far away—North Carolina—though it's doubtful he'd be much help even if he were on the scene. Sam's distance is more than miles. It's been up to Clare, with help from her aunt Bernice, her mother's sister, who was the maid of honor in the wedding.

Bernice lives within a few miles of the lake cabin, where the event will take place, and is something of a natural organizer. At first, Clare felt guilty asking Bernice to check into this detail or that one—she, with her own husband confined to a wheelchair, after all, probably had her hands full—but Bernice took charge with such enthusiasm that Clare's reluctance soon passed. In fact, Clare has recently begun to worry that Bernice has made larger work of the whole affair than it really needs to be. She thinks this again when Bernice calls with her latest brainstorm: a mock wedding.

"You know, they never had much of a wedding, Clare." Bernice's voice is more lively than Clare remembers it being. "It was Depression time, and the start of the War.

Dad said a wedding or a reception, but not both. They picked a reception. I would have, too, given a choice like that."

"It sounds like a lot of work for you, Bernice. If I were there to do more . . ."

"Your mother will love this, believe me. And there's help here. I've already asked Joan to be the bride and she's found a wedding gown at the secondhand store. Something we can use and just toss. It's the dry cleaning that's expensive, you know. You wouldn't have an old formal around, would you? Something that would fit Jeanine? I want a lot of bridesmaids and groomsmen — it's what your mother would have done if there had been any money for it — and I want them all to be the younger generation. The grandchildren — Jeanine and the cousins. That's closest to how your parents looked at the time. I would have spit nails if my kids had married as young as your folks did. You know, maybe it's Jeanine that ought to be the bride. It's her grandparents, after all. Do you think?"

Clare takes the deep breath it seems Bernice should need. "Well, you've already asked Joan. Are you thinking kind of a re-enactment of their wedding?"

"With a few liberties taken." Bernice laughs, full of secrets, then lays one out in view: "I was thinking of having the bride and groom on roller skates, chewing bubble gum. Do you know your mother was only seventeen? When it's time for the kiss, they could each blow a bubble and stick them together."

Bernice laughs wickedly. Her summer has clearly taken on a fresh purpose.

"Someone could take the part of your grandfather," Bernice goes on, "carrying a shotgun. It's no secret to anyone about your brother Sam anyway. Or would that be in poor taste? Clare?"

Hearing Bernice talk so openly about this piece of family history is a shock to Clare, even after all these years. A secret guarded as tightly as that one was can never become a joke—not after fifty years, not after a hundred. There was still some capacity for scandal in those days, and Sam's "premature" birth was something Clare's mother never talked about. She certainly never talked about it with Clare. Sam was ten years old before Clare was even born. When she finally figured it out, quite inadvertently, Clare was well into her twenties and understood clearly the unspoken rules of family pain. She, too, kept quiet.

"I don't think everyone knows about Sam," Clare says. "I don't think Jeanine does."

"Well, you're probably right. No point in stirring up that old ash pot, I guess. Do you think it would be too tacky to use a roll of toilet paper for the aisle cloth?"

Clare hears her uncle Howard quoting Bernice the long-distance rates and then Bernice begins her goodbye, a long, drawn out affair, dotted with *I must go* and punctuated, finally, by Howard's warning that the dog is circling by the door, ready to pee the rug.

❦

When Clare tells Paul and Jeanine at dinner about Bernice's plan for a mock wedding, Jeanine's taken with the idea. "I want to be the soloist. Tell her I'll sing. There has to be music. What did they sing for weddings in those days?"

Those days sounds centuries ago.

"How about 'I Love You Truly'?" Paul suggests. He sings a couple of lines in a deep baritone that wouldn't be half bad if he'd quit horsing around and just do it. But he horses. Lots of vibrato and where he doesn't know the words he hum-de-dums. But Clare can see on Jeanine's face that she's planning.

After dinner, Clare gets down an old photo album and shows Jeanine a picture of Clarence and Roberta on their wedding day. There was no album of posed shots—the bride showing a garter, the groom eating cake—just this one picture, taken by a friend who later died in the War. The bride and the groom face each other, hands clasped, heads turned toward the camera. Just their torsos. They stand without legs before a stained glass window. The photo, of course, is black and white, so the colors can only be imagined, but behind their shoulders and between their faces, the images are clear: Eve, shoulders tangled in hair, legs in serpent; Moses, robed and laden with stone tablets; Abraham, knife poised; Jacob, Rebecca, Joseph, Esau, angels, angels, angels.

A literature professor Clare had in college once told the class that all the stories ever told are in the Bible. All the stories since are retellings, just more holding points along that original story line dropped through time. It made Clare think that, if she only knew what to look for, she could find out her future by reading the Bible. If every story ever told was there, the story of her life was there, too. She secretly hoped it was in *The Song of Songs*.

In the photo, the bride's smile is faint and proper. The groom is appropriately somber. He holds the hand of a woman he's about to marry. Inside her she holds their son, growing toward birth. Behind them are all the possible human stories, told in bits of colored glass. One, if they could find it, was theirs.

13

The notice announcing auditions for the centennial
show appears in the newspaper mid-May. "*One Hundred Steps Toward the Future:* A Celebration of the Centennial of Mirage, Arizona." Clare's contribution to the ad
is in small print: "Auditioners should prepare a song."

There's a planning meeting the same week. They meet
in Ty Greggory's office at the community college around a
table so small their knees knock underneath. The script
writer is there, along with the orchestra teacher from the
high school, who will be conducting the show's orchestra,
and Nate and Clare.

Ty is a large man. He takes more than his fifth of the
table. The office is further crowded by his penguins. Large
and small, carved, stuffed, or inflatable plastic, they are
there, Clare supposes, to be unusual. Conversation pieces.
A little Arizona Arctic. While Ty goes on about Clare's
inspired lyrics, she imagines pulling the plug of the inflat-
ed bird and making him the first penguin in flight. Nate's
knee rubs against hers three times during the meeting. She
counts them: three.

He walks with her to her car afterwards. It's gotten dark
while they were inside, but it's still warm. Hot, really, with

no breeze. When Clare opens the car door, Nate reaches around the door and rolls down the window. Clare gets in and Nate closes the door and bends down to the open window. "The music will be great. Familiar, rousing, and customized." This is an exact repetition of what Ty said in the meeting. Nate says it theatrically, deep and somber. Clare wonders, who is he mocking? Ty or her?

Clare looks at him. His face is about three inches from hers and full of mischief. He's just a boy, or he's a man playing the part of a boy because he thinks it makes him irresistible.

"Great," he says again. "Trust me." It's more than lyrics he's talking about now. His eyes tell her.

"Why should I?" she says.

His face is daring a cream pie — or a kiss — to make it a target. He grins and makes a sound Clare would remember later as delight.

She wishes for a pie, but settles for her palm. She presses it firmly against his nose and holds it there until her other hand can get the window up. He steps back, still smiling, and throws her a kiss as she pulls out.

She refuses to look at herself in the rearview mirror. She doesn't want to see this, but she feels it nonetheless: the intricate muscles of her face pulling upward into a smile.

☙

It's not as though she's looking for a lover. It's not as though she has any reason to. Paul is always there for her.

Always dependable. Always reasonable and kind and generous. Paul is . . . always Paul. There are a lot of reasons to love him.

He's asleep, holding her, when she thinks: delight. It was delight, that sound Nate made. She kisses Paul lightly under his chin, then takes her discovery to her side of the bed where she can remake it, just for the pleasure of it. There's some small intention also to think about that pleasure with some more objective part of herself, but she falls asleep before she gets to that. It comes back to her full-size, though, when she wakes during the night with Nate in her dream and Paul in her arms.

14

Since the dinner, instead of coming to take Jeanine out somewhere, Jeffrey's more often been coming over — to watch TV, do homework, swim, or just hang around. He takes his shoes off now and opens the refrigerator himself when he wants a Coke, and this week when she did the laundry, Clare threw in the towel he leaves hanging from one time to the next on the wall by the pool. Once, when Clare looked in from the kitchen, she could see just the backs of their two heads — Jeanine's and Jeffrey's — over the back of the couch, and she thought how they could be brother and sister, just home from school, eating chocolate chip cookies and watching Batman cartoons.

Tonight Jeanine's rehearsing and Jeffrey is an audience of one. From the bedroom, where she's retreated, Clare recognizes the familiar song Jeanine's been preparing for her audition.

Clare begins a letter to Bernice. The thanks, the news, and then her idea. She's decided to make a photo collage for her parents as an anniversary gift. She thought of it the night they had the wedding picture out. She'll start with that, mount it on a background, and surround it with other photos—events and faces significant to these fifty years of marriage. She has some pictures, but she needs help. It's a lot of years she's been gone. The last eleven years are hardly there in pictures at all. There are a few from the one visit they made back home nine years ago, but that's it. She needs Bernice to scrounge a little on the Minnesota end. There still wouldn't be recent pictures of all of them together, but if Bernice could find some of her parents, Clare could piece them in near ones of Jeanine and Paul and herself.

From the Singing Room, Clare hears another song—strange in the immediate context, but then familiar, only from a time further back. Jeanine's voice, clear and precise: "*I love you truly, truly, Dear.*"

Then another, low and exuberant. Jeffrey's. "Truly, Babe. To the max."

Jeanine: "*Life with its sorrows, Life with its tears.*"

Jeffrey: "Boo-hoo." A cartoonish honking of a nose.

Laughter and shrieks from Jeanine. Quieter voices. Silence. Then the whole song, uninterrupted.

I love you truly,
truly, Dear.
Life with its sorrows,
Life with its tears,
fades into dreams,
when I feel you are near,
for I love you truly,
truly, Dear.

It seems too simple a message to begin a thing like marriage. Innocent. Embarrassingly unadorned. It needs a blanket thrown over it, just for decency, or a bucket of cold water splashed in its face.

There are a few things these young people should know about this song and about life in general. The things are perfectly clear to Clare just this moment. She opens the bedroom door with the urgency to say them — quick — while they last, but when she walks toward the Singing Room, they leave her completely. There, in front of a music stand Clare bought for Jeanine to encourage her toward the rarer, finer things in life, are Jeanine and Jeffrey, locked in a common, simple embrace. It feels like news to Clare that male and female bodies fit together this perfectly. Despite the fact that her imagination has put them together in just this pose many times, the embrace looks rare and fine, and seeing it steals her strength away.

Jeanine's fingers ripple like a mysterious underwater creature through the curls at the back of Jeffrey's neck. Watching, Clare feels their slippery softness on her own fingers and she feels the tug on her own scalp as Jeffrey's hand, fingers spread, slides through Jeanine's hair, separating it into three strands as if for a braid. It occurs to Clare that any other male body would fit just this tightly against Jeanine's. And any other than Paul's would mold itself to her own just this way in the moment of an embrace. It seems too simple a fact of life.

❧

"They were kissing tonight," Clare tells Paul when he gets home. He goes immediately to the bedroom, already unbuttoning his shirt. It's ten o'clock and he's been working since seven this morning.

"God no."

"Yes."

"Who?"

He exaggerates the impact of the little punch she gives his arm. "Jeanine and Jeffrey. Who else?"

"Who else? Hell, anybody. It's a common activity. Come here. No point in us missing out."

He kisses her tentatively, like an experiment, then again, for real. His hands give her bottom a hug. "You thought he's never kissed her?"

"Well, no. Of course I didn't think that." She's pulled away, gotten objective. "I thought he had. That he does, I mean."

Paul begins undressing.

"Seeing it is different, Paul. Seeing it—it makes you think."

"Think what?" He pulls off his socks and throws them, in little inside-out wads, into the hamper. Clare thinks of the woman who wrote Dear Abby recently, complaining about her husband's habit of turning his socks inside out, tabulating the hours of her lifetime spent turning them back after washing them. Later, another woman wrote that her husband did the same thing, and now that he was dead, she'd give anything to have his socks, and presumably her husband, with her. Things like socks are small, too small to break the back of a marriage, but the small things are significant in that they wear you down for the big stuff. When the big stuff comes around, like your daughter becoming a woman, you could be caught exhausted by that little stuff. Then what?

"You're going to have to stop doing that with your socks."

"What's that?" Paul asks, peering cautiously into the hamper.

"Turning them inside out. It's exhausting me. I'll have to start leaving them that way. You'll find them in your drawer still in those little wads. They won't get dry that way. They won't even get clean." For some reason, her voice has taken an edge.

"Oh. Okay," Paul says, unruffled. "Why did Jeanine and Jeffrey kissing remind you of socks? That was dirty socks, wasn't it. Dirty socks?"

Clare ignores this. "I thought, seeing them, any boy. Any man. There's kissing and kissing and kissing." Clare's throwing her arms in every direction and her voice is urgent.

Paul takes note. He thinks before he speaks, and it puts confused lines on his face. He almost whispers: "How many boys-men are we talking about here?"

Clare stares, as if she's heard the most off-the-wall words. "What?"

"I've lost track. Is it Jeanine and Jeffrey we're talking about or just humans in general?"

"This is funny? You think this is funny?" She pushes past him and out of the bedroom. He follows close behind, so close that when Clare, on impulse, breaks her driving stride and takes a deliberate step backwards, she tramps down pretty hard on his bare foot.

"Clare!" He limps — affects a limp, Clare thinks — and this annoys her too. When he grabs her shoulders and turns her around, she won't look at him. "How'd he kiss her, for God's sake?"

"Hush. She'll hear you."

"Where is she?"

"She went up to bed."

Clare takes Paul's hand suddenly and leads him into the Singing Room, over to the music stand. "They were here," Clare whispers, "like this." She takes Paul at the elbows and maneuvers him into position. Then she puts her arms around his neck. His circle around her back, his hands resting again on her bottom. They give a squeeze.

"Here?" he says. His breath is warm on her cheek.

She shakes her head very slightly, no.

"Here?" he says, moving his hands to the small of her back.

She nods, yes, and brings one hand to the back of his neck. He pushes out his lower lip, registering the fact of Clare's fingers playing with his hair.

"She plays with his hair?"

Again Clare nods.

"Clare? I'm not dressed right for this, am I?"

She looks down at his underwear — all he's wearing — and smiles. "Shh. Be good."

Then he looks into her eyes in a way that makes Clare remember Minnesota, a convertible and stars. "Here?" he whispers, his mouth and the words little flutters against her cheek.

"No," she says, a warning and a revelation. "Here." She puts her mouth to his. They're Jeanine and Jeffrey. They're anyone and everyone. There is kissing and kissing, all over the world.

15

In the morning, Paul is gone before Jeanine starts her waltzing in the kitchen. Clare can see it's waltzing, and she can see Jeanine thinks she's disguising it by incorporating the steps into her normal course from cupboard to refrigerator to table. She's also humming. Elton John. "Healing Hands." Well. It's not hard to guess whose hands. Just what does she think they're healing?

Clare's tired of clues. What she wants is a few words of clear communication. She wants them direct, not echoed, and now. I *saw* you kissing in the Singing Room last night, she could say. I *heard* you singing that sentimental love song as if it were meant just for Jeffrey. I *know* a thing or two about these things. You *can't* fool your mother.

Jeanine's gathering up her books for school and Clare notices her notebook is covered with the word *Jeffrey*. *Jeffrey* written in curlicues. *Jeffrey* written in large block letters. *Jeffrey* in script, in cursive, upside down and with three-dimensional shadowing. "Jeffrey's notebook?" Clare asks innocently, though she knows better.

Jeanine rolls her eyes. "No-oh," she says, in two syllables. You silly old woman, her eyes say.

"So it can be returned if lost?"

"Mo-om." Her smile is vanishing.

Clare doesn't quit. Whatever this is, driving her, it's relentless. "So he can be returned if he wanders away?"

Jeanine's eyes flash. "Don't rag me, Mom. Just don't rag me." She piles her books furiously on top of her notebook. A horn sounds outside. Jeffrey. Jeffrey in his car. Jeffrey in his car with the privacy windows. Jeffrey with his curls in his car with the privacy windows. Jeanine turns sharply on one heel, like reversing directions in a tango. She slams the door on her way out.

Clare sinks down into the nearest chair at the kitchen table. At her elbow, on a faded placemat picturing Cinderella, three soggy Cheerios swim in Jeanine's cereal bowl. Clare feels tears pressing behind her eyes. Clare, you bitch. Clare, you fool. You silly old woman, Clare.

❦

Clare has six students today. She notices during the second lesson that the piano seems out of tune. In fact, she imagines she can hear it becoming worse and worse through the afternoon. This is silly, of course. It couldn't possibly go that bad that fast. But Clare feels herself listening for flatness to the point of distraction. When the last student leaves, Clare is tired, as if she's worked eight hours instead of three.

She goes to the desk, searching for the piano tuner's business card. She doesn't find it. She finds instead a letter from her father, postmarked in April. It's a startling sight. She can't imagine how it got left in the desk and the fact that it somehow did shakes her. It's unopened, of course. She holds it up to the light, to be sure it's the real thing. *Love, Dad* is visible through the envelope, at the edge. The other words fold onto each other, make themselves unreadable, but still she knows what they are. They're the same words that were in his letters when she used to read them. They're the words that would break her heart if she even let them begin.

She takes the letter into the bedroom, opens the drawer and lifts the sweater. She puts the envelope in place behind the May letter, her hands shaking, and closes the drawer.

She'll call the piano tuner now and set an appointment. It's a small, unencumbered action she can take and a problem will be solved. She reaches for the yellow pages. She finds the phone number for the piano tuner there. She dials and waits for a voice. The one that comes isn't real. A machine tells her to leave a message. She checks her watch. Of course. It's after five. She waits for the tone, but when it comes she can think of nothing to say.

16

The one trip they took back to Minnesota, two years after Michael died, a year and a half after they moved to Arizona, was taken with the deliberate purpose of returning to the site. Going to the source of their misery seemed the only way to subdue it, and they needed to subdue it. Once it had seemed the only escape from the pain was to leave that place, to go as far away as possible. They did that promptly, within months, and to no avail. Slowly it began to seem necessary to return, to face the past squarely, and stare it down. It was ruining them, eating out their insides, making Clare weep in bed and Paul startle at things too small. It had to stop.

It seemed an act of self-preservation, taking that trip — critical and urgent — but it was no cure. It came clear then that no matter where they were, there was no escape. In Minnesota, at the lake, they were where they lost their son, and he wasn't there. In Arizona, they were away from where he died and still, he wasn't there. It was his absence they needed to change and that was the one unchangeable thing.

Jeanine was six. They went by car. They were at the lake one week, which included the Fourth of July holiday.

The old tires were still slung over the support posts of the dock as bumpers for the boat, but the boat was covered with the canvas tarp the whole time they were there. They didn't take it out. The weather was warm and stormless. Jeanine wore a little Snoopy life preserver every moment she was outside. By the end of the week, she had tan lines where the vest crossed her shoulders. "It's no different from wearing a seat belt while riding in a car," Clare told Paul.

The strategy for getting through the week was not to talk. Everyone knew this without anyone saying so. No mention of the accident. No mention of Michael. Just a healthy dose of good times, please, everyone. The eternal life preserver violated this code. Clare could see this, but it couldn't be helped. She needed it, like her father needed the silence. They'd have to accommodate each other.

They did. Jeanine wore her vest and Clare confined herself to whispers, to Paul, in the nighttime darkness of the back bedroom, the one that had once been purple, and just once, on the beach, under the glow of Roman candles, to a stolen glance at her father's uplifted face.

The Roman candles made a sound like hot embers falling into water as they shot their reds and greens and whites into the night sky. Beyond the fireworks, there were stars that night. Millions and millions of stars.

Clare remembered her father, one July Fourth when she was eight or nine, setting a bottle rocket in a piece of pipe, lighting it, and diving to the ground as it shot, too quick, directly for his head. It happened so fast, Clare couldn't be sure afterwards it had happened at all. But her throat was clinched shut and her father's knees were green with grass stains and, up in the sky, there was a burst of silver. These things seemed convincing evidence that her father had almost lost something essential just then. An eye, a limb, his life. Almost.

July Fourth, the summer he died, Michael had a sparkler. He'd just learned to write his name, and he was waving the sparkler like a glittering pencil, forming the letters of his name out of light. Clare's father had shown him how to do it. It infuriated him that one letter disappeared before he could get the next written. He wanted his whole name written across the night at once: Michael.

It may have been that name her father was searching the sky for that July Fourth they made their visit, his face lifted as if in prayer. Clare was sure, when he felt her watching and met her eyes momentarily, that whatever thought he'd retrieved from the darkness, it was one very near her own. Michael.

But no words. No words all week. They were all happy. The happiest week of their lives. Smiles and laughter. Happiness like fog. Like a sedative. Happiness like water in their lungs.

She and Paul and Jeanine went back to Arizona. At night, every night, Paul held her. "He was five and blond and blue-eyed," he would begin. "He was our son. His name is Michael." And he'd tell her one of the stories. Michael when he got his hamster. Michael screaming on the Ferris Wheel. Michael about to feed Jeanine raisins when she was four days old.

Clare loved Paul then like she'd never loved him before.

He knew this one thing that was everything about her: Michael was gone from this earth and she couldn't bear to have him taken from her heart besides.

17

The auditions for *One Hundred Steps Toward the Future* are the last Saturday in May. Clare arrives early, out of nervousness and the need to avoid Jeanine's nervousness. Jeanine was flitting around last night, clearing her throat and singing a jumbled mix of phrases from one song, then another, undecided at the last minute on her audition number. Clare tried to help, but Jeanine found a reason to reject every piece of advice she offered.

Paul was no help at all. He had discovered this week that one of the loan units under his management had not been processing their charge-offs according to plan, so it looked as though they would miss forecast this quarter. And he had been using temporary secretarial help all week. His secretary resigned with three days' notice, leaving a trail of mistakes that just kept presenting its effects day after day. He spent the evening sacked out on the couch, mumbling such tepid antidotes as, "They're both great, Jeanine. You can't go wrong. Any song, you'll do fine." There wasn't enough adhesive to anything he said to give Jeanine even the opportunity for a counter-argument.

She saved these for Clare. The two of them made a complete circle, propelled by Jeanine's Yes But's, arriving right back at Clare's original suggestion, that Jeanine sing the piece she'd intended to all along. Combined with her own anxieties about the auditions, it all unsettled Clare so much that her goal this morning was to get out of the house early, alone, before Jeanine could ask for a ride. It would be silly for Jeanine to come this early anyway.

Paul can drop her off on his way. He's playing business prospect golf today with the bank president and two representatives of a Phoenix dairy company. Or she could come along later on her bicycle. For now, Clare wants this time to think her own thoughts. It's the only thing that will settle the confusion in her head.

Sitting in the auditorium of the community college, before the lights are on, her thoughts run a frantic course from reassurances to plots to get herself out of this. She thinks of Paul this morning, shaving, telling her it would be fine, she'd be fine, everything would be fine. The words came out in a garble, his face pulled taut against the blade like it was. Maybe he picked these bland, calming words because anything more alarming would have caused his jaw to jump. He would have been delayed, calming her after all and sticking dampened scraps of Kleenex to the cuts on his face. It would have been most time efficient to just pacify her right off. On to coffee, the newspaper, and tee time. She's wishing him double bogies before long: how dare he rush her through her hour of need?

She doesn't think kindly of Nate this morning either. Flattering her into taking on this job. And she doesn't think kindly of herself. Being suckered into this. Naive and self-important. Look what it's gotten her. In an hour,

this place will be filled with people, all with their expectations, and it will be her job to make them happy, full of
community spirit and on cue. It'll be fine? She'll be fine?
Everything will be fine? How could he be so simple?

She's sitting about two-thirds back in the center section, three seats in from the aisle, mentally composing her
apologetic resignation, when she sees Nate come in the
side door near the stage. There are four steps there coming
up to the aisle. He takes them in two strides, hands in the
back pockets of his jeans, then stops and looks into the
dim auditorium. "Hey," he says, surprised. "Clare."

He comes up the incline of the aisle, his strides long
and easy, the walk of a man with no ambivalence. There
are no superfluous movements.

He sits down. Not the aisle seat, but the one by Clare.
She sees now as he does it that she's left him that choice.
Where he sits surprises her less than the realization she's
set it up. She's left two empty seats and put her purse and
cassette player on the opposite side of her.

He smiles. Another reason she should be out of here. It's
risky business letting her heart leap around like this. In her
heart, there are superfluous movements. It's dangerous feeling fifteen when you're not, when there's a big difference
between fifteen and what you are. At fifteen you can afford
to be frivolous. At forty, you're twenty-five years into other
things. You have a lot to preserve and these things take
preserving. Clare knows it. At forty, you've had time to see
this. One day your husband suddenly becomes patronizing
and you're called upon to become forgiving. It's not so
solid as you once thought. In fact, it's fragile, all of it.

"What the hell are we doing here?" Nate whispers, close, like a confidence. So — now he's her pal.

Clare's careful with her mouth. She'll allow no smiles, not even a hint of one. She feels him watching her, though she picks something other than him to look at, and she remembers his saying, about this mouth that feels like an independent, living creature, that it was beautiful. "You tell me," she says. She looks at his face just a moment, then at his arms. The sleeves of his T-shirt are rolled up to the shoulder, and the way he's sitting is like a pose, with his arms folded across his chest, his biceps standing out, flexed.

"Because we're good. We're the best and they know it." He says this with conviction that shows a lot of teeth.

"Yeah. Right." She looks at him now, really looks. He doesn't let her eyes go easily. She feels it all over, like sunburn. This man. This show. She gets up then, with a stamp of her feet, takes her purse and the cassette player. "I'm going," she says. "This isn't for me."

He stands up too, turns and puts his hands to her shoulders. "Oh, no. Sit down now." He puts a little pressure to her shoulders. His arms are muscular still, outstretched like this. "Clare."

She faces him, the purse and player to her chest.

He opens his eyes wide. His voice has such a range, and now he picks a deep, whispered tone, with some kind of urgent intimacy in it. "You're going to leave me in the lurch? Clare?" He watches her a moment, then takes his hands and finally his eyes away, giving up or confident now she'll stay. He sits down.

After a moment, so does she. The purse slides to the floor. She just lets it go. The cassette player rests like a weight in her lap.

Nate slouches down in his seat, his knees reaching to press against the seat in front. He turns his head toward her, not lifting it from where it rests against the back of his chair. "I'll be awful without you," he says.

Clare looks at him. He's wearing a stricken look. "I might be awful, period," she says.

"You'll be great," he says.

Lights come on and Ty Greggory moves across the stage, slowly. He waves at them. Clare watches Nate's knees come down as he slides upright and puts his feet on the ground. "We're the best," he says again.

He keeps saying it throughout the day. When Clare comes around from backstage after listening to Jeanine's audition, wondering if she's been objective, Nate's there to tell her they're the best. It's what he means by the thumbs up he gives her as he's demonstrating a dance step to a group on the stage. And while they watch the final cut, which includes Jeanine, Maureen Connolly, and Mrs. Daley, run through lines from the Building City Hall scene, he says it again, scrunched down in their seats, like this morning. "We're the best." And his smile.

Clare knows he's perfectly aware of the power of that smile. He knows exactly when to give it, when to take it away, in order to make women respond in some perfectly predictable way. Well, not Clare. The thing he doesn't know about older women is that they're smarter than he is.

❦

At six o'clock, Jeanine and Clare get into the car and head home. "Is this a pioneer woman of Mirage, Arizona, I'm driving home?" Clare asks.

"Townsfolk, that's me. 'Where is that Tommy Mayer?'"

"You say that?"

"In the scene we read through." She draws one leg up under her on the seat, with more bounce and flounce than is usually her way.

"I'm glad you got a part. You'll have fun. Singing and dancing—what could be more you?"

Jeanine's taken a hairbrush from her purse. She flips down the sun visor, where there's a mirror, and brushes through her hair. She snaps her wrist just as she gets to the end of each long stroke. "That choreographer is gorgeous. Why aren't I taking dance from him?"

Clare recovers quickly. "That's why. Jeffrey would be furious." Clare gives Jeanine a smile that's as wicked as she can manage with the adrenaline pumping through her.

"Well, he can show me all the moves he wants," Jeanine says dreamily, lying back against the seat. She closes her eyes. Her hair is spread out around her shoulders, black and wavy. She looks like Sleeping Beauty just before the Prince's kiss.

Jeanine turns her head and opens her eyes. "You were great," she tells Clare.

This surprise is more pleasant. Clare smiles, in a way she thinks of as motherly. "I was?"

"Yes," Jeanine says, matter-of-factly. "I was watching the ones just ahead of me. You were very professional. And sincere."

"Thank you. That's just how I'd want to be."

"Well, you were."

After a moment, Clare says again, "Thanks, Jeanine. Really, it means more to me to hear that from you than from anyone else there."

"Well, there were people saying other stuff."

Clare feels the bottom loosening, ready to fall out. "What?"

"Well, just something I heard. Gossipers, you know. That Mrs. Daley, for one."

"What did they say?"

"Stuff about you picking your own daughter. That it wasn't fair. I set them straight, though."

"Oh you did?" Clare tightens her grip on the wheel, then realizes she has and relaxes it.

"I told them you were completely partial."

"Partial."

"Uh-huh."

"Did they know it was my daughter they were talking to?"

"I don't know. That's funny, I guess I thought they did, but maybe not."

"So you told them I was partial."

"Yeah."

"Didn't you mean impartial? Like fair? I wouldn't pick my own daughter unless she was good?"

"Right."

"That's impartial."

"Oh."

Their corner-eye glances meet and Jeanine giggles

about halfway, then folds her lips in against it, waiting. Clare looks at her again, sort of parental and severe, a look that's never worked with Jeanine, then laughs herself.

It's a good thing, a laugh like that with your daughter. When you're forty and fifteen, and so is she, and there are men like this around and you're partial, well, it's the only thing, maybe.

They laugh and then laugh again at new private thoughts. Some of her thoughts are funny and some are not, but Clare laughs at them all. It's such a pleasure not to have to sort.

❦

Paul phones from the clubhouse of the Desert Mirage Country Club soon after Clare and Jeanine arrive home. He's had twenty-seven holes of golf and two hours of beer with the dairy company folks, courting an equipment leasing agreement that's been prominent on the bank's prospect list for months. "How were auditions?" he asks. The word for his voice is *weary*.

Clare tells him they were fine. Everything went fine. She startles herself with this brevity. Almost apologetically she adds, "Jeanine is a townsfolk."

"That's great. That's really great."

"She's happy."

"Clare, they've invited us to dinner and I think I could sew this thing up, given another couple hours. Them, their wives, us."

"Oh, Paul. I'm so tired."

"I know. Me, too. Now they want to buy a spiral ice cream machine. Dinner, quick, then home to bed. Just two hours of charming."

"I don't think I have two hours of charming."

"Clare, you don't even have to try."

"Where's dinner?"

"Alfredo's. I'll leave now, come home and change. Can we say thirty minutes?"

"All right, Paul. Thirty minutes."

18

Alfredo's is an odd mix of elegance and ruggedness. Log walls and a bare wood floor, candles stuck into empty wine bottles, but white linen tablecloths and six pieces of silverware per setting. The pasta is homemade and the Chianti rich and one of the wives, Melody, is a beautiful woman.

Her dress is black. It may be that color, or perhaps the soulful look in her face, but from the first glance, Melody strikes Clare as a wounded woman, a woman in mourning, though what would someone so young have to mourn? Melody's husband is at her elbow and he looks into her eyes when he talks to her. He smiles. What could there possibly be to mourn? It's a mistake, a complete misperception, Clare's sure now.

But that face. That dress. It cuts a sharp diagonal across her throat and chest, leaving her right shoulder bare and strangely vulnerable in the candlelight. Her hair is long and nearly as dark as the dress. When it moves to cover the bare shoulder, Clare breathes easier. Something is restored, and then Melody tilts her head again and it's reopened.

It's the same way with the pendant. Melody wears a silver chain with a diamond on it that dips in and out of the upper edge of her dress as she moves. Twice Clare's seen Paul watching it, the in and out, the peek-a-boo. He's sitting just across from her, from Melody, and he's no longer weary. It's his profile Clare can see, sitting next to him as she is. She knows him so well she can see when his eyes are lowered and when they're not, almost without looking, with looking only a little. She knows his breathing, the rate of his speech, the height and width of his gestures, and now, with Melody across from him, they are all accentuated.

Clare knows. There is no subtlety too minute for the senses of a woman who's been well loved. If the men who love these women knew this, well, it's just kinder that they not know. Really, who could stand to know he'd been stripped this bare?

It seems ungenerous even to watch these disclosures Paul's making. Like reading his mail or paging through his sketchbooks. Two times she's looked at him and Clare won't look again.

It's harder to avoid the pendant, in and out, catching light, a tiny star. Clare wishes for the chain to break, for the diamond to fall into Melody's plate of fettuccine, for her to eat it and choke. But then Clare imagines Paul, his arms wrapped around Melody from behind, his good and gentle hands, warm to the fingertips, fisted and pressed into the deep black stomach of her dress. Then the fine china and silver and the candles in their bottles cleared away and Melody, beautiful and still, laid out on the white linen cloth where no wine's been spilled, and Paul sharing breath with her, a girl with a star in her throat, and Clare sees it's better just to finish the meal, to go home and go to bed, shut their door against this savagery and reach for each other in the loving dark.

They do. They do just that. At first Clare is watchful, wanting to know if she's herself or an impersonator in Paul's arms, but soon she lets down the vigil, forgetting who it was she might have been, probably unable, if asked at just that moment, even to say her own name. And then Clare asks Paul for something he's not done for a while, how long was not so apparent to her until just now, and now it's urgent. He hesitates — it's so unexpected to-night — but there are these few sure things we can know about each other, and this is one Paul knows about Clare.

"He was blond and blue-eyed and five years old," he begins, like the first sounds after emerging from under water. Like a familiar refrain in a song so long you can only pretend to know the words. He tells her about Michael riding the carousel in the amusement park. His fourth birthday. He was wearing a paper crown with the number four on it in glitter. He rode a purple horse because someone else got to the black one first. He held the brass post with one hand and nearly stood in the stir-rups on the up end of the horse's motion. Clare rode beside him on a horse of her own and thought how nice it was to have this moment to be a little girl on a carousel with her own son.

It was like a *Candid Camera* sequence she'd seen on TV once. A grandfather and his grandson were at the park when they came upon a yellow cardboard box labeled

"Fountain of Youth." The grandfather decided to go inside. A moment later a boy walked out, dressed just like grandpa, and asked the grandson to play with him. There was a moment of hesitation — disbelief — but then the grandson went with him, an act that delighted Clare. My God, what faith.

There was a certain faith on the carousel that day, too. Clare could see her son moving in opposite ups and downs beside her, and on each revolution, they could both see Paul, standing at the gate with Jeanine in his arms. Carousels have always given him motion sickness. When a gust of wind took Michael's crown, they watched Paul chasing it, balancing Jeanine on one hip, and laughed. By the time they came around again, Paul was back at the gate, holding the crown, smashed, in his hand. Clare saw Michael's face reflected off the mirrored center post the horses circled: disbelief. The carousel stopped then and Paul told them about the boy who ran up and stamped on the crown just before Paul reached to pick it up.

"That was an incredibly mean thing to do," Clare says now, in the bed, the water below them moving in ripples. "Have you ever heard of anything meaner?"

"It was pretty mean all right. Right up there in meanery." He runs his stubbly chin over her bare shoulder, then kisses it.

"Where do you think that kid is now?"

"The crown stamper?"

"Yes."

"Beats me. Probably on the carousel. Probably elbowing out good little boys and girls to get the black horse."

Clare laughs, small, through her nose. "Before the crown business, while we were riding, I was thinking of putting Michael on for another ride so he could have the black horse. I wish we'd done that."

Paul kisses her hair, twice.

"You liked Melody," Clare says then.

It's Paul's turn to laugh, but gentle, careful. "I should hope so," he says.

"What?" Clare pulls away from him, sets the bed sloshing.

"She's a beautiful woman. What do you take me for, a rock? A fern? A protist?"

This is straight from the biology review Jeanine was studying this week in preparation for finals. They had a laugh over the arrangement of the textbook, building up slowly to the final chapter: Human Reproduction. Very funny. However, Clare refuses to be pulled off course.

"You know what I mean." Her best effort at wifely. What a thing to attempt.

"Do you know what I mean?"

Paul will just never cooperate in a good argument. He can't do indignant and enraged. He goes for the tender underside. "What?" Clare ventures.

"Clare, there are beautiful women out there. Everywhere." He walks his fingers quick and ticklish over her belly. "Is this news?"

"No. Of course not."

"Well then?"

"Well then you're supposed to exercise restraint."

Paul laughs again, not so careful this time. More like

glee. "Clare, I *do*. Have you ever known me not to?"

"I don't suppose I'd be the first to know a thing like that."

Paul takes her up in a bear hug, even the growl. Then a kiss, very human. "Wouldn't you?" he says.

Well.

Paul settles into the pillow, takes her in his arms, ready for sleep. He lets the bed get still before he says, "There are lots of good-looking men out there, too, Clare."

"Yes, I know." She thinks of Nate on the stage this afternoon — his energy, his smile — and she's a little annoyed at him for coming into her thoughts at such an inopportune time.

Paul pulls his arm around from her shoulder, looks at her. "You knew this?"

"I'm not a protist."

"I know. That's what worries me."

"Don't worry," she says. "Restraint."

"Is that all? Restraint?"

"What else?"

"It just sounds so much like abstinence."

"Oh?"

"Abstinence didn't work."

"I have a fifteen-year-old daughter. I don't want to hear this."

"The facts."

"Anyway, it did. It worked. I abstained from everyone but you."

"Were there that many?"

"I'm too tired, Paul. Good night."

"Good night."

Shift and settle again. The waves.

"Clare? Do you still believe in fidelity?"

Hesitation is more telling than words after questions like this. Clare's already hesitated, just thinking of it. Fidelity. It's a lot to ask of anyone. But "Yes," she says, sleepily. It's midnight and feels like three A.M.

"Me too."

"Over and over," she adds. A simple yes seems so naked.

"Fidelity over and over?"

"Belief over and over."

"Good. Okay. Good night."

"Good night, Paul."

19

It's nine o'clock before Clare and Paul get out of bed the next morning. Nine o'clock before they wake up. The hour is so startling to the little crack of eye she's opened toward the clock that Clare throws back the covers and sits up with a suddenness that shows no regard for the courtesy co-occupants of a waterbed must show each other.

"What?" Paul gasps, his arms instinctively encircling his head.

"It's nine o'clock."

"That's an emergency?" He turns back into the pillow.

"We haven't slept this late forever," Clare says, somehow breathless. She'd be hard-pressed to say how long. Factually. Truthfully, the morning she's remembering probably began somewhere nearer to six o'clock, but waking suddenly and alarmed like this reminds her of the first time Michael slept all night. Clare was so accustomed to a two A.M. feeding that she was convinced before she was even fully awake that Michael must be dead in his crib, suffocated or starved. It's that panic that's back this morning.

"Thanks for that up-to-the-minute report," Paul says into the pillow. Then he turns and reaches for her, wanting his early morning embrace, daily as coffee.

But it's no longer early and Clare's already got one leg out of bed, and now, besides, she's remembered her dream. My God. Small wonder there's panic. Jeffrey. Jeffrey on a white linen tablecloth with a diamond in his navel. Good, good God. It was abstinence and fidelity and such things she was thinking of when she went to sleep. That and what had Jeanine and Jeffrey done last night to celebrate Jeanine's part in the show, and then she dreamed of Jeffrey. Jeffrey wearing a crown and nothing else but the diamond. He—good God.

She pulls away from Paul and away from the bed like it's a madhouse and he's another phantom waiting to bite her neck. That's what he'd done in the dream. Jeffrey. Bitten her neck.

"Oh, no. Oh, no, come back here," Paul says, holding tight to her hand. He tugs on it playfully, rolls over and wraps his other arm around her thigh. She feels his stubbly chin against her back as she tries to pull away. He insists. So does she. It's a sweet, gentle struggle and a sweet, gentle nip he gives her bottom with his teeth.

And now there's nothing else to do. There's nothing else for Clare to do but collapse on the bed with her laughter and this man of hers. It's a crazy life. Your daughter's boyfriend biting your neck and your husband biting your butt. A crazy, crazy life.

❧

"What did you and Jeffrey do last night?" Clare asks Jeanine in the kitchen.

"Last night," Jeanine says, as if she's struggling to remember. She's peeling an orange over the sink. "Last night? Well, you're just going to have to get up earlier. You can't expect me to remember that far back." Her voice has a parental tone that stops Clare for a moment.

"What does that mean?"

"Staying in bed all morning. Shame on you."

Clare looks over at Paul, sitting at the table. He's reading the newspaper, unaware that their parental mystique is evaporating moment by moment.

"It was a long day yesterday. We slept in," Clare says, feeling childlike and found out.

"Yeah. Right." Jeanine pops an orange section into her mouth, then smiles, lips closed. She chews, swallows. "Your . . . dreams? . . . must have been pretty funny. Do you know you were laughing right out loud?" It's no smile. It's a smirk.

Clare feels her own mouth standing open and fixes that. She wants to paddle Jeanine's behind, though this is something she's never done so deliberately, never more than an impatient swat, but maybe now's the time. And Paul—he's still reading. Can't he see there's an emergency here? He should be sending Jeanine to her room. Washing her mouth out with soap. Another thing they've never done. But he's reading the sports and then suddenly it's too late for these measures. Instead, what Clare wants now is to hold Jeanine, rock her in the bentwood rocker, tell her stories about magical, undying things: princesses and singing dolphins and falling stars. But the bentwood rocker's gone to the Salvation Army and this daughter of theirs

117

is . . . well, she's someone new. She was five and then she was ten and now she's fifteen and she thinks she knows about laughter in her parents' bedroom. She's practically a stranger. No wonder Clare feels so exposed. The only decency is this: Jeanine is wrong. She'd never guess. The things Clare had laughed at? Jeanine is too young to guess.

20

Sunday afternoon, Clare goes to the garage and takes out the eighteen by twenty-four inch piece of plywood Paul uses every Christmas to level their tree. She supposes she'll regret it in December, but right now it's just what she needs for the photo collage she's making to give to her parents.

She takes the plywood into the yard and begins sanding it, which brings out a wonderful wood smell but also makes her sneeze. This is the way the basement used to smell when she was a child, those weekend afternoons her father would spend in his workshop, building the doll cradle for her or, another time, stilts for Sam.

The workshop of the old two-story house in town was really just a workbench against one wall of the laundry room. It had a fluorescent light fixture overhead that rattled whenever the clothes dryer was running and no matter how recently it had been swept, there was always a film of sawdust on the floor. It was something her mother complained about, said she could feel sawdust in the sheets just from washing them in the same room.

Once Clare had broken out in a rash that covered her body just like a shirt and a pair of shorts, starting and stopping where the clothes did, and her mother said it was from wearing clothes with sawdust in them and that was when her father built the wall. A ten-foot partition of two-by-fours and sheetrock that never got finished beyond that point and that separated Sam's dart board from the piece of tape on the floor that he stood behind to throw the darts.

Both parts of the room became too small to be functional. You hit your elbows on the wall whether you were operating the Skilsaw or transferring wet clothes from washer to dryer. Peace was a senseless commodity in their house, strange and twisted. Sam was already old enough then to recognize that, to know he should take the dart board somewhere else and keep his mouth shut. Clare was young enough to be surprised when she took a pinch on the arm as Sam passed her, hard in the face, his pockets stuffed with green- and red-feathered darts.

But the smell of sanded wood is still pleasant to Clare. There is a certain contentment in stroking her hand over the surface of the board and having her fingers turn white, a little gritty. Maybe she is like her father this way, though it's startling to think of. It's been some time since she's considered being like her father in any way.

There are four black circles stained into the wood where spilled water collected one year under the legs of the Christmas tree stand. Clare rubs at them, but without much success. Probably it won't matter. They'll be covered anyway. She envisions this board completely covered with pictures from the fifty years of her parents' marriage. She sands a little more, then runs her hand across each of the four stains and smiles at what she sees. Four shadows, hidden but permanent behind the Kodak glossies: Paul, Jeanine, herself. And Michael.

❦

Sunday evening, Clare has the board laid out in the middle of the family room floor. She has the wedding picture of her parents positioned at the center of the board and a few snapshots scattered around it. She is surrounded by her own photo albums, the large padded envelope full of old pictures her Aunt Bernice sent, and Jeanine's notes for her biology final, from which Clare's quizzing her. Jeanine is sprawled on the couch, her legs dangling over its back and her hands in close proximity to a bowl of popcorn. Paul is outside racing the quick Arizona sunset, trying with hooks and plastic-coated wire to persuade a bougainvillea to climb the wall. The light will be gone soon. The water in the pool has already taken on the opaqueness it has in darkness.

"What's the function of the umbilical cord?" Clare reads from Jeanine's notes.

"The transfer of nourishment and oxygen from mother to child via the mother's blood," Jeanine recites over a mouthful of popcorn. She licks her buttery fingers, then wipes them across her pants. She swings her legs off the back of the couch and sits up. "I've got this stuff, Mom. Really. We had it all in sixth grade anyway."

"How could you have?" Clare asks. Her eyes fall on the diagrams of male and female anatomy.

"Well, practically. It's that way with everything. Math. English. There's only so much to teach and all those teachers. All those days of school. Mostly they teach the same stuff over again and just throw in a little bit new each year. You always start with number lines and nouns. It never gets interesting until at least January."

"Oh," Clare says, unable at the moment to think of any better response to her daughter's theories on education.

Jeanine stands up and a few pieces of popcorn fall out of her lap onto the floor. She picks them up and eats them. "All's they told us new was about birth control."

So. In January of their sophomore year, this was the new thing kids were ready for: birth control. "That's a pretty important thing to know, isn't it?" Clare says.

Jeanine shrugs. A photograph on the floor catches her eye. She bends over and picks it up. "Is this you?" she asks. "Whose horse?"

Clare takes the picture and tries to place it. Its of her. She's nine or ten years old. It was taken at the lake cabin, that summer she had the short pixie haircut and hated herself for three months while it grew out. She's on a horse. That would be the Mattinglys'. "It *is* me," Clare tells Jeanine. Jeanine sits down on the floor, crosses her legs. "Our next-door neighbors at the lake cabin had horses. Claudia was my age. Well, a year older actually. She liked to boss me and tell me shocking things."

Jeanine smiles, recrosses her legs. "What shocking things?" she asks.

"Ghost stories mostly, I think. That's what I remember. And something about badgers coming up from the woods and into the cabins at night. That they'd chew their way right through the walls. I was afraid of that for two months at least, until your grandpa told me he was painting the cabin with a special indestructible paint that couldn't be chewed through. I suppose the cabin just needed paint anyway, but it seemed very heroic at the time."

"I can't wait until we go for the anniversary," Jeanine says. "I can't remember that place at all."

Clare picks up the photo again, takes a closer look. "I wonder if there's one here of Claudia." She takes Bernice's envelope and dumps it all out on the floor. She picks up the pictures one by one, lays them aside, and Jeanine picks them up next.

"Here's Michael," Jeanine says, "dressed up like a cowboy."

"That's Sam," Clare tells her.

"He looks just like Michael."

Clare takes the picture, a glossy black-and-white snapshot with scalloped edges. Sam in a cowboy hat and boots and a vest made from a brown paper bag, fringes cut unevenly all along the lower edge. There's a star crayoned at his chest. He's smiling, missing teeth in front. There is a resemblance to Michael. It's something Clare's never stopped to consider before: her son looking like her brother. But it's definitely Sam in the picture. The photo is old and Michael never lost his teeth. "It's Sam," Clare tells Jeanine again.

"Is he coming for the anniversary?" Jeanine asks.

"I don't know for sure. I hope so."

"I think I've seen him about twice ever."

"Don't be silly. You've seen him more than that." Clare feels the latest installment of the Family Deprivation lament coming on. It's a guilt trip Jeanine throws at her now and then, one that always works. Her parents' annual invitation to visit at the lake cabin is always good for a round. *You never take me to visit my grandparents and you won't let me go alone.* "You saw him when Stace got married. You saw the whole family."

Stace is Sam's oldest son. He married a woman from Venezuela four years ago and they all went to Sam's place in North Carolina for the wedding. "You had bronchitis, remember?" It was true. You could hear Jeanine coughing all through the videotape of the ceremony. "Your grandma bought you that peach satin dress and you got grease on it helping decorate the car. That was before pictures and you had to stand with that part of your dress behind my skirt so it wouldn't show."

"That part I remember. You about fried me."

Clare truly feels that, in her entire career as a mother, these moments of wickedness have been few, but they seem to be the few Jeanine recalls. Recalls and reminds Clare of, like she's calling in a debt.

"Here," Clare says, paging through one of her albums. "Look." She's found the picture of Jeanine and Paul and herself posing for a family portrait the day of the wedding. "See there? How you're cozied up beside me? That's so the grease wouldn't show."

Jeanine looks. "My nose was red," she says.

"The bronchitis." Clare turns the page. "Here you are dancing with your Uncle Sam, whom you never see because your parents are so mean."

Jeanine opens her eyes wide and twists her mouth to one side.

Clare pulls back the cellophane on the page and peels the photo out of the album. "I'll put this one on the collage. Documentation."

"It was a pretty dress," Jeanine says. Her tone is conciliatory, as if she's making some large admission.

Clare looks at the picture again. Jeanine, arms raised high to circle Sam's neck, satin bodice pulled snug across her small, just begun breasts. A sash at her waist, then the skirt flared wide and fluid over her thin, stockinged legs. Even in this still-life view, the legs are graceful, dance their natural medium. One of Sam's thick hands cups Jeanine's as if it's a little bird. He's solidly into middle age, has unbuttoned the top button of his shirt, though he's left his tie in place so it's hardly noticeable. The look he gives Jeanine is paternal. All three of his children are sons.

"Who are these kids?" Jeanine asks, another picture in her hand.

"Oh," Clare says, something between surprise and a nostalgic sigh. She takes the photo. "We used to put on these plays, we kids at the lake. This is Claudia," Clare says, pointing. "Her two sisters, me, some kids from up the hill. I can't even remember their names. This one was cross-eyed."

Clare takes one more look, then hands the picture back to Jeanine. "Claudia was always the director. She was the oldest, ten or eleven, and I told you, she liked to boss. I was nine that summer. We'd dress up like that, whatever we could find in the closets. We'd make programs and everything and we'd charge our parents to come and see it. Really. We sold tickets." Clare flips idly through pictures, not really looking at them now. Then she sits back, leaning on her hands. "Once we sang this song. *Catch a falling star and put it in your pocket. Save it for a rainy day.* Perry Como or someone. Anyway, Claudia got me believing you could really do it. Catch a star and keep it. We'd sit out on the dock in the dark as long as our mothers would let us, dangling our feet in the water and waiting for the chance. It was wonderful. Just watching the sky. Out of all those stars, there'd have to be one. Sometime. We had a glass jar, the kind your grandma used to can tomatoes. We were going to catch it in that. We took turns holding it. I just remember the waiting and how exciting it was. Wanting the star to come and wanting it to come while I had the jar. I could even imagine it in my pocket, how it would make my leg warm and how I'd have to keep it a secret and how I'd take it out some starless night, like in the song. I wondered if I'd be able to have it back once I took it out."

Clare catches sight of Jeanine and her intent listening and realizes how she's gone on. She gathers some pictures quickly into a pile. "Well, enough on that. You'd better get your studying done and go to bed. Should I ask you some more on this?" She picks up the biology notes.

Jeanine leans back on her hands and stretches out her legs. "Nah. I got it."

"What about the birth control?"

"Got it straight."

"You know, Jeanine . . ."

"I know, Mother." Her look runs a direct course to Clare's face. She pushes herself up onto her knees, then stands.

It's always *Mother*, Clare's noticed, *Mother* when Clare tries to talk to her about sex. "I mean, if you should ever . . ."

"Gotcha," Jeanine says, sharp and quick. She slaps at her bottom as if she's been sitting in sand or sawdust or cut grass. She gathers up the notes and folds the pages in half. She looks down at Clare, still sitting on the floor, surrounded by pictures. "I like thinking of you on that dock. Waiting for the star and all."

"I hadn't thought of that in years."

"Perry Como?"

"Before your time."

"How does the song go?"

Clare gets up, stretches at the waist, smiles. She thinks a minute, catches Jeanine's eyes and starts in softly, singing, "*Catch a falling star and put it in your pocket, save it for a rainy day. Catch a falling star and put it in your pocket, never let it fade away.* Something, something, I forget. *If love should come and tap you on the shoulder, one starless night.* Da-dum, da-dum, another line here. *You'll have a pocket full of starlight, pocket full of starlight.*"

Jeanine's joined her on the repeated line, and starts in without Clare, singing it over again. She forgets *never let it fade away*, so Clare puts it in and then hums the missing line. They're singing *pocket full of starlight* in harmony when Paul comes toward the patio door carrying a lighted flashlight. It's gotten dark. Jeanine's sharp breath makes

Clare look and she, too, sees the light moving toward them, and thinks the same thing: a star. Jeanine squeezes Clare's arm tight and they break into laughing as Paul comes in the door. "What," he says, taking in the two of them. He's dirty and sweaty and the bougainvillea's given him a struggle. One of the scratches on his arms is deep enough to be bleeding. "I'm funny?"

This brings on a fresh burst of laughter. Paul stares a moment, but very soon concedes the impossibility of making sense of this. He throws them one skeptical glance over his shoulder and leaves them to this women's work.

❧

Jeanine goes to bed and Clare piles the photo albums and pictures onto the board, carries it into the Singing Room and slides it under the piano. She picks up the picture of Sam in his cowboy costume and looks again for Michael in his face. Five years old is too young to lose teeth. Some do, but Jeanine was six when she lost her first one. Left it in a bite of carameled apple at the state fair, fished it out, carried it home in a paper napkin and put it under her pillow for the Tooth Fairy, who took it and left fifty cents.

Another time the Tooth Fairy had been less conscientious. Another parental lapse Jeanine could bring up when she needed one: the morning she came running from her bedroom with a fallen tooth in the palm of her hand and the news that the Tooth Fairy forgot to come. But Clare was quick. There's a small measure of redemption in quickness. She convinced Jeanine that the fairy probably didn't know the tooth was out, since it had happened so late in the day, that she should give her another chance. Please.

She wondered then: What do other parents do with all those sad, rootless teeth? After they take them from under the pillow, leave the quarters, what about those little cast-offs from their children's mouths? They can't possibly keep them — imagine finding them in a drawer. There's only one thing to do. Drop them into a wastebasket at least half full of Kleenex wads. They'll disappear like pearls dropped through clouds and you'll be able to believe what the children do — that the Tooth Fairy's taken them off and given them to a baby somewhere, waiting for his turn.

Clare thinks of sitting on the dock in the dark, the water and the air so equally black you can't see where one ends and the other begins. You feel it. You put your legs down until they're cold and then you know they're in water. If you sit very still, they grow numb with the cold and the hanging down and you have to tap your feet together under the water just to be sure they're still there.

That's what she and Claudia would do. They'd sit there on the dock, their feet in the water, waiting for a falling star. The jar would be there, in one of their laps, and all that hope and expectation. They would be watching the sky, waiting, and then there would come that numbness, that cold, encroaching fear that, underwater, just beyond what they could see or feel, something awful had happened. A shark, or a minnow, or something else, shapeless and mysterious, had stolen their feet away. It was a desperate, helpless dread that they savored for just a few moments. For just a few moments, they would let their hearts sink, they would feel themselves completely in the grip of that feeling, and then they would tap. They would tap their feet together — three times, that was the rule — and they would be whole again. Complete girls, all parts and senses intact, and lifting upward again into the sky, waiting for the star.

In White Bear Lake, Minnesota, there is a child who can see now with Michael's corneas. A little boy from St. Cloud was saved with his kidney. In drowning there is no disease, no trauma to the body if it's recovered quickly. Sometimes — especially from a cold Minnesota lake — it can even be revived by miracles of science. But not always. Sometimes not even by love and wanting. Jeremy, the child who was given Michael's heart, died after two years.

Clare gets up, goes to find Paul. Her throat is tight and her eyes blurred. She can't find him. He's not in the bedroom and doesn't answer when she calls his name. Then she goes to the patio door and sees him. He's on the diving board, poised, in his moment of meditation before the spring.

It's a sharp, taut love she feels for him just then and it leaps out of her with the tearing force of birth as she watches him dive. She feels it push a foot hard against her womb as Paul's propel him off the board, up into the dark to bend like a fish and begin his descent. Her tears come out with the love, slickening its passage.

Clare unbuttons her blouse, takes it off. She doesn't decide to, but just does this: takes off all her clothes. She opens the door and steps outside. As she walks to the diving board there's night air touching her like she's never been touched before, all her life. Her body is alive and there's more of it, more surfaces, more joints and bends, than she's known before.

She thinks of hitting the black water, of the cold, the numbness, the disappearing. She thinks of the weight of her heart and how it could hold her under, drown her, but she steps onto the board, sees that Paul is watching her, and feels his eyes move warm over her like the night air turned tepid. Paul doesn't say anything. He waits. He watches her. She raises her arms and feels her breasts tighten. Her feet grip the board and then push off. She dives, thinks for once she's kept her legs together, thinks how she's learned this finally, by cold and nakedness.

She doesn't surface until she's found her way to Paul, standing in the shallow end of the pool. She thinks she feels starlight glowing on her bare bottom as she swims, but tells herself this is silly. Starlight we see, not feel. She knows this, but still it feels that way. She thinks she hears something, too. Whispers, muted and echoing. There is some logical explanation for the sounds, too. The pool pump is running or Paul is moving, making ripples that only seem like singing.

Paul's arms make a circle she comes up into. Her face breaks through the water and he allows her one breath before he covers her mouth with his. His hands move down her back, neck to thigh, all those starlit parts of her, feeling like nothing else she can imagine.

"Clare," he says, his breath warm against her face. "You've forgotten your swimsuit."

"Yes, I know."

"You're swimming naked."

"Yes. So are you."

"No, I'm not."

"Yes, you are. Soon." She loosens the cord at the waist of Paul's swim trunks, then tugs until they are at his ankles. She tries to pull them away with her toes, but he won't lift his feet. She tickles, which makes him squirm, but he won't lift his feet. It's a game now. He kisses her, holds her, tickles her ribs for every stamp she gives his feet, but will not, won't lift his feet, so Clare pulls away, rounds her back, goes under and gets those trunks. Maybe he lets her; it's hard to be sure. Maybe he fears she'll drown, laughing underwater like that. She takes them, gets far enough away that he can't grab them, and then she flings them far and wide.

He watches them go, but it's Clare he comes after. It's a sweet pursuit that ends on a step at the opposite end of the pool. "I suppose you know. We're in a pool," Paul says.

"Yes, I know."

"You could get hurt doing a thing like this."

"You wouldn't let me."

He pulls her to him quickly then, holds her, holds her. She feels Paul and floating and Paul and water and Paul. Paul.

Later, Paul is standing in the yard with a towel wrapped around his waist, shaking the eucalyptus tree whose upper branch snagged his trunks when Clare sent them flying. Clare lies on the lounge chair, a towel damp around her, hair dripping. She watches the sky, and Paul. He shakes the tree and it sounds like a thousand wings in flight. The tree trembles and quivers, like a woman naked in water with a man, like her. All the branches move against the sky so that it looks as if it's the sky that's moving. All those stars, shaking and falling. Coming down, falling.

21

Clare is sending her last student for the day out the door when Sally Brandt arrives with fast food tacos. She called at noon and Clare invited her. Paul had business in Phoenix today and won't be home until late, and Jeanine is having dinner at Jeffrey's. Clare hands Sally a beer and they go out to the patio.

Sally's come straight from work. She takes the wide leather belt off her dress, rolls it up and lays it on the patio table. She kicks off her shoes, slides her panty hose down her legs and stuffs them into her purse. She sits down with her knees apart, hikes up her skirt so it hangs like a curtain between her legs, and sighs. "My back starts aching at four o'clock every day. Just like clockwork. If I feel my back aching, I don't even have to look at the time. It's between four and five." Sally works as a paralegal.

"You'd better start going in at seven and leaving at four then," Clare says. She cranks out the umbrella over the table.

Sally laughs and opens the Taco Bell bag. She spreads a napkin for each of them and puts the food on the table. "Jeanine done with school?"

"Tomorrow's the last day."

Sally's children are grown and she has a grandchild who has single-handedly filled all the display surfaces of her refrigerator with scribbled drawings of unrecognizable objects. His name is Seth and, Clare noticed when she last saw Sally's kitchen, he likes green and sharp, angular lines.

"How's the centennial book coming?" Clare asks between bites.

"Done. Just went to the printers. We had to allow a month for that. I'm still getting letters, though. People have the most amazing and the most boring stories. This one I got today was pretty good. I might have used it if it had come sooner. Someone named Hilda Perkins. Here. Listen to this." Sally sets down her taco and opens her purse. She takes several sheets of lined stationery from an envelope and reads Clare the entire letter.

The woman is eighty-six, living in a nursing home in Tucson, but she lived in Mirage for many years, until her husband died eighteen years ago (heart attack) and she moved to Tucson to be closer to her daughter (obstetric nurse).

The story is about the daughter, about her miraculous escape from death as a year-old baby. It seems the woman's husband (Cyril) was getting a late start to a doctor's appointment in Phoenix (didn't really want to go). He'd been fixing fences on their property (west edge of town), came in, cleaned up (dilly-dallied), and just left himself too little time. When he went out to the car (Ford), he was rushing in earnest. He left at some speed (bat out of hell), enough to raise dust in their gravel driveway (paved in '55).

Hilda noticed shortly after this that Rosemary, the year-old baby (in need of diaper change), was nowhere to be found. Hilda sent the older children searching and went herself to check the two most feared places the baby could be: the well and the outhouse. If she had fallen in either one, she could be drowned. One of the older boys (Stewart) actually had fallen down the hole in the outhouse once (rescued, clothes burned, shampooed with Hilex). But Rosemary wasn't found in either place. Hilda went to the phone and called her neighbors, Sherwood (tightwad) and Grace (saint), and the sheriff. And then she phoned the doctor's office in Phoenix to leave the message for Cyril to get (his ass) back home even faster than he'd left it.

Grace took care of comforting Hilda (whiskey) and the children (saltwater taffy). The sheriff was just getting his search party organized when Cyril called from Phoenix. He was bringing Rosemary home, in somewhat the same condition as Stewart after falling down the outhouse hole (that diaper). Cyril had found her when he arrived in Phoenix, standing on the running board on the passenger side of the car, clinging to the door handle, and almost asleep.

Apparently, she'd been standing on that running board when Cyril got in the car and drove off, and (wasn't it miraculous) she hung on all that time (thirty miles). She was returned to her mother safe and now has three children of her own, who all have children, too. It's the most miraculous thing that's ever happened to anyone in Hilda's family (twenty-one great-grandchildren in all).

"That's an amazing story," Clare says. "Can't you include it somehow?"

"How?"

"I don't know."

Sally goes back to her food and beer. "Actually, Stewart's story may have been better. Can you imagine?"

"Yes. God. It's too bad you can't put it in. About Rosemary."

"It doesn't have any historical significance though."

"It has human significance, Sally, don't you get it? It was extraordinary good fortune. Really, a miracle. You need to hear about one once in a while to keep believing in the possibility. You go too long without hearing about something extraordinary happening and, next thing, you've forgotten it can."

"Well, we did use the picture you liked. The one of all the children, in rows, dressed up. Remember?"

"Yeah. You found out their names?"

"No. We couldn't even find out why they were dressed up, posing."

"So why did you use it?"

"It seemed important to remember them. There was something significant enough about the day to deserve all those fine clothes and a photographer. The caption will just say that no one can remember why these children were assembled or any of their names."

"I like that."

"Yeah, I thought you would."

22

Jeanine decides on the last day of school that things are ending on a note a little too close to ordinary. "We're not graduating, we were too young for prom, it's like, turn in your books and so long. I want to have a party," she announces to Paul and Clare at dinner. "Tomorrow."

"That's coming right up," Paul notes.

"Not till afternoon. And nothing fancy. Swimming, burgers on the grill. You don't have to do anything."

"Where are these burgers, right now?" Clare asks.

"Well, just drive me to the store then. That's nothing. Probably you need to go anyway."

Clare raises her eyebrows. It's the called-for thing, even though Jeanine's right. They're out of a few necessities. Margarine. Kleenex. Dreyer's Pralines-n-Cream.

"You basically just want to rent the hall, then, do I get it?" Paul asks.

"What hall?" Jeanine says.

"You wouldn't want me to cook these burgers, would you?" Paul says.

"Oh, thanks, Dad. Yeah. Of course."

"It's a good idea," Clare says. "We can put the volley-ball net up in the pool if you want to. I'll make you some brownies. Just don't spread the word any further than your own friends, okay?"

Clare and Jeanine clear away the dishes and then head out to the store. They come back with eight sacks of groceries, twenty plastic squirt guns, several bags of small balloons, and a huge set of disguises: plastic noses, eyeglasses, red smacker lips, fuzzy mustaches, and face paints to draw on anything else not in the set. "This is going to be great," Jeanine says, silly in glasses and mustache.

Clare thinks she's right. She puts a pair of big red lips to her mouth and goes to the couch to give Paul a kiss. He gives her the google-eyes-crazy-person look, then takes the lips away with his own mouth, drops them onto the couch and kisses her real ones.

"You guys aren't going to act silly and stuff tomorrow, are you?" Jeanine says.

"Silly?" Paul says. "Like how?"

"Like that."

He checks himself over, head to foot, under each arm.

"Like that, like that, like that," Jeanine squeals, shaking her whole arm at him.

"Like this?" Paul says again, all innocence. Then he sobers, pulls his arms close to his sides and lowers his head. "No," he says quietly. "No, of course not."

"Good," Jeanine says, forcefully. "Good. Just remember you said so."

"I'll flip my burgers as inconspicuously as possible and leave by the side door," Paul says.

Jeanine has to double-check to see if he's teasing. His mouth turns up just slightly and she wraps her arms around his neck and squeezes hard. He's taken the big red lips into his hand and slips them quickly to his mouth and kisses Jeanine. She shrieks and slaps his arm, runs her feet quickly in place. "Like that. Like that," she says again, laughing.

But Paul's already hidden the lips and assumed his innocent bystander pose. Then he frowns, as if he's just arrived on the scene, sweeps the look over Clare, too, as if she and Jeanine are at some sorcery again, as if it may be dangerous here, unsafe for man or beast.

❦

By three o'clock the next day, the food is nearly ready and the bathtub is full of red and blue and yellow balloons filled with water: huge, mutant bath oil beads in technicolor. Jeanine has spent two hours stretching their tight, rolled-back openings over the faucet, turning on the tap just enough to fill the balloon, not so much as to send it spraying all over the bathroom, tying the wet, slippery necks closed, and laying them, gently, in the holding tank. There are, she announces wearily to Clare, one hundred and twenty. She holds her reddened fingers out for inspection and sympathy. Clare obliges.

Already Clare can envision colorful fragments of balloon being shredded in the lawn mower, clinging like surreal blossoms to bushes and trees, clogging the filtering system of the pool. The thought makes her feel old. It's a parent thought, a tired and forty thought. She's too young—she knows she is—for weariness like that. At fifteen, anticipating a night like this, she would have been thinking other things. Much different things. At fifteen, at Jeanine's age, she would have been thinking: Is my skin soft? More lotion? Does my hair smell nice? Would it feel nice, against a cheek? My breath? Lips chapped? Think of three never-fail questions for conversation voids. Him. His interests. Will he kiss me good night? Once or twice? If we get the chance, should I let him touch me? Why not? Why *not*?

Clare imagines those thoughts stirring around in Jeanine's head as she watches her walk upstairs. Time to primp and preen now. Time for all those thoughts; it's part of it. Clare takes tomatoes and onions from the refrigerator. No, fifteen was exhausting. All that agonizing. It's much easier now. Forty, tired, concerned with broken balloons, brownie frosting, burger fixings.

Clare rinses the tomatoes in the sink, lays them on the cutting board. What if word of this party has spread further than Jeanine's own friends? What if complete strangers show up when her back is turned? Parties could be that way. What if they arrive drunk? Would she even recognize crack? And what does one say upon discovering naked teenagers in one's bedroom? Would they listen or laugh if she tried to throw them out? And where, where is Paul? Why doesn't he get home here? Suppose he gets delayed. Held up. Unavoidably. Detained. A fine thing that would be. Sole responsibility. Brownies, burgers, *and* behavior. All of it. Fine. Oh, fine. Flip the burgers. Flip on the lights. Lights are good. Good help for sole responsibility. Would sophomores laugh at that? Twitter? They're juniors now. Older every minute. Older and smarter, more daring, more stupid. And Clare's standards, she rather suddenly realizes, are twenty-five years old. Twitter, twitter. Lights? Like that's going to make a difference?

And what do the parents of these young people expect of her? How dare you allow my daughter to untie her string bikini and be impregnated in your hedge! Where were your clubs and whistles?

The tomato she's holding under the faucet is overripe, and Clare's thumb breaks through its skin. The seedy red flesh bursts out, slippery in her hand, and the acidic juice stings her skin. She lets the tomato be washed down the garbage disposal and then she holds her hand under the cold water, lets it grow numb, lets herself be hypnotized by the sound and sight of the stream of water, its constancy. The water separates around her fingers, like a rope coming unbraided. Like tendons, twisting. She thinks of Paul's legs, muscles flexed, poised on the diving board, then underwater, wrapped around her. Those were the same muscles that were working under Nate's jeans the morning of the auditions, when she saw him on stage, dancing. The same muscles she, or Jeanine, would use to dance, to dive, to hold a dear someone near. Our bodies, so alike.

Clare comes up on her toes, standing in front of the sink. Her feet are bare, the bones delicate, toes descending in an even line. They're pretty, the way hands can be. The way neither often are. She comes up on her toes, feels the muscles in the back of her calves tighten. She pulls higher, until she can feel the flex in her thighs, and thinks of diving, legs together, straight. With form. She comes down from her toes, sets her feet in first position, second. These rote pieces of ballet we never forget if we've been taught them by someone who has let us into her heart. First. Second. Mrs. Bonet, up the hill, at the lake. She had the cross-eyed girl and the braid thick as a snake swinging against her back. Sophia: the cross-eyed girl. Grace. Grace was the thing Mrs. Bonet wished for all of them, six little girls, each summer, up the hill, grace. The thing that emerged like magic, that entered their hands and feet as they pressed them to the barre. A brass rail attached to Mrs. Bonet's wall, the length of the room. It looked cold and was always warm. Warm and smudged with a million fingerprints. Toeprints. Six girls, all graceful, every one. They drew it out of the barre and Mrs. Bonet's European voice, absorbed it into their skin, like strength, like pleasure.

Once, listening to Mrs. Bonet count in whispers and delicate tongue sounds, Clare thought of putting her mouth to that barre, letting it touch her lips hard and warm, fill her right at her center with that precious radiance, but she'd been afraid. Poison, electrocution, something awful. A mouth was too tender, too close to life, to put to a risk like that. She saw she'd have to seek the grace with more remote parts of herself. Extremities. Hands, feet. Calloused surfaces. *Plié. Demiplié.* A pulling stretch. Tension and connection. A brass rail to hold her. Mrs. Bonet saying first, second.

First. Second. Clare raises her arms to complete her legs' movements. Water runs down from her hand and drips off her bent elbow. The faucet's still running, making its sound, its metal neck cold, straight, polished.

Demiplié. Back straight, knees apart and bent, she sinks lower. *Plié*. Clare feels the stretch, the grace, and Paul's arm, from behind, laid solid between her breasts, his hand cupped over her shoulder. He's startled her, and her body sends out an emergency rush of adrenaline. He brings her up, her legs straighten, and she turns to him.

"It's about time," she says.

He reaches over and shuts off the faucet, then takes some chips from a bowl ready for the party. "How's it coming?"

"Set. You made me worry, though. I thought I'd have to handle this all alone. You're late."

"Small fires all day. The world's borderline crazy, Clare. I don't even know the rules anymore. I want a beer."

"Poor baby."

Paul takes a bottle from the refrigerator, opens it. "Are you prepared to handle booze, drugs, and sex tonight?" Clare asks.

Paul tips his head back, shuts his eyes as he drinks. He gives her such a look. "Oh, Clare. Tonight? Can't you behave this once?"

"Funny. You're funny. The party."

"Oh, right. The party. Water balloons and disguises."

"Right. But juniors." Clare's started with the onions, peeling and slicing. "I think you have to consider these things."

"Why?"

"To be prepared."

"It's not going to happen." Paul pulls out a stool from under the counter and sits.

"Not in our town, not in our neighborhood, not in our house?"

"Clare—" He runs his hand through his hair, leaves it standing on end, damp with sweat.

"It'll be up to you to throw them out. You're the man and I'm not strong enough."

Paul takes a look around the kitchen, another long swallow of the beer. "Is that what you were doing there when I came in? Working up the muscles?" He tries to hide his mouth in the beer bottle, but Clare can see he's laughing.

"You won't think it's so funny when Jeanine's in the bushes with her suit off."

Paul hooks his heels on the rungs of the stool. He puts a second hand on the beer bottle, as if it may slide away from him. "Why would she be?"

"Why do you think? S-E-X. Ever heard of it?"

Paul laughs now, but it's too bold a laugh, the kind doubts hide behind. "Once or twice. I liked it."

"Yeah, well," Clare says, as if this may be enough to say. "So have they."

"Who?" Paul says. He's baiting her now, trying to dispel this gravity that's settled in the kitchen. Clare knows his methods, knows them all, she thinks. Which ones will infuriate her, which will succeed in making her laugh. But he still lays them out tentatively, testing, as if they're new, as if he has no idea how she'll respond. His uncertainty is endearing.

"The kids," she says. Plainly, simply. "The people coming in an hour to our house."

"To have sex. Those people?"

She slaps at him and the two hands on the bottle prove to have been smart. "Go put that volleyball net up, won't you?"

"Volleyball, too?"

Clare wipes at her eyes, which are watering from the onions. "Go on."

Paul gets up, sets his empty on the counter.

From upstairs, Clare hears Jeanine singing. *It's my party and I'll cry if I want to, cry if I want to, cry if I want to.* "Paul," she says, "listen to that. Listen to her. Where would she learn that?"

"You're asking me?"

"Do you know how old that song is?"

"Actually? No."

"Well, it's old. *Old.*"

"Okay. Is that good?"

"Good? Just old, that's all."

"Okay. Okay. I'll go put up the net now."

"Okay." Clare sets the plate of hamburger fixings in the refrigerator. "Paul," she calls after him. He turns, his hand on the doorknob of the patio door. "Did you know this? Baby ostriches. They sing in their shells. Before they even hatch, they sing, and the parents sing back. They actually learn to recognize their parents' voices before they hatch. I read it in Jeanine's biology book."

Paul watches her a moment. "Nope. Can't say I knew that. In the shell, huh?"

"Yeah, just singing."

"It's interesting," he says and opens the door.

146

"It's extraordinary, don't you think?"

"Sure. That too." He gives her a funny smile: will you be all right here? I'll hurry back. Then he goes.

Clare stations herself near the door as Jeanine's guests arrive and recognizes all but one, but this one Jeffrey introduces as Mark, a friend from Domino's Pizza. They got off at the same time, and here they are, dressed in identical orange and blue pizza delivery shirts and smelling faintly of pepperoni or perhaps sausage. Mark shakes Clare's hand and shows her a winning smile. Jeanine takes them in. Clare sees Jeffrey plant a kiss on Jeanine's mouth. His arm circles her waist and they bump hips. Jeanine introduces Mark to her friend Stephanie, who smiles and later pelts him repeatedly with water balloons.

The evening is like that. Playful and fortuitous. The disguises are a hit. Paul takes videotape of a water volleyball game played by Marx Brothers and vampires and kissy faces and when they watch it later, it's only bumping and innocuous touching Clare sees. No true groping, except after the ball. The water balloons last about five minutes and one lands in a potted plant near the grill, splattering Paul's legs with wet dirt. It's Stephanie who's thrown it, and when Paul takes chase with a water pistol, Mark's right there to defend her.

Funny, Clare thinks. Just how much of love and life is like that. Luck and chance meetings and a million small things that could have gone another way. Someone takes a water gun inside and leaves water spots on every glass surface in the house and a pair of lacy panties is left mysteriously behind, but no one gets truly hurt or unhappy or embarrassed, which is no small claim. Even Jeanine, whose father's been silly, is forgiving. Generally, it's a good time. Even for Clare and especially for Paul, who is, Clare's reminded, such a kid.

23

Rehearsals for *One Hundred Steps Toward the Future* begin in chaos. During June they were to have been Wednesday evenings and Saturday mornings, but when the first Saturday comes, Clare receives a phone call early. Nate. Would she help notify the cast? Ty Greggory has had a heart attack just the night before. A mild one, but serious enough to put him in the hospital, serious enough to throw doubts on the likelihood of his directing the production. The only news now is that he's doing okay and no rehearsal today.

"You got the list of everybody, right? Phone numbers?" Nate says.

"No. No, I don't."

"Ty sent it. Last week."

"Not to me."

"Oh, well, I'll read them off to you then. Half or so. No. Wait. Tell you what. Meet me. Meet me at the college. My office? We can make calls from there and then put a note on the stage door for anybody we don't reach. Can you meet me? Fifteen minutes or as soon as you can."

His call woke her. Clare glances down at her nightgown, at Paul still curled up under the sheet. Fifteen minutes? "All right, Nate," she says. "You start. I'll be there quick as I can." She hangs up and leans over Paul to see if his eyes are open. They're not. She gives him a quick hug and throws the sheet back on her side.

"Leaving me to meet another man," Paul says, his voice still sleep-thick. She loves that voice. She loves, she decides just now, how he looks as he's waking up: eyes kind of hooded, stubble like some revelation on his face, mouth soft, yielding. He looks, she decides further, vulnerable. In some rare, immensely appealing way, he looks vulnerable. It's arresting. It makes Clare pause, think. Think how we clank around in these bodies all our lives, feeding them, resting them, trying to take care of them and make them last. Taking the pleasures as if they'll never stop, enduring the pain as if it will. We start to love some curve of a hip, the way an arm stretches and covers some part of us that needs covering. We start to love these bodies and to think they are us, that we are truly flesh, bones, lips, fingers. We let ourselves forget we're not. That we're separable, each from the other, each from our own bodies. We forget that it's no small thing to discover each other each morning, still there, still inside, still present and operating, and besides that, still loving. No small thing.

"And he's going to start without you?" Paul says. "I don't like it, Clare. It sounds kinky."

"Oh, stop, won't you?" Clare gives his shoulder a push, then another. "Ty Greggory's had a heart attack."

Paul pulls himself up onto one elbow. "Seriously?"

"Yes. Last night. He's okay, but not up for directing the show, I'm sure."

"What'll you do?"

"That's the question. I don't know." Clare's pulled on a pair of shorts and a T-shirt. She sits down on the edge of the bed and ties her tennis shoes. "I don't know how long I'll be, Paul. Let Jeanine know—no rehearsal today."

"Okay."

She brushes through her hair, pulls it up and off her neck with a banana clip. The kiss she gives Paul is quick. He pulls her back for another. "I may take Jeanine for some tennis," he says.

"Good. Good, do it," she says, and then she's off.

❦

Nate slams down the hood on Clare's disabled car, wipes his hands on his pants, and gives her the news: "I don't know, Clare. I'm no mechanic, sorry. But come on. I'll give you a ride home."

Clare was surprised when she came out of Nate's office and the car wouldn't start. There hadn't been any indication something was wrong. It was fine and then it was dead, just like that, but Nate's news is just what she expects. It's true: he's no mechanic. She only let him look under the hood to humor him. She takes her purse and notebook from the front seat, shuts the door, locks up. "Thanks, Nate," she says. "You've been sweet, but really—I'll call Paul. He'll come get me." She wonders if Paul really did take Jeanine to play tennis, if they'd be back yet if they'd gone.

Nate puts a foot up onto the front bumper, slides his

hands into his back pockets. "No, come on. I'll give you a ride. It's no trouble. We've got to settle this thing anyway. About the show."

They've been around once already on this. Sure, Clare sees now. Sure, that explains all this solicitous behavior. He's regretting what he said, assuming he'd be the one to take over the show. Now he needs to do something for her, to make amends—fix her car, give her a ride. *Ply* her.

"Do you want to call a wrecker from my office?" Nate says. He's come around from the front of the car to where Clare stands by the driver's door. His sleeves are rolled up to the elbow. Clare can see a long streak of something black running up his right arm.

"No, I think what I'll do is call Paul. He'll know what's wrong. I can use the phone in the lobby."

Nate narrows his eyes and brings his teeth down hard against his tongue. "Okay," he says. "Okay," in case she hadn't heard.

"Okay." She shifts her purse on her shoulder.

Nate shoves his hands into his pockets, then takes them out. "Clare," he says. "Clare, come on. I'm parked right over there." He puts a hand to her elbow, points vaguely toward the Arts Center with the other. Clare can see the sign they've tacked up on the stage door. Nate's hand on her elbow feels substantial and a little perilous. She feels color coming into her face. It spreads across her chest and then moves up her throat, into her cheeks, and there it is, hot.

"Listen," Nate says. He starts walking. His hand at her elbow puts her in motion too, so easy, no thought required. She shifts her notebook to her left arm, the one Nate is beside. "You could do the show with me," Nate says. "You and me. A collaboration. It makes perfect sense."

"Perfect sense?" Clare says. Nate's significantly taller than she is and his stride is long. She has to hurry to keep up, and today this feels like a disadvantage. "How could I collaborate with someone who still believes in perfection?"

This takes him off guard. "You don't?"

"Perfection?"

He slows down a little. His hands are back in his pockets. He considers and then, "Nah," he says. "Not perfection *exactly*." He takes a check of Clare's face, looking for a clue, she supposes. Clare watches the ground, not giving any. She sees he wants her approval, and she doesn't know why, but it's touching nonetheless. She wonders what it *would* be like, directing the show as a team.

Nate stops walking and for a few paces Clare goes on. Then she stops, but doesn't turn to him. He goes to her, comes to a stop at her left side. "Do the show with me, Clare," he says.

She takes two steps further down the sidewalk, turns and looks at him. "Do the show with *me*," she says, then turns and begins walking again, faster, across an intersecting stretch of sidewalk.

"Clare," Nate calls to her. "Clare?"

She stops and turns.

"We're over here," he says, turning the corner where the sidewalks meet.

All right. All right. He's felt foolish. She's felt foolish.

It's even up. Clare backtracks, makes the corner, comes up to Nate's side. "Where's your car?" she says.

"Oh, no car," he says, angling off across the grass to the side of the Arts Center building. Clare follows him to a bike rack, watches with her hands on her hips as he flips through the combination on his bike lock.

"A bike?" she says. "A bike? Oh, perfect."

He looks up at her from where he's crouched, removing the lock. It's a grin — almost a grin — on his face. "Perfect," he says, but quietly.

"Forget it," Clare says. "What do you think? I'm going to climb up on the handlebars? Sit on the crossbar? What?" She needs a breath and takes it. "I'm going to call Paul," she says, then strikes out across the grass, her steps long and deliberate.

Nate gets on the bike, rides down the sidewalk in Clare's direction. "Clare. Clare, wait," he calls.

She doesn't. She doesn't even turn.

"Do you want to use my phone?" he asks.

Clare says nothing.

Nate turns the bike off the sidewalk, into the grass, comes after her. "Clare, don't be silly. It's easy. Come on. I'll give you a ride."

"Easy?" Clare says. She makes a right-angle turn. So does Nate, at her side, wavering with the slow speed on the bike.

"Perfect?" she says, turning again. There's no sense in her course now. She's headed right back toward the Arts Center and nearly running. The speed makes Nate's job easier. He follows.

"Do the show with you?" she says. She comes to a hedge and hesitates only a moment before pushing right through it. It's waist high and too thick for a bike to pass through. Nate finds this out by trying. He leaves the bike there finally, tangled in oleander, follows Clare on foot. She's kept going and has a good lead on him by now. He runs. At first she does, too, but then, feeling a little ridiculous, she stops, feet apart, hands on hips. "Do the show with you?" she says again. It seemed important to speak first, anything.

Nate stops, more breathless than Clare. He looks at her a moment, just looks, taking an assessment of things. "You with me. Me with you. What's the difference?" he says.

She takes his hand then, starts walking again, deliberate as before, back to the hedge and the bike, leading him. "Is it stuck?" she asks.

"I can get it out," Nate says, and with a little patience, he does.

"I'll ride you," Clare says, putting her hands to the handlebars.

"What?"

"Do you want the handlebars or crossbar?"

Nate puts his hand to his forehead, runs it down over his face. He smiles while it covers his mouth.

"Well?" Clare says, holding the bike. She knows she's not being fair. They've so distracted themselves with the scramble for the upper hand that it's no longer clear what the issue is. The tussle itself was seductive, and Nate's even more charming off balance than he is in that poised position of control he so loves to inhabit. Clare takes a deep, slow breath, the kind you need before beginning to sing.

"This won't work," Nate says. "You'll be too short for the seat and I'll be too tall for the handlebars. How about if I get the point and ride you?"

Clare considers this, fingers the handlebars, the seat of the bike. What did he mean by that? How did they come to be standing here, out of breath, having a discussion about how to travel together on a bicycle? "I haven't done this since high school. Probably junior high," she says.

"I'll be careful," Nate says. He puts his hands to the handlebars. Clare takes hers away. Nate throws a leg over the bar, then holds the bike steady for Clare. "Sit on the crossbar. It's easier."

Clare tries it, tentatively, her notebook under her arm. With the bar pressing against the backs of them, her thighs spread, soft and fleshy. She tugs at the hem of her shorts, trying for another inch of cover, and Nate has to catch the bike as it jerks to the side with her movement. She's too old for this. She knew she was. She lays the notebook across her lap.

"Ready?" His face is close, his arms curved around her to reach the handlebars. The black streak is still there, running up his right arm. "Here we go."

Nate pushes off. They waver once as they start and Clare feels the weight of Nate's chest and arm pressing against her shoulder. She doesn't dare shift on the crossbar, but turns a little more toward the front. The bar is hard and uncomfortable under her until its pressure makes her numb. The wind whips her hair, makes her eyes burn, so she closes them.

Without sight, her ears are alert. She hears the sound of the tires over pavement, a dove, Nate breathing. His breath comes faster and his effort tells her they must be picking up speed, though this is hard to be sure of with her eyes closed. Her legs dangle uselessly, disconnected from her by lack of circulation. She tries to feel whether there's more wind against her face, moving through her hair, but this she can't measure. There's only Nate's breathing, coming faster. One sign.

"Can we do the show together?" she says, eyes still closed. She doesn't look. She listens.

"Yup," he says, a little breathless. "Yup, perfect."

Then, because she's entrusted this man to move her through space with his own exertion, or because she's forty and it can't wait forever, or because she's a fool, she says, "Shall we use my music?" Her heartbeat is a throb behind her eyes.

"What music is that?" Nate says.

They're approaching Roadrunner Park then and Nate turns in and they sit in the grass near the carousel and as her legs tingle back to life, Clare tells him. She has the sheets of music and lyrics in her notebook and she waits to see his facial expression before she decides to show them to him. It's a wide leap she's considering here, and his face recognizes that and urges her on. She shows him and again she watches him, her heart pounding. He reads. He reads and turns pages a long time and sometimes he smiles. He looks up at her a few times. He picks out the melodies, humming. The carousel circles and circles, taking passengers on and letting them off, its calliope music faintly in the air.

One risk enables the next, and she decides as she watches him that she will sing for him if he asks, and he does. She sings a few lines from each number. He joins her on the refrain of the last one, a reprise of the opening song. His voice is clear and mellow. The sound of him singing her music stirs her and she stops singing and listens. Her throat tightens and she feels that if she looks at him she'll either cry or kiss him, and so she doesn't look.

"It's good," Nate says, a quiet, intimate voice. "When did you do this?"

"I've had it a while. I've had it since before I gave Ty the other lyrics. I just didn't say so."

"Let's use it. Do you want to use it?"

She breathes deep. "The orchestration isn't very good."

"I think it's perfect."

She looks at him. She's got it under control now, but she sees that if she'd looked at him a moment ago, it would have been the kiss, not the tears. "Okay," she says. "Okay, then. Let's use it." It's a thrill and a fright.

"Good," Nate says. He smiles. He gets up then and goes to the bike. "Come on. I said I'd take you home, so that's what I'm going to do."

24

They do phone calls again and get the music to the orchestra conductor for his adjustments and Wednesday night the cast assembles in the Arts Center to observe mercilessly Clare's imminent nervous breakdown. It's worse than the day of the auditions. Tonight she's physically shaking. She snapped at Paul completely unprovoked before she left home. This after he spent all Sunday afternoon replacing the battery in her car.

Even Jeanine had the good sense not to talk to her during the ride to the college. They rode with the radio turned up high, tuned to a station Jeanine regularly ridicules for its oldies music, but tonight she listened without complaint and when Clare looked at her, she smiled serenely. The smile was practiced and controlled, and it infuriated Clare. She switched the radio to the sports talk station and caught a glimpse of a wrinkle in Jeanine's eyebrows, but still no response. Only that annoying packaged smile.

Clare's mouth is entirely dry. She's a wreck and Nate is calm and collected. She's an agitated woman in an antiperspirant commercial, and he's the serene guy on the next channel, promoting life insurance. She hates him for it.

And now, because she's so jittery, she's letting him take over. He spoke first, announced to the cast the plan. In fact, he's doing all the talking. She's nodding. She's standing on one foot. She's letting him put his arm across her shoulders as he explains what her role will be, what scenes they'll be rehearsing tonight. In fact — and this not only infuriates her, it worries her — she's wanting that arm, she's taking security from it, comfort. Nate is getting everyone in position for the opening number and she is trying to remember: *Where* did she leave her spine?

"Clare," Nate is saying. He hands her the score. She thinks he does it impatiently, that he snaps the sheets a little, that they touch her hand a fraction too sharply. She avoids his eyes and takes the music.

She looks to the high school orchestra, assembled in shorts and T-shirts in the orchestra pit. They hold trumpets and violins and French horns and wear suffering faces. Clearly, their mothers, fathers, teachers have coerced them into being here. Stephanie is there with her flute, looking glum as the rest, though she brightens a little at seeing Clare. This is a bunch of kids thinking of getting into their cars, Clare thinks, their fathers' cars, cruising Main Avenue, stopping at the Snow Swirl for hot fudge sundaes and scrawling obscenities on the walls of the bus stop shelter. They're planning how they will kiss each other there. Touch sensitive body parts. They have their own history to make. Why, they're thinking, did I ever take up the cello? I could have played basketball and put myself above all this. I could be eating yet another unclaimed pizza with Mark, Stephanie's thinking. Maybe a deluxe.

The cast looks strange, too, bumping together on the stage. It's their legs Clare can see best from her angle, down in front of the stage, near the pit. They're bare legs mostly. People keeping cool. Sandals, tennis shoes. Mrs. Daley's varicose veins are blue and bulging. Clare looks for a familiar pair of legs: Jeanine's. She finds her, toward the back of the stage, barefoot. She's lifting to her toes, coming down, up, down, getting ready for something strenuous. Her calves flex and release. Her toes, nails crimson, wriggle. She's more ready than the evening will demand. Clare tries to see Jeanine's face, but it's hidden from her view by shoulders, Hawaiian shirts, ponytails.

Clare rises up on her own toes and feels the pinch of a sandal strap pulled too tight. She bends and unbuckles them, kicks them off. Up, down, up, down. Limbering up. First position. Second. She bends over at the waist, reaches for the backs of her ankles, stretches. When she comes up and shakes her hair back, Nate is looking at her. He gives her a smile that fills her up. He's confident she'll come through. Definitely, that's what his smile means. She gives him one of hers and he takes it, puts it away somewhere inside him. It's sweet, seeing him do that. Now that she's seen it, been surprised, and understood, it's sweet. It's a lot of work to stay mad at him, and she has so many other things to do.

※

After rehearsing the opening number, Nate sets up for the Building City Hall scene. Clare goes through the musical number for this scene with the chorus and the orchestra. It's feeling better now, more natural. Jeanine is part of the chorus, and though her voice is indistinguishable, blended with the others, Clare can see her mouth forming the words of the lyrics and it's a soothing sight.

Nate details the choreography next, which will center on a boy throwing painted styrofoam bricks up, one by one, from a wagon on the stage to the workers stationed on scaffolding above him. The boy is Frankie Lawson, one of Clare's voice students. Nate has Frankie go through the motions alone several times and then he calls for the others to join in and for the music.

Clare is surprised to note that Nate has a very precise conception of how this number should go. When they decided to use the new music, he told Clare he could use some of the same dance steps and would just improvise on the rest. If what he's doing is improvised, he's very good at it. He goes to Frankie, bends his body into position as if he's made of wire: the curve of his legs, the arc of his arms throwing the bricks. He signals the orchestra conductor and Clare. When the music begins, Nate leans over Frankie from behind, moves him like a rag doll, showing him the rhythm, the way a father will show a son how to step into a pitch, swing.

They move like one body, teacher and learner, and it's like magic to Clare to see Nate's vision of the scene transfer to Frankie. He takes it in — through his arms, glued to Nate's? Through his face, open and receptive? It's mysterious, and Clare can't be sure. She can only see that Frankie's received Nate's feel for the scene like an electrical charge. He moves with new energy and so does Nate, leaving Frankie now on his own.

Nate's both intense and agile. He moves quickly, with urgency, giving directions and encouragement to the cast, his movements his own sort of dance on the stage. His bare feet pad and slide across the hardwood surface. From where she stands, Clare can see his feet arching, and though he's wearing a pair of loose-fitting pants, she can imagine his muscles from ankle to waist flexing taut.

The faces of the cast are opening up to him. Their feet seem to lift more easily and with new assurance as they glide smoothly through the pattern he's demonstrated. Frankie's bricks sail evenly from wagon to scaffolding plat-form and when Mrs. Daley comes through the door of the plywood general store façade, Jeanine is in position to take her arm and whisper into her ear as they approach the wagon at center stage. Nate claps his hand to Jeanine's shoulder with a squeeze of approval as she passes.

It's that vitality he has, that vitality Clare's seen in Nate before. It's overflowing. He's infecting everyone on the stage. He's infecting Clare. Passion like that you have to admire. When you see it, being scattered like wildflowers, you wish for a few petals to fall on you, or close enough that you could pick them up, hold them, smell their fra-grance and see if it's how you imagined it would be.

❧

"You were good," Nate says to Clare as everyone is leav-ing. They're wheeling the wagonload of bricks off stage, one of them on each side of the wagon.

"I'm wondering if we need a few more voices on the refrain of that City Hall number," she says. "Did it sound thin?"

"I didn't think so." They park the wagon against the back wall and Nate picks up a brick that's fallen out and tosses it back in. "Do it though if you think you need to," he adds, an afterthought.

"Well, I will," Clare says. "If I think I need to."

"Good."

Clare feels how they've shifted, from contentious to deferential, how they're trying to find a comfortable fit in this partnership. "Yeah," she says. "I'll consider that. I'll hear it again Saturday."

Nate settles against the wagon, slides his hands into his pockets. "You were good."

"So were you. With Frankie, showing him. You were good."

"I think we should work up each of the scenes, the musical numbers that go with them and all, and then get our old-timer in to narrate, put it all together the last few rehearsals. Don't you think?"

"Sure. That'd be the way. First the parts, then the whole."

Against one wall backstage Clare sees several plywood cutouts of 1940-ish cars, large enough for two people to carry and walk behind. They're for the parade scene, the soldiers coming home from the War. The cut-outs were Clare's idea. She goes over to them. "Hey, they're done," she says, flipping through them.

"Yeah. They look great. Will you come have a beer

with me?"

"Well, we ought to paint a baby on the side of one of these cars."

"A baby?"

"A one-year-old girl, riding on the running board."

"Well, sure. If you think so," Nate says. "Why would we do that though?"

"It's one of the most amazing stories Mirage has and nobody knows it. A survival story. A miracle story, really, the best kind."

"Let's go get a beer and you tell me."

"A baby rode thirty miles on a running board with a dirty diaper, almost falling asleep."

"A Coke if you'd rather."

"Her father didn't know she was there."

"Can you?"

"Never fell off."

"Can you go for a beer? Or a Coke."

Clare hears him, considers a moment. "I suppose Jeanine is waiting for me."

"She was good in the City Hall scene. She has a good sense of herself on the stage. She moves well, I mean."

"Well, she dances."

"So do you."

"What's that?"

"Dance."

"No."

"What was that little warm-up I saw you doing earlier? Your vocal cords run down the back of your legs, do they?"

Clare has to laugh, then backs away. He's checking to see, checking her legs. "Wait. Wait a minute," she says.

She comes around to the front of the curtain, looks out into the auditorium. Nearly everyone is gone, but standing in the back are Jeanine and Stephanie and the blue and orange pizza guys. "I'll be right there, Jeanine," Clare calls.

Jeanine looks up. "I've got a ride, Mom. With Jeffrey," she says. Jeffrey raises an arm, waves. So do Stephanie and Mark. "We're going to Mark's. I'll be home later."

So will I, Clare starts to say, then doesn't. "Okay," she says instead.

Clare comes backstage and Nate is there, wearing a different shirt and with his shoes on. She wonders how he happened to have this other shirt and where he changed—right here? "So you're free?" he says, bending to tie his shoes.

"I guess I am," she says. "These are the only clothes I have though." She pulls at the hem of her shorts. She's put her sandals back on.

"Looks like enough to me. Looks good, if you want to know."

Clare feels her cheeks grow warm. "So what kind of transportation do you have tonight?"

"Let's just get it straight up front, huh?" he says and laughs. He laughs twice, as if there's been a second thought, one not expressed. "I have my bike, but let's just walk. Let's go across the street, have a drink, and come back for the vehicles."

"Sounds like a plan. Sounds good."

They go to a place called The Mad Hatter and Clare has what Nate has, a tap beer. It's the only brand of beer she can think of: a Me Too. They slide into a booth whose table seems narrow. Nate, at least, seems close, especially underneath where his long legs are in her space. There are hanging plants over the booth and one keeps catching in Clare's hair. She brushes it away a few times and then Nate reaches over and breaks off three or four inches of the offending vine. He sets the broken piece, three leaves on a ragged piece of stem, on the table. Clare can't help it. She looks at it, she supposes, with horror. Nate takes in her reaction, then dumps some cellophane wrappers out of the ashtray, fills it with beer, and floats the piece of plant in it. "There," he says. "You can take it home with you if you want."

Clare drinks her beer slowly. She tells Nate the story of Rosemary riding the running board, and then she tells him the story of the brother: Stewart down the outhouse hole. Nate likes the Stewart story better. He suggests they rig a trap door on the stage and have some kid—Frankie, maybe—fall in during one of the scenes. Unexplained. Just have him fall in, and only he and Clare will know why. A joke built into their show, just for them.

"No one else will know," Nate says, but his eyes have softened from the brightness they had a moment ago. Clare has the time to see this: he leaves them on her until he's sure she has. Then he lifts his bottle and drains it.

They walk back to the Arts Center, to the parking lot. Clare's is the only car left. "What's become of your car?" she says as they approach hers.

Nate laughs softly. "It's at Collision America. I'm finally having it repaired. That crunched bumper was about the only thing Susanna left me. I had a hard time parting with it." He laughs again, more ruefully this time.

They're standing at her car and Nate leans down and kisses her. On the mouth, just that naturally, as if he's done this every night and every morning for years. He doesn't linger; it's quick. But he's kissed her. Kissed her again, and despite his nerve, his boldness, his audacity, his impudence, his outright balls, all right, it's good. It feels good.

He hands her the piece of broken plant, delicately, as if it matters. "See if that starts," he says. "The car."

"It'll start," she says. She takes the wilting leaves. "New battery."

"Well, just see. I want to know you got going okay."

Clare unlocks the door, gets in. Nate brings his face to the window and she remembers another night, him looking through that window, waiting for a kiss. She doesn't roll it down. She turns the key in the ignition. The car, of course, starts up. She gives him the thumbs up, mouths "Bye."

He returns the gesture, waves. She puts the car in reverse and he starts off walking. She wonders, watching him, where his bike is parked. Maybe he needed a ride. She watches a minute. He's heading toward where he had his bike on Saturday. He walks fast, energetically, and it reminds her of him on stage tonight. He's so full of life he bounces. He hasn't lost any of it, he's that young. Why would he want to kiss her?

25

"It's too bad," Jeanine says the next morning. "After you spent all that time writing lyrics for those *Oklahoma!* songs, then he doesn't even use them." She pours Clare a cup of coffee and brings it to her at the table. It's a gesture of care Clare appreciates even if its cause is mistaken. "Where did he get this new music?"

"Don't you like it?" Clare says.

"Well, sure. It's okay. But what happened to yours?"

Clare just shrugs.

"Who wrote the new stuff?"

Paul looks up from his newspaper and cereal. Clare shrugs again. Lying—even the kind that is really just withholding information—is unnatural for her. She hopes she can get by without having to actually say anything untrue. She hopes a few more waggles of her shoulders will be enough.

"They aren't going to use your lyrics?" Paul asks.

A shrug and a negative nod of her head and something to say that is true: "They were awful anyway."

"I'm sorry, Clare," Paul says. He says it so sincerely that she is almost ready to tell him the rest of the story. He gets up then and takes his car keys from the counter and his briefcase from beside the couch. "I'll be home at six," he says, and collides briefly with Clare's lips as he passes. Jeanine goes into the kitchen for the coffee pot and comes back to the table to refill Clare's cup.

❧

Bernice is talking ninety miles an hour about the mock wedding, and even though Clare has let the salad she was making when the phone rang go, she still feels she's not taking this all in. Mexican wedding cakes. Frogs. A ring from a Kerr canning jar. A green furry pillow for the ring bearer. Ugly. Electronic keyboard or tape? Roll of white paper towels as aisle cloth, more tasteful. Motorcycle.

"Motorcycle?" Clare asks, just to stop the flow.

"We need a motorcycle. Stace has one, but it's a long way to bring it. I'll try to borrow one here. They just have to ride off on it after the ceremony, no great distance."

"Who does?"

"The bride and groom."

"On a motorcycle?"

"Sure. That's what your parents did, you know. Your father had a motorcycle and that's how they left. Your mother rode on the back in her wedding gown. She threw her bouquet as they started off."

"Clarence and Roberta did this?" Why was she using their names? To see if they fit this new image of her parents? To double-check whether she and Bernice were talking about the same people?

"Yes. Your mother and father."

"I never knew it."

"Your father was a wild one, Clare."

"He wasn't either."

"Not your mother, though. She just went along."

"That's not true either."

"Well, you don't want to hear it, but it is."

"They left on a motorcycle?"

"Right."

"I really love that. Put it in the show."

"The show?"

"The wedding. Find a motorcycle if you can. I really love that."

"Okay. And Jeanine wants to sing?"

"Yeah. She's been practicing. 'I Love You Truly.'"

"That's not what they had."

"Well, it's close enough."

"It was a religious ceremony. 'The Lord's Prayer.' 'Song of Ruth.'"

"Whither thou goest I will go?"

"That's the one."

"Play it while they take off on the motorcycle. Play it on the keyboard."

"That's not funny."

"Sure it is."

"It's not how it happened. Are you trying to make this into a spectacle?"

"You think it isn't already?"

"That's not funny either, Clare. Maybe you'd like to organize this, long distance. Maybe you'd like that better."

"I'm sorry, Bernice. I appreciate all this. Really I do.

You're doing a great job. What are the frogs for?"

"One frog. It jumps into the punchbowl."

"That's funny?"

"It really happened that way. You didn't know this either? What has your mother told you about her wedding?"

"I like that, too. A frog in the punchbowl. Is this before or after we drink the punch?"

"Really it happened before. We thought Oscar Warren did it. He was your mother's other boyfriend. We can put it in after if you want."

"No, put it in before. Just leave it there the whole time maybe. She had another boyfriend?"

"It might be kind of unsanitary to drink punch that has a frog in it."

"Okay then. After. Bernice?"

"Hmm?"

"Stace is coming then? Is Sam?"

"They're all coming. Everybody will be here. The first time in eleven years that we've all been together in this place."

"Bernice?"

"Yeah."

"Thanks again. For everything. You're a dear."

"Don't you forget it."

"I won't. I don't."

❧

Clare doesn't see the June letter from her father when it arrives. She's been rushed that day and has thrown the whole batch of mail on the desk unopened. It's Paul who finds it, that evening, after they've had dinner and are getting ready for bed.

"Here's your mail," he says. He comes into the bathroom and hands the envelope to Clare. She's standing at the sink in her nightgown, washing her face. She sets down her washcloth and takes the letter. He's handed it to her with the address side down. She turns it over, sees what it is. She feels Paul watching her, studying her, and is careful with her face, with what she shows him. She sets the letter down on the vanity, picks up her hairbrush and pulls it through her hair. Her strokes are careful, even. She moves her arms in wide, sweeping arcs. She brushes her hair more than is necessary. Really none was necessary, not for her hair.

"A letter, I see," Paul says. A safe beginning. "From your father?"

"Yeah."

"What's he saying these days?"

"These days?"

"In the letters. With seeing you soon and all, I'm wondering — what's he writing?"

"Don't pretend, Paul," Clare says. She states each word separately, with an effort. "Not that. If you have something to say, then say it." Her eyes come up and meet his as she finishes. They're burning with something that hurts from the inside out.

Paul comes to her. He opens his arms, tries to take her in. She turns away, but his arms close around her anyway. She stands stiffly with her back to his chest, the hairbrush tightly in her hand. His arms are securely around her, but they don't warm her at all. "You ought to read the letters," he says softly, into her hair.

"Why?" One-word responses are what she feels she can manage. One word at a time.

"Because he's your father and he's written them."

"Don't."

"Clare, you're going to see him in a month. For the first time since Stace's wedding, and you certainly didn't resolve anything then." He brings his hand to the side of her face, lifts her hair back, and she feels uncovered. She turns away, her other cheek pressing against his shoulder. "It's been eleven years, Clare. Let it go."

She struggles in his arms, but he holds her. "*Don't*," she says, through closed teeth.

Paul takes his arms away, tries to turn her to him. She resists, turns away, crosses her arms tightly over her chest, a hand on each shoulder. "Have you thought about what you're going to say to him?" Paul asks, letting her be.

"Nothing. Nothing! That's the way, isn't it? Don't we all just pretend nothing happened?" She's gone back to the vanity, is brushing her hair again. Furious, snapping strokes that fill her hair with static electricity.

"He's an old man."

"*Don't!*" She shouts it and then she slams the brush to the vanity top and the handle snaps cleanly in two. The bottom half is still in her hand. The half with the bristles flies into the air, hits her squarely on the right cheekbone, and drops into the sink. She stands there for just a moment, hair wild with static, stunned. She sees herself in the mirror and thinks that: stunned. Next she sees her face crumple and it's like watching someone else. The woman begins to cry and Clare thinks that, too: a woman, crying. She hasn't summoned the tears or even felt them approaching. They're there in the mirror like something unattached to her. She feels their wetness on her stinging cheek and it's as if someone's thrown water on her. She's been hit and then sprinkled and now there she is: a woman with hair standing on end, one cheek red, and water — tears — running down her face.

"Are you okay?" Paul asks.

She looks at him but doesn't answer. She doesn't know the answer, can't imagine what it is. She looks at him and his face changes. It looks that way it did before he said *Clare, oh Clare*, and she thinks she'll hear that next: *Clare, oh Clare. Clare, oh Clare.* It's all he could say for an eternity after her father came up the dock with the sheriff. The storm was passing by then, the thunder distant and the wind subsiding. The weight of his news and all those soaked clothes, perhaps, pulled her father's mouth open. Gaping, trembling. His eyes were dark and sunken. He told them with a voice that didn't even sound like his. Clare thought first the sheriff had spoken, but it was her father. It was. *Clare, oh Clare.* Paul said that next and pressed her face to his shoulder. A rescue team was searching. That was what the sheriff said. But little hope. Thirty minutes. Her father didn't cry. He never cried. And Paul only said her name, again and again, and held her.

Clare throws her hands to her ears, holding her name out, hears a sound anyway. Hers. That woman, crying.

"What'll I do?" Paul says. His voice is small, far away. That face.

"Cry, can't you cry? Haven't you got anything to cry about?" Someone shrieks this and Clare thinks she knows who it is. She didn't know she could be this cruel, but it may be her own voice. From the look on Paul's face, someone's hurt him. Someone's dug deep and unearthed some things he didn't want to see again. Remember? Remember this? Someone's done that. Clare. It's her own voice: Clare's.

Paul goes to the sink, picks up the piece of the broken hairbrush and drops it into the wastebasket. He comes to Clare, takes her hand and opens her fingers one by one until she releases the handle of the brush. He drops that in the wastebasket, too, then walks out of the bathroom. Clare goes to the wastebasket, looks in. Both pieces of the brush have disappeared, hidden under wads of Kleenex. When she turns around, there's Paul. He has an icebag. He puts one hand to her head, steadies her. The other, with the icebag, he puts to her cheek.

26

"When Michael was four years old," Clare tells Jeanine, "his preschool put on a program for the parents." Jeanine's asked about another of the photos Clare's added to the collage. "It was 'The Soda Shoppe Bop,' or something like that. Fifties music and the kids in poodle skirts or tight pants and greased-back hair. That was Michael's costume."

The picture shows Michael in blue jeans and a white T-shirt, sleeves rolled to the shoulder, hair slicked back and dark glasses. He's standing with legs apart and thumbs hooked in his belt loops, and what's making Jeanine giggle is that his fly is unzipped. "I know," Clare says, laughing herself. "It was like that through the whole show. Your dad was trying to give him a signal, but he just didn't get it. At least when he did his little impromptu bit he had the guitar in front of himself."

"Impromptu bit?"

"The whole group sang a song at the end of the show. They lined up on these risers, the whole class, on one side of the stage, in front of a microphone. There was a mike on the other side of the stage, too, and Michael just helped himself to one of the cardboard guitars, stepped up to that mike and started singing the song. Singing and swaying. No one stopped him. They let him have his moment of glory, and he lapped it up. By the end of the song, he was throwing kisses."

Jeanine laughs. "Throwing kisses? That's too funny."

"A four-year-old greaser with his fly unzipped."

Jeanine laughs her gasping, hilarious laugh, the rare one, the one Clare most loves. Clare thinks how she hasn't heard it in a long time, this laugh, how if Jeanine were nine or ten, she'd just take her up in a big bear hug right now. She thinks maybe she will anyway. She is about to when Jeanine stops laughing, slips her arms around her, and whispers, "What was the song? What did he sing?"

Clare thinks a minute, then says, "I don't know. I can't remember. Isn't that awful? I just can't remember."

"I can't even remember *him*," Jeanine says. "I can remember things you've told me, and these pictures, but I can't remember anything like a feeling for him."

Clare puts her hand to the back of Jeanine's head, strokes her hair, long down those angel curls, down her back. She lays a kiss near her ear. "I'm sorry," Clare says, and it's not enough to say. I'm sorry you lost your brother? I'm sorry he's gone? I'm sorry we can't remember? "I'm sorry."

"I'm sorry, too," Jeanine says. Her words are as palpable against Clare's throat as her own were inside it.

It's not enough. None of it is enough.

27

When Clare arrives for rehearsal Saturday morning, the Arts Center is quiet and rather somber. She's early. There were no other cars in the lot yet. Jeanine has spent the night at Stephanie's and will be coming with her. Clare walks through the lobby with the subdued manner of someone alone in a large place ordinarily filled with people. A place like a church on a Monday morning: recently emptied, hymnals not yet straightened. With any imagination at all, a place where you can still hear whispers and see the little streams of gray rising above extinguished candles. You tiptoe in a place like that and Clare does. She pulls open a door to the auditorium and goes inside. There's light—one, a spotlight—on the stage. The rest of the hall is in complete darkness.

Clare hears scuffling she can't immediately identify and her heart leaps, throat tightens. She grasps the back of a seat by the aisle where she's standing and listens. The sound is up front. On stage? Feet—padding, tramping, sliding. Her eyes are on the spotlight when Nate moves through it. He's there and then he's gone and it's just the feet sound again in the dark. There's no music, but he's dancing. She thinks that's it: he's dancing. She waits for him to pass through the light again and the anticipation is a pulse behind her eyes. The sound of his feet and the bright empty circle of light and the expectation that any second Nate will appear in some bodily shape she can't anticipate make her heart drum. She slides into the seat on the aisle, sits low, hiding, spying, and can't take her eyes off the light.

He comes then, makes a pass through, like some primeval creature crossing the moon, and then he's gone, nothing but disembodied foot poundings. Clare tries to catch the rhythm of his feet, tries to imagine the music in his head, for she's sure now of this much: he's dancing. And she waits for the next pass. And the next, her breath quick and short.

She feels her senses straining: her eyes for vision, her ears for music. She puts together a picture in split-second flashes: he's dancing, in gym shorts. No shirt. Barefoot. Whatever he's hearing is intense and rhythmic and allows him no slowdown. It's nothing from the show. It's nothing from anyone else's memory even, maybe. It could all be improvised movement, all his, the private song of his heart. Whatever it is, it's building, mounting at a pace that drives his feet faster and then faster.

As he crosses the light again, Clare wishes for him to stop, to freeze for a moment and show her his face. What does it look like? Passion like this. She sinks lower in her seat and begins to feel she shouldn't watch him. That it's intrusive and even dangerous. But she wants to. She wants to, with an illogical intensity. Just now she'd trade precious things for this vision if she had to. His body is pure beauty and he's filled so full, so full, of this energy that draws her. It's powering this dance. She can see that much: how it's powering him. She watches and watches for the clues: what is it that's inspired this dance? What is it? She wants to know.

Clare thinks of that first night of rehearsal, of Nate teaching Frankie his brick-tossing dance, and she wishes she were up on the stage right now, learning this dance of Nate's. She wants to mold herself to him, like Frankie did, and be moved across the floor under his volition, until she, too, can hear the music. She wants to spread herself over him like a weightless sheen of sweat and tune the song in her heart to this one in his. It's so alive.

Nate finishes finally, stops, as Clare's been wishing, in the spotlight, head raised. His chest is pumping hard, his mouth is open, his body covered with perspiration. But he doesn't look spent. He looks triumphant.

Nate leaves the stage, walks behind the curtain at the left side, and Clare takes her chance to leave unnoticed. She goes out into the lobby, feeling spent herself. She's trembling a little and there's a clammy coolness on her chest. She wonders what she would have done if he'd noticed her there, watching. If she would have asked him what he was dancing and if he would teach her. It occurs to her now that possibly he did see her. Possibly he saw her, knew she was there. Had he meant for her to see this dance?

❧

The rehearsal goes very well, well enough that afterwards at The Mad Hatter, Nate's talking about starting to put it all together next week. They have lunch this time. Clare goes feeling she can, that she can go this once more without the going becoming a routine. A third time and she'll really have to think about this, but this time, this once more, it's okay.

Over hamburgers they laugh and talk about the show mostly, and Clare thinks this time that she likes Nate's laugh. There's something unrestrained about it. It comes from very far inside him. She likes it. She notes that—that she likes it—and that's when she realizes there is this list inside her. Things about Nate she likes. Things about Nate she looks forward to seeing, hearing. Things that have happened that she likes to remember, that she replays in her mind. She's doing this, she sees today at The Mad Hatter, and it's hard to believe. Spending thoughts on this boy of a man, his laugh, his kisses, his dancing.

Stopping to think about that, with him across the table from her, she sees herself first as a starry-eyed young girl and then as a foolish old woman. It shakes her that she can't be sure which she is. Neither feels precisely true and that's what keeps her from telling Nate that she saw him dancing. There are things she'd like to know about that, things she'd like to ask him, but just now she can't. She has nowhere to put the answers. She's full up with his laugh and this confusion about what she is. Of the two, the laugh is the more engaging. For now, she'll have lunch and the laugh.

When Paul holds her in bed that night, Clare thinks for the first time in a long time of her list about him. It's sweet to have been reminded of it, and to travel through its entries before sleep. Paul, seventeen, in a convertible, asking her to come to his house for dinner. Paul, twenty-two, at their wedding reception, dancing with her Aunt Bernice whose shoes were too small. Paul going to work on skis after a blizzard his first winter at the bank in Minnesota. Paul biting his tongue and taking orders from her father as they assembled the crib for Michael. Paul the Lamaze coach kissing her first on the mouth and then on the belly after Michael's birth.

Clare's eyes fly open. The room is dark, the moon a full disk of light behind the shade at the window. The moonlight casts the moving shadow of a eucalyptus tree against the shade. Paul is still holding her and she still can't see it. She was trying to remember and couldn't call it up: Michael's face as a newborn. Her stomach floats gravity-less inside her. She can remember Jeanine, just born, her head molded to a point, the way she put her thumb into her mouth moments after birth. She can remember her doctor double-checking the decision she and Paul had made that two children would be the size of their family. She can see Jeanine on her stomach, sucking her thumb, the doctor asking as he prepared to wheel her off to surgery, Are you sure? She said yes, and now she can't even remember Michael's newborn face. She can't remember. "Paul," she whispers. "Paul."

His sleeping face is two inches from hers and there's no response.

"Paul," she says again, and he's far, far away from her. Here, in her arms — she could put out her tongue and touch his face — she can't reach him. He's as distant and close as death. She shakes him hard with the urgency of it.

His first reaction is to squeeze his arms tight around her, tight enough, almost, to set her stomach down in its place. He makes a sound like a heavy breath made audible, then opens his eyes wide right into hers. "What?" he says, louder than he'd need to. She's right there, right there.

She sees she's shaken him harder than she needed to. She's shaken him far down inside himself.

When she doesn't answer right away, he sits up, pulling her along with him. The bed sloshes and they fall against each other. His nose bumps against her bruised cheek. "What's the matter?" he says. The words are dry, breathless.

"Can you remember Michael's face as a baby? Just after he was born, what he looked like?"

Paul looks into her face a moment, then turns his face away and runs his hand through his hair. "He looked like a baby," he says finally.

"But what did he look like?"

"He was cute. A beautiful baby boy."

"I can't remember what he looked like. I can't see him."

Paul watches her, takes a breath. "Well, that's how. Cute. His eyes were blue."

"Every baby's eyes are blue."

"You could look at a picture."

"Don't you see? I can't remember." She realizes she's shouting at him.

"Come here." He lifts his arm from around her shoulder, slides back down under the sheet and pulls her with him. "Come here." He presses his body to hers. She can feel every point where they touch: chests, stomachs, hips, legs wrapping legs, his arm behind her neck, and then lips. He moves immediately to come inside her, which takes a gentle insistence. But he's right. It's the exact right thing. Her body sees it, too, and unfolds.

28

When the third trip to The Mad Hatter comes, it's easier than Clare thought it would be. Three doesn't seem such a significant number anymore, or it matters less that coming here may become an expectation. Actually, there's something comfortable about it being a standing date, about not having to decide each time, is she coming? She comes, and Nate knows by now what she wants to drink. The brand of beer or that she wants sugar if it's coffee. She likes that he knows these small things about her and she likes that he's the only person she knows who dips french fries in mustard.

By the last week of rehearsals, it's even become comfortable that he kisses her when they say goodbye. Just a friendly sort of kiss, no embracing. Her cheek or her mouth, but even when it's her mouth it's the sort of kiss that belongs on a cheek. They've gotten the scenes into their sequence now and the old-timer narrator is absolutely the right connector. The pharmacist who plays the part has acquired a cold and it's given his voice a gravelly quality Clare's hoping he keeps until after the performance. It suits the character perfectly.

The music, she's decided, has the potential to be flawless and probably is beyond being anything worse than fair. The most she'd hoped to feel at this point was relief and a minimal amount of confidence that she wouldn't completely embarrass herself, and what she has instead is something coming close to pride in this centennial show. She's done more than she thought she could, done it better than she expected to. It's a little bit of a surprise and, more surprisingly, it's no surprise. Now that it's about to happen, it's as though she knew all along she could do this well, that of course, she would. That there was ever any doubt seems impossible.

Paul hasn't seen a full rehearsal of the show yet and probably won't before the real event this weekend. He's coming to the end of the heaviest part of the yearly cycle now, reviewing financial statements for businesses with December 31 year-ends. And he's still getting together the proposal for the dairy company. It's a project that's gotten under his skin. Clare can always tell that by how Paul's legs jump around at night. The degree of mid-night sloshing in the bed is directly proportionate to the stress level Paul's working at during the day.

She's been sleeping lightly herself. She's been tired—extra rehearsals this last week and getting ready for their trip—but restless with the anticipation of it all. She's taken to brushing a coat of varnish onto the collage each night just before going to bed. The stroking motion is soothing and the lacquer smell reminds her of her father, building first the doll cradle she had as a child and later the cradle Michael and Jeanine slept in as babies. Still, once in bed, she'll often wake up and feel the water moving and realize her heart is pounding. Beating wildly like she's just had the scare of her life. And that's the thing. Despite her daytime confidence that the show is ready, that it's going to come off with no major hitches, she feels afraid.

At those moments when she wakes up in darkness and feels her heart and Paul's legs racing through some dream, she can't imagine herself as the composer and director of the music in this show and she has to take herself through a mental routine that re-establishes in her mind that it's true.

She starts with envisioning herself standing on a stage. Then she puts the cast all around her, in their costumes. Then the audience, in their rows. In this vision, the air conditioning is always out—the audience fans themselves with their programs. All these programs, waving. The house lights go down. The cast members open their mouths and no sound comes out. They just open their mouths and let them gape, visions of shock, terrible news. Then they all look at her. They're waiting for something. For her to do something. She feels as if she knows what it is, but she can't think of it. Can't think of it and can't do it. Everybody's frozen except the audience. They're fanning and fanning.

Then Nate arrives on the scene. Rushes in, he does, rushes from behind the curtain, out of breath, and he's a presence. Clare's relieved to see him: she can feel relief moving through her just ahead of the annoyance. That goes through her too, slower and more persistent. It puts a grip on her and twists hard. He stands there, triumphant, like when he finished the dance she watched that day in hiding, and she's mad at him for appearing so calm, so in control. But it's Clare that everyone is looking at. She has to do something, anything, so she makes an announcement: *No fanning will be allowed. No fanning in the auditorium. No fanning on the premises. It's distracting as hell and must stop now.* She says this and Nate snickers, but the audience — all of them — put down their programs.

The show begins. There's sound and movement on the stage and all of it is stunningly perfect. She and Nate watch from behind the side curtain. She sees him stealing glances at her, looks not meant for her to see. She looks at him too, when he's not watching, when there's shadow on her face. What she sees is that he's vulnerable, too. He's got his heart fully invested in this show and no real sense of what a dangerous state that is. It's such an innocent thing to do, to be able to do. She feels that she should warn him, that she should say something to him about investing your heart so completely in anything. Here the scenario stalls. She never does figure out what to say to him, but she stays on guard because now she sees that he, too, needs someone to watch over him, someone to take care.

※

On Wednesday night, when the rehearsal comes closest to perfect, when Mrs. Daley's shrill soprano is nearly sweet, when Maureen Connolly carries off her solos with sheer competence, when the dancing appears effortless and inspired and Frankie Lawson tosses his bricks with perfect regularity, it's Clare who kisses Nate. On the street corner, waiting for the stoplight as they leave The Mad Hatter, she wraps her arms around his neck and kisses him solidly on the mouth. His hands settle, one on each of her hips, and when she takes her mouth away, he's looking directly into her eyes. He watches her a moment, eyes narrow, then tips his face up toward the stars and lets go one of his endearing laughs. He laughs and then he takes her up in his arms, takes her up and kisses her the way she's known a man like Nate is capable of kissing. He gives her the kiss she's been imagining. In fact, he gives her more than she's been imagining. And now she has new things to imagine.

29

When Clare arrives home, it's eleven-thirty and Paul is there, sitting in the grass by the driveway, his suit coat and shoes piled next to him. He doesn't get up when she pulls in. He sits there, knees bent, arms draped forward over them. It's an ominous sight, him there like that. The house is probably burned out in the back, somewhere she can't see yet. Or Jeanine is lying in an emergency room bed, lacerated and unconscious. Her father — this thought pulls so tight across her chest she can't breathe — has died, waiting to hear some word of forgiveness from her.

Clare parks in the garage, hurries out of the car, and feels her legs weaken under her as she runs toward Paul. Still he sits there, with some sort of deliberate calmness that feeds her dread. He hasn't even looked at her yet. "Paul?" she says. "What's happened? Tell me."

He looks at her finally, stands up, gathers his things. "Battery went dead on my garage door opener."

The simplicity of it is almost unbelievable. Clare still feels herself braced for more. "Didn't you have a key?" she says.

"I haven't had a key since Sally Brandt came to water the plants the time we went to California."

"Why didn't you go buy a battery?"

"I haven't been here that long. Really, fifteen minutes. I thought you'd be coming any minute. Actually, I thought you'd be here. You're late tonight."

She can't look at him while she says it. "Last ditch efforts with the show. Isn't Jeanine here?"

"I thought she was with you."

"Well, she was. At rehearsal, she was. She left with Jeffrey afterwards."

"Well, she should be here any minute then, too."

"Yeah." Clare takes a glance up the street. It's dark except for the circles of light under the streetlights. It's garbage day tomorrow and every driveway has a plastic trash can at its side. Paul has put theirs out too. It's there by the driveway, in place, on time.

She and Paul go into the garage and on into the house. Rehearsal's been over since ten. Clare's had time to drink a beer, kiss a dancer, and mislead her husband. What could be taking Jeanine so long?

☙

It's midnight when she arrives. Paul's been quiet, has hardly spoken since they came in. He comes out, though, from the bedroom when Jeanine comes in the door. Clare realizes as she summons up the words she'll say to Jeanine that they've become lenient. With summer, with the evening rehearsals, they've been less than consistent in enforcing a curfew for Jeanine. Summer, rehearsals, and their own distractions. Add that, Clare thinks. Add that.

"It's late. Where have you been?" is what she decides to say to Jeanine.

"We had a Coke. Jeffrey and I," Jeanine says. She walks past Clare and then Paul, on into the kitchen. Paul follows her. Clare comes too. Jeanine opens the refrigerator and stands looking inside for a while, then closes it.

"Long Coke," Paul says, and Clare bristles more than Jeanine.

Jeanine merely shrugs, looks at them, first Paul, then Clare. Clare feels the look is piercing, but realizes she's not being entirely objective. She's on alert herself. "Have you been here waiting?" Jeanine speaks it like code and directs the question to Clare.

"A while," Clare says. She'd like to spank Jeanine for the look she gives her then.

"I've been here," Paul says. "And the rehearsal's been over since ten, so we know you've been somewhere else."

Clare takes this in and her face grows hot with the knowledge that Paul is saying this as much to her as to Jeanine. There's nothing else she can do there in the kitchen but hold tight to her composure and remember what it is that's happening: she and Paul are disciplining their daughter. She's come home late. She's pretended to have been somewhere she wasn't. She's spent two hours with Jeffrey, having a Coke or doing the things you do when you're fifteen or sixteen, alone, and in darkness. Fifteen, sixteen, thirty or forty.

Do she and Paul really believe they can impose some kind of moral standards on Jeanine with a curfew? What does the attempt say to her, really? We see you growing up, we hope you'll get through with as little hurt as possible, without permanent damage? Or, start your misbehavior earlier so you can make it home by eleven? The truth may be it's all uncontrollable. Probably curfews are for parents, to let them feel they tried. To give them something measurable to insist upon. To give them the obligation to be home enforcing it.

Jeanine opens the refrigerator again, takes another long survey of its contents.

"Close the fridge," Paul says.

"I'm hungry," Jeanine says.

"Close the fridge," Paul says again. He's raised his voice, and it pushes Clare's composure to the edge to hear it. "Close it now." Clare's heart pounds.

"Well, excuse *me*," Jeanine says, her tone snotty. She has no sense, this girl, at moments like this. She gets under the influence of an emotion and just lets it take her. It's scary to be reminded of that just now. How she jumps onto a feeling and rides it wherever it takes her. "Excuse me for living," she shouts, and Clare's heart turns a somersault. She senses they're about to capsize, to plunge into something so dark and deep they'll never be able to emerge from it as the same people. She's beat against the silence that has surrounded this pain but now, faced with seeing it broken, Clare at least acknowledges the capacity silence has to insulate, to place some distance between pain and its survivors.

Jeanine slams the refrigerator shut and tries to push past her father and out of the kitchen. Paul stops her. He takes hold of both her arms and physically stops her. She pushes once more, makes a sound like a little shriek, then glares at Paul. He still has her. He holds her arms just a moment longer, looks at her, and Clare knows he wants even more to grab onto *her* like this. He'd like to grab Clare and demand, Where were you? Don't you remember? We have a deal here: bind each other's wounds. Wounds. Bound. Bounds. People who've been through what we've been through don't get to live in the present anymore. They live in an aftermath of the past that goes on forever.

Paul takes his hands from Jeanine's arms. "I was here once," Jeanine says. There's accusation in her voice. "Where were you?" She says this to Paul, though just the words, spoken to anyone, are enough to turn Clare cold. Yes, where was she?

"I was at the Arts Center looking for any member of my family with a house key," Paul says. "Neither of them were there, but Mrs. Daley was. 'Well, you just missed them. We just got done,' she says. So I come back home, wait, wait some more. You weren't here." He's saying it to Jeanine. Clare checks and that's who he's talking to.

"I was, too," Jeanine says hotly. "We came here right after, but no one," she directs an incriminating look at Clare, "was here."

"And you didn't have your key either?" Paul says. He's beginning to sound like an investigator.

"I don't even own a key!"

"So where did you go then?"

Jeanine's face takes on a dangerous look and Clare thinks, here it comes. Here it all comes. Grab a breath, we're going under. Jeanine throws her hip to one side and narrows her eyes. "We went straight to Roadrunner Park and fucked our brains out."

Clare laughs. It comes out spontaneously, with a choke, pure overflow of tension. She thought they were about to release themselves on each other, pull off an arm or a leg, drag it through all the bitter accumulations of survival and then fling it at the one to blame. *To blame.* But instead, it's this other thing—the sweet, physical enactment of rescue and reconnection. It's the plunge she's feared Jeanine would take this summer, but now that it's been named and projected against some of the other options, it seems less damaging than before. The laughter is partly relief and, of course, the wrong thing to do, but Clare's already done it before she realizes that. It's such a ridiculous word to come out of Jeanine's mouth: fuck. So disallowed, but so exactly on target.

Well, Clare's shattered the interrogation completely and it's as if Paul just now remembers she's here, or perhaps he turns to her because he doesn't know what to say next to Jeanine, a daughter who's just flung the F-word into his face. "Where did you go?" Paul says.

"Not there," Clare says. "I am not a witness."

Now it's Jeanine laughing.

It's awful. They can't tease him like this. Not now. An emotionally draining experience can be like three martinis in how it makes you giddy and disposed to inappropriate responses.

"So where then?" His voice is serious. He wants to know.

It's not as though there's anything in particular to hide.

Really. Why shouldn't she go for a drink? Nate's a friend and they have a job to do. She's let this take on too much weight. It's nothing. Nothing at all.

"I know, I know," Jeanine says, waving her hand in the air like a schoolchild.

Stop. It's got to stop.

"I went to The Mad Hatter with Nate," Clare says, before Jeanine can say it. "We had a drink and talked about the show." There. She's said it and it sounds reasonable. Paul's heard it and he looks reasonable. If he's remembering that she once told him Nate wanted her to be his lover, it's not showing on his face. Probably he's forgotten it. Probably he didn't really hear it in the first place. Just now he's heard her say she went for a drink with Nate, they talked about the show. A business drink, that's all. That's what she's said. Later I kissed him. Then he kissed me. He's been kissing me for some time now, but this kiss was different. I liked it. I might do it again. I know, I can't understand it either. That's what she hasn't said.

Jeanine doesn't say anything. Not *Again*? or anything like that. She looks at Clare, though, and then she looks at Paul looking at Clare, and the kitchen seems suddenly small. When Jeanine's eyes return to her, Clare has the feeling she's just entered into some sort of pact. She and Jeanine, a silent agreement.

"I expect you home at eleven o'clock weeknights," Paul says to Jeanine.

He's not going to say anything at all about the activities in the park? He assumes it was a lie, something said deliberately to hurt him? Or is this another wave of silence come to wash out this latest assault on their fragile peace?

To Clare Paul says, "I think we need more keys around here."

It wasn't true, what he'd said, either. Fifteen minutes. That's what he told her on the driveway—that he'd been waiting fifteen minutes. It was longer than that. There was more than that to say.

❦

Clare's been lying awake for an hour when she remembers the collage. She holds her hand against the bed to minimize the sloshing and gets up. She goes to the Singing Room, opens the can of varnish and applies another coat. The collage is on the floor and Clare crouches next to it, rocking from knees to feet, forward and back, as she strokes the brush from top to bottom of the board. When she's finished, she sits down there on the floor and smoothes her nightgown over her knees.

The varnish was thick and milky when it went on. She could see all the brushstrokes and it clouded over the faces in the pictures like gloom. As she sits there, it dries and clarifies, slowly, the faces emerging as if through a membrane. Her parents on their wedding day. Jeanine dancing with Sam. Michael at the Soda Shoppe Bop. Clare watches —she feels she must—until all the faces are visible again.

30

Now that her younger students are out of school for the summer, Clare is able to schedule their lessons earlier in the day. The day after Paul is locked out, she finishes teaching by three and, before rehearsal, she goes to Ace Hardware and makes keys. It's a self-service operation. Clare reads the instructions, then places her key in position on the machine and starts. The sound is horrible, the sort of grinding that goes right to your heart and scours it out. The machine grinds and jumps in a way it doesn't seem it should, and Clare has the thought that it's breaking down. There's something wrong with the machine. It's not only not going to make her two spare keys, it's going to chew up the one she's given it. Her only one. It'll be mutilated. They'll have no keys. If the battery in the garage door opener dies today, they'll never get into their house again.

The machine whines into a high-pitched squall and gives off a burning odor. Clare is about to shut it down when she sees it's copying the grooves and ridges of her house key. All right then. She decides to go for another — one for Paul, one for Jeanine — and sets the machine to work on the second key.

It's a little startling to think they've been making do with one house key. It could have so easily been lost, misplaced. It's strange that no one's been locked out until now. They've moved in such a pattern, she and Paul, knowing when the other could be expected home, trusting without question that the door would be open when they needed to go in. They've been relying on that, believing in that. It's a wonder a family could have survived this long in so innocent a position. Innocent or precarious. But still, a part of her is reluctant to move on from this stage, to become a family with three keys.

The keys are solid and warm in her hand. As she stands at the check-out waiting, she runs the tip of her thumb along the ridges of the keys, seeing if she can tell whether they're all alike. She pays for them and it seems not enough. It seems unlikely they could be this inexpensive.

Near the check-out is a display of pool products: chlorine tablets and skimming nets and hanging over it all, on ropes suspended from the ceiling, is an air mattress built for two. Double-wide. Below, on the shelf, are more, still in boxes. On the box are a man and a woman, both young and tanned and beautiful. They look as if they're having fun. That old easy thing. There, on the box, together on their double-wide mattress, they're floating and having fun. They make it look as if this air mattress would be the thing to have, a good purchase to make. She and Paul could float together in the pool, lie side by side, touch hands or whole bodies. They could lie there at night, when the water's black, when the stars are out. They could whisper. Float. It's on sale, too.

Clare takes one from the display, goes back to the check-out line again, waits. The box is heavier than she'd expected. It's a lot of mattress, flattened out and folded, to put into such a small box. At home, she'll pump it up. She'll do that before she goes to rehearsal. Afterwards, she'll come straight home. Paul will be home by then. Even if he works tonight, he'll be home by then. To be sure, she'll call him at the bank, tell him. There's a new air mattress in our pool. Double-wide. Come on home. We'll float and kiss. It'll be fun.

Clare pays again, goes home, and gives Jeanine her key. She puts Paul's on the dresser where he'll be sure to see it. Then she goes out to the garage for the foot pump. She carries it to the backyard and begins pumping up the mattress. This takes a while. It's a big mattress. It's blue and has six round indentations for putting drinks into. Six? Clare pumps it up and puts it into the pool. It's nearly as wide as the pool is at the narrow part of the kidney shape.

She calls Paul at the bank. He's out. She leaves a message for him to call, but by the time she has to leave, he hasn't. She thinks of calling him again, leaving another message. "Come straight home." It sounds too alarming. An emergency. Some horrible thing happening to them. She'd better explain. "I've bought us a double-wide air mattress. Hurry home. Let's try it out." Too silly. His new secretary would squint her eyes and say *What?* and then Clare would have to say it again, the whole silly thing. "There's fun at home. Get there pronto." Paul would stuff that one into his pocket quick and look around wondering who's seen. Finally she doesn't call. He'll come. Eventually, he'll come. She'll be there when he does.

❧

Nate is wired. When Clare arrives at the Arts Center, he's motoring around backstage a hundred and sixty miles an hour and emitting that energy that's undiluted magnetism for Clare. She feels tired already. Just the sight of him and she's worn out, no reserves left. She takes a breath, holds it in her lungs for its tranquilizing effect, and goes to him.

"Rehearsal every night the rest of the week," he says, pulling off his shoes and socks. He does this standing up, jumping on one foot, then the other. He gives each sock a shake and stuffs them into his Reeboks. The shoes he takes and throws ten feet from where they're standing in the green room. They hit the wall and drop into the corner.

He looks at her watching the flight of his shoes, plants a quick kiss on her mouth. She's sure he hasn't bothered to check, but she does: there's no one watching. "We need it, Clare." He turns his face from her the way a boy will from his mother when a smile arrives on his lips at just the moment when it most shouldn't. "Rehearsal," he says, a loud whisper. "This show. We're not ready."

It's urgent with him, she can see. The mischief is gone from his face. He's got his heart invested so far into this thing, it's, well, it's humbling. It's so rare.

If she sets her eyes just so, so her field of vision begins just below the bottom edge of his shorts and reaches down to his feet, she can imagine it's been his clothes he's flung against the far wall. They're in a heap there in the corner. He's here, next to her, without them. She looks at his bare feet and that's what she imagines. It fills her up with things she wants to know. Does he care for her? Why did he and Susanna split up? Why does he kiss her? Does he kiss other women? And while we're on it, who? When? Where? How? Why?

It's exhausting. Looking at him, listening to him. It's like heavy exercise on an empty stomach. Two days without sleep. Two weeks without sex. All the stuff that wears you down and makes you want. It's the wanting that's exhausting her. Wanting and wanting and wanting.

❦

After rehearsal, Jeanine leaves with Jeffrey. It's become a regular habit Clare's grown to anticipate. Nate's grown to anticipate it, too. That and that Clare will go with him to The Mad Hatter.

Well, tonight she won't. Tonight she's had enough tortuous thoughts. Tonight she's going home. Fun. Fun tonight. Fun tonight in the pool. Fun tonight in the pool with Paul. Morally responsible fun tonight in the pool with Paul.

This dancer. He's full of the things she's been wanting and trying to name. Seeing them in his eyes, she can recognize that: there they are, my things.

She's going home. She tells him that: "I'm going home."

"You are?" he says. "Right away, you mean? Now?"

She has to smile. Underneath it all — the flash, the winning ways, the bravado — he's such an innocent. He's so young. It's something she ought to remember. She ought to think of that all the time, write it in lipstick across her mirror, hang it with a magnet on her refrigerator: Be careful of this dear heart. He's so young.

"Yup," she says, and the word pulls tight around her heart. It's his word. She never says this, never has until now. Once more: "Yup, I'm going home. I'm going home now." She doesn't stop to consider her next act. It may not have prevented her if she had. She puts her hand to one of his cheeks, a kiss to the other.

He takes hold of her arm as she turns away from him. She turns back and he looks at her. "You were good tonight," he says. "Your music is really terrific."

Clare feels that sinking feeling again — doubt seeping in around the edges: he's luring me. Watch out because he's no child. He knows how to play this scene. He has all his steps down. "Thanks," she says, "so were you." He smiles and she's a little ashamed of her suspicion. She's leaving now. She's going. Right now she is. "Bye."

"Yup. Bye."

31

Coming into the driveway tonight is a lot like coming in last night. Paul is not really sitting there in the grass, but Clare remembers him being there almost as vividly as if he were. She repeats last night's thoughts, too. Fear for Jeanine's welfare. For Paul's. She thinks again of that other harrowing eventuality: something happening to her father. Certainly, she recognizes the possibility. He's seventy-two years old. But it seems too horrible, too mean even for Nature that something would happen to her father before she sees him. She feels almost secure in being in a kind of grace period. Nothing could happen now, not these few days before the anniversary. Besides, she's home earlier tonight. Ten o'clock. She's come directly home. She's exercising restraint. Responsibility. There ought to be some grace for a daughter in that.

Jeffrey's car is parked at the curb. Clare presses the button on her garage door opener, expecting to see Paul's car in the garage. It's not. Clare pulls in, parks. The house is quiet when she comes in. There's one lamp on in the family room, and four shoes, Jeanine's and Jeffrey's, tossed in the corner by the couch. Clare calls once, "Jeanine?" and gets no answer. She begins to think of where they may be and doesn't like what comes to mind. She doesn't call again, considers whether to be quiet and surprise them or noisy so as to warn them they're not alone. It's a tough decision. It's a tough decision for tonight.

In the kitchen, some evidence they've been there. Watermelon rinds on plates with lots of seeds floating in pink juice. One fork. Empty Coke cans and a napkin scrunched up in a wad. A note in Jeanine's handwriting: "Dad called. Home at eleven." Who will be home at eleven? Paul or Jeanine? Can't anybody be explicit anymore? Is she already here? Jeffrey's car is outside. The shoes in the corner. Where are they? Upstairs in her bed. Too bold. Upstairs in the bathtub. You can be driven to boldness when it's necessary. The car is stalled outside. It wouldn't start. No gas. Things like that happen. They've walked somewhere. Out to look at the stars. To the Circle K for a can of gas. To a private spot dark enough to hide them for a while.

Clare walks into the family room and shuts off the lamp. She sees them then. Sees their movement glistening on the surface of the pool. In the darkness outside, the moving water catches diffused light from street lights and the windows of neighbors' houses. The neighbors themselves are safely inside their homes playing Scrabble with their children and eating popcorn. The houses are solid and warm and she is here at a window watching her daughter and a just-become young man laugh and wrestle in the pool. In the pool on her double-wide air mattress that she pumped forever and hasn't even used herself yet. She's made a decision now: she'll be quiet so as not to reveal she's seen them. She's seen enough. There's nothing more she needs to see. There's nothing more she wants to see. What are they doing anyway?

Clare turns the lamp back on, retraces her steps right back out of the room. She goes out to the Singing Room, puts a wall between her and the patio door, and sits down in Paul's chair. She hadn't even used it yet. Her air mattress. Clare leans back against the chair's head cushion and thinks she can smell Paul. The evening Paul, doused with a day's worth of work, worry, and wonder. Wonder? Or the morning Paul, after a night of sleep and an early-morning tangle with her. Sunday mornings, in the kitchen before a shower, she could find him with her eyes closed, with her hands behind her back, she could.

"You guys kissed for half an hour," Michael told her one Sunday as she made pancakes. Dollar-sized pancakes was what he liked. He used to play with them on the plate, arrange them into patterns. In a line like a caterpillar, or one big and two littles like the face of Mickey Mouse. "I came to your room and you were kissing." Smack-smack. He did that into the air. "In a half hour, you were still there, still kissing. I looked on the clock. Half an hour." It was hard to tell if he was more satisfied with himself for telling the time — this was new — or for his message, which he seemed to consider a kind of revelation. This was very close, this Sunday, to the time of the accident. Very close, Clare makes herself think, to the end of his life. She thinks and can't remember: what he made out of his pancakes that morning. What was it? She wants to know and there's no memory of it in her. Nothing to call up. Gone.

Clare turns her face into the chair's cushion, lets its fabric stroke her cheek, breathes deep. Clare feels sure now. She thinks of it for no reason and there's complete certainty in her heart: she didn't dry her hair after the time in her parents' Roman tub with Paul. She didn't and her mother said nothing. And almost certainly her father didn't buy that story Paul told him about using the pillows in the car for traction. How could he believe that? He pretended. He closed his eyes or he closed his ears. It occurs to Clare now that her father was like that always. Keeping the peace. Placating. Building a wall between the sawdust and the clean laundry. Avoiding conflict. If things were not all right, he'd act as though they were. As if pretending—done intently enough, with enough belief, with enough endurance—could force the wrong things right. Could take back angry words. Could pick up the clothes off the kitchen floor and put them back on her mother. Could bring back a drowned grandchild. Clare knows, knows it in her heart, that those letters in her drawer are those kinds of letters. Pretended. Pretended normalcy. Life-goes-on letters. The weather, the routine daily events. No mention of problems or mistakes. Certainly no mention of the Big Mistake. Drive it out of their lives with silence. Never say its name. Don't breathe it. Don't. Shh. Quiet. Gone.

Clare gets up out of Paul's chair and goes back into the family room. She turns out the lamp. She could alert them to her presence with light, she thinks. She wouldn't have to make a sound, just on-off, on-off a few dozen times. They'd notice.

She leaves it off. She goes again to the window. There they are on her new, never-used-by-her air mattress. Still there. Still kissing. Jeffrey is standing chest-deep in the water, Jeanine is stretched across the mattress on her stomach. She's wearing half a bikini. They're joined, chest to chest, mouth to mouth. In the light provided by the neighbors, Clare can see Jeffrey's hands. They move down Jeanine's white-white back like years, like memories, and disappear into the black water. He loves her. He thinks he loves her.

≈

This is the big stuff, Clare thinks as she listens from the bedroom to the sounds of Jeffrey leaving. Ready or not, here it is. The door opening. The door closing. Probably there were less audible sounds in between. Whispers. A kiss. Finally the car, completely functional after all, starting up, driving off. This is it. Ready or not, time to talk. How long until eleven? Would it be easier with or without Paul?

Clare goes out into the family room. There's Jeanine, wrapped in a towel, hair dripping, standing at the window Clare left a short while ago. Committing it all to memory, Clare thinks. Going over it all in her mind, getting the pieces into place.

Jeanine sees her. "Oh, you're home," she says, the obvious thing. "Did you have fun?" Clare hears no sarcasm in that, no hidden agenda at all.

Fun? Clare thinks. No, I guess fun's been tabled for

tonight. No Mad Hatter with Nate. No pool with Paul. No fun at all. "I've been home a while," Clare begins. "I've been here. I saw you in the pool. You and Jeffrey."

Jeanine looks away, looks out at the pool, for evidence, perhaps, some indication she was there and seen. Then she looks back at Clare, squarely, unblinking. "Oh?" she says. She looks away, fingers a strand of her wet hair, pulls it across her face, lets it go.

"Yes. I've been home a half hour or so."

They've come to lean on time as a code, Clare realizes. They talk of curfews and tardiness when they mean sex. There needs to be some means of separating yes from no, right from wrong, so we draw a line and call it midnight or call it ten P.M. It's an easier name. We all know what it means. We can all say it. It's much easier to say *half hour* to your daughter than *half naked*. Jeanine, you seem to be on the edge of midnight. Once you pass ten P.M., it's hard to go back. Think about it. If you and Jeffrey are having minutes, you need to be smart, or there may be hours of misery ahead. If you're going to be late, you'd better be careful. We need to talk about stop watches. Alarm clocks. The time seems right for this. It's the right time. It's time to be right. It's time to be, right?

"Jeanine, sit down, will you? Let's talk a minute." There, it's starting already. Talk a minute. "Sit down." Clare sits down, shows her: See? Easy.

Jeanine comes to the couch. She sits on its very edge, only one leg on it actually, as far from Clare as she could be. She folds her arms over her chest and Clare realizes there are no straps on her shoulders. The towel is wrapped over her breasts, tucked tight under her arm, and her shoulders are bare.

"I know you don't like to talk about it, but I don't want to see you in trouble." In trouble? "If you and Jeffrey are involved—in sex, I mean—" (as opposed to what? crime? illegal bribes? narcotics?) "you need to be smart. Think ahead. Even if you're not, but may be soon. It's hard to be dispassionate when you're passionate."

Jeanine gives her a look, sidelong: you're bizarre, Mother.

Clare takes a breath, starts again. "Okay, now here's what I really want to say. Think about this. It's sweet and kind of irresistible, but think about this. It's an intimate thing. What happens in your body is nothing compared to what happens in your heart and there are no pills, no precautions against that. You have to think before you invest your heart like this." Clare stops for breath, then says the truest thing: "It will change you." The prospect of that change and that risk closes up Clare's throat for a moment. It shuts down her brain and turns her fingertips cold. All she can think to do is say it again. Her voice is quieter this time and quavers less than she was afraid it might. "It will change you."

Jeanine softens her glance ever so slightly. She lets her arms go loose, drops her head a minute, then looks again at Clare. "I love him best and for always," she says. Her voice is steady, but not defiant. Each word is studded with conviction.

It's just the thing, isn't it? The thing we want our children to believe at fifteen? That there's someone they can love best. Someone they can love for always. It's the sort of thing that, when you hear it at forty, makes you doubt, makes you start the next sentence with a drawn-out *well*. . . . But what else would we want them to believe at the start? What else? You couldn't punch a hole in that if you tried. No one would believe you. No one fifteen. Not even yourself maybe. Don't you, somewhere inside, believe it still?

"You think that," Clare says. She watches. She watches this girl-woman child of hers.

"I know it," Jeanine says. "It's the truth."

Well. . . . Well, we say for thinking time, well. It's true then. She says it's true, she believes it's true, it's true. She loves him. Best and always.

The things a mother can do are these. Take her to the doctor and the drugstore. Do the physical things to prevent pregnancy and disease. Say the other stuff you need to say that she won't hear. Know that. She won't. But say them for yourself. Say them and see if you can tell. Are they still true?

❦

Paul is on time at eleven. Jeanine's gone to bed and Clare's had time enough to think how he'll hate this. He'll hate this news of Jeanine. He'll hate what Clare tells him will happen next. He'll want to talk some sense into her. Jeanine, and probably Clare, too. He'll want to take charge and change all this, get his family back on track. And he'll want to hang Jeffrey by his heels and leave him to starve. Clare surprises herself with a flash of sympathy as she considers this fate for Jeffrey.

"You're here," Paul says when he comes in.

Still here. Still kissing. She does—kisses him. "Here I am," she says then. "I'm here." She kisses him again. Take these pleasures whenever you can. Take them. Hold them to you tightly. You must.

She looks at him. Looks hard. She memorizes his eyes, his mouth, and takes his scent into her nose. She brushes her face against the stubble on his, leaves him some trace there, some sensation, some validation. "It's me, Paul. Clare." She takes him in, makes him sit. She tells him the news of the day.

Paul takes the thoughts she's given him to the window, the same window, what is it, a family look-out point? He looks out, to the yard, the pool. "I think it's smart," he says finally. "I wish she weren't doing what she apparently is doing, but if she is, I think you're right. Think of the chances we took as kids. We were just damn lucky."

"You do?" Clare says. She's come to the window, is standing close enough to bring an arm around his waist. She doesn't do this, not now, but she's that close to him there at the window.

"I didn't think you would. I was afraid you wouldn't."

"What else can we do?"

"Well, you could talk to her. Tell her don't do it. Ground her. Take away her allowance. Spank her and send her to her room."

"I wish. Keep her there for three years. Six."

Clare puts her arm around him now. Now's the time. He brings his head close to hers and looks out into the yard. "No," he says, "it's the right thing. What else?"

Clare shrugs, her shoulder bumping Paul's.

"Is that the air mattress? Where did we get that anyway?" Paul asks. "It's big."

"I bought it. I bought it today, for us."

"Us? You and me?"

"Is there someone else?" *She said that?* "I bought it at the hardware store."

Paul rests his chin against the top of Clare's head. He lets it slide down the side of her face until they're cheek to cheek. He tries to look at her, eye squashed against her face, then presses his mouth to her neck and gives her a nip.

"She took it and used it before we even had a chance," Clare says. She feels tears, hot and quick, in her eyes. She blinks them back, puts them away. "You're a good man, Paul." She tightens her grip on him, hangs on. "You're a good father."

"Clare?"

"Hmm."

"What would you have done if I hadn't agreed with you on this?"

She doesn't hesitate. "I would have gone ahead anyway."

He looks up to the ceiling, down to the floor, smiles. "I thought so," he says. "That's what I thought."

Clare nods, sets her mouth firm. "That's what," she says.

"You didn't think I would."

"I thought you might not."

"What did you think I'd do?"

"Hang Jeffrey by his heels and leave him to starve."

"Oh, Clare. Clare, that's a great idea. It's just the thing. Let's. Let's do it."

She presses a hand to his chest, pulls away from him. He grabs her arm as she turns away. "You have to help me. How will I get him up there by myself?" He's trying to hold her, trying to keep her there. Clare pushes at him, laughing, then breaks away for just a minute before Paul grabs her again, takes her down on the couch. He trips — Jeanine's shoes are there — as he does this and comes down on her a little harder than she expected. His breath and the distinct moan he has for back pain come into her face. She watches him as he rolls his eyes back. Then he closes them and brings his mouth down to hers. He moans again, and this time Clare knows he's faking. "I'll never walk again," he says between kisses. "You'll have to do it yourself. Hang him up, but tell him I wanted to be there. Tell him it's from me, too."

"Okay," she says. Kissing is just the sweetest thing. "But I get everything that falls out of his pockets."

"That's fair. I want to know what all it was, though. Everything." His mouth presses new urgency into hers. He delivers a long, insistent kiss and then he pulls away from her just enough to see her. Really see her. He looks a while, with his mouth still open. "Clare? My God, come here." He puts his hand behind her head, lifts it from the couch. "Hurry. We're getting old, aren't we?"

"You hadn't heard?"

"I'm serious. Come on. Let's get to bed and go to it. You're going to have fun tonight." He pulls himself off of her, gets up, pulls her after him. "Quick. Come on."

There's only one response to a request like that. Clare gets up. She goes with him, fast as she can. It's midnight already. Already she hears the clock. Twelve strokes.

32

The next morning, Clare infringes. She knows that's what she's doing, but it can't be helped. The end will justify the means. She listens for Jeanine's song, for the news of what's going to happen next. She stands outside the bathroom door. She goes so far as to put her ear to it, and she listens. It's a critical time. A mother needs all her reinforcements at a time like this. She needs to know.

Eternal Flame. Oh, wouldn't you know? Wouldn't it just have to be? Twenty minutes of hot water given to a song like that. "*Do you feel my heart beating? Do you understand? Do you feel the same? Am I only dreaming, or is this burning an eternal flame?*" Jeanine sings. She drops the bar of soap once or maybe it was her knee hitting the side of the tub, but all the rest of the time, she sings this song, over and over. *Eternal Flame.* Isn't that something on Kennedy's grave?

At least there are questions in this song. Questions are good. Questions, in fact, are eternal. Does she realize that? But why couldn't she be singing *Wait?* Or how about *We All Sleep Alone?*

The news that evening is that the gravelly voice so perfect for the old-timer narrator has been acquired by

Maureen Connolly, who plays the part of Lucy Bradford, a founder of the first hospital in Mirage. The part includes two solos. Maureen can just barely speak, so singing the solos is out of the question. It's bad news. It's Wednesday, it's three days until showtime, and what's worse is that Maureen's understudy, Sharon Benedict, has tearfully confessed to Clare that although she knows Maureen's musical pieces well, the prospect of having to speak — and possibly forget — lines terrifies her. Clare tells all this to Nate before the start of rehearsal.

"It's okay," he says. "It's all right. In fact, it's perfect." They're backstage and he's taking off his shoes and socks again, getting ready. Does it always have to be this way? Isn't there somewhere else he could do this than right in front of her? And now he's got to say this, too: perfect. She glares at him. That's enough. He must know this much about her, doesn't he?

He smiles his bad-boy smile, sheepish but as if he already knows he'll win her over. "You do it," he says simply. He looks at her, a sock in each hand. He shrugs. "*Why not?*"

She turns away. Her heart is thumping. No no no. She tells him: NO.

"Why not?" he says again, as if this phrase can never be used up. How many times does he think we get to say *Why not?* in a lifetime?

"Because I'm not. I'm not singing in the show. I have a job to do and that's not it. No."

"But this is what we need you to do. What could be more important than that? Who will do it if you don't?"

"Do we have to have so many questions? The answer is no. The answer to all questions is no." A loud cymbal crash punctuates her sentence. Clare pulls the stage curtain aside and sees a drummer out in the orchestra pit bending over to retrieve the cymbal from the floor. The cast is starting to gather, too. The chatter is spirited tonight. There's anticipation, hope, dread, something, building. There's been a feeling this week of pulling together, of summoning up the best inside yourself and putting it out there for the show. The final leg. It's Nate who's inspired that, Nate who has pumped them up. She's been here every night, she's lent her expertise, but it's Nate who's driven them.

Even so, there's just no way. Sing? Solo?

"So you don't think you want to do it," Nate says. He's standing, legs apart, arms folded over his chest. He's wearing a T-shirt and patches of sweat are already visible under his arms. His face is careful. It's obvious he sees the need for some caution. He says this, he watches her a moment, and then he kisses her. Right now, with musicians dropping things out in the orchestra pit, with townspeople and soldiers and prominent historical figures walking around on the other side of that curtain, he kisses her. Right now, while she's angry, riled, ready to strike out, he kisses her. The man is reckless. She knew the caution had to be a fluke. What he really has under that sweaty shirt is recklessness. And she'd like to get some of it. It's what she's going to need if she's going to do this. If she's going to sing, it's the thing she needs.

❦

Clare sings Maureen's part during rehearsal. Only for rehearsal, but she does sing it then. The silences and Nate's eyes were impossible to ignore. But she also makes it clear to Nate: she's shopping. She's looking for someone else. That's her job. She'll handle this, she will.

Afterwards Jeanine and Sharon and several others tell her she was good, that she should go ahead and sing for the show. Do it, they tell her. Why not? That's what Nate tells her, too: you were good. Do it. Why not?

That's the part she can't answer. The *Why not*. Now that she's done it for the cast, it ought to be an easy thing to do it for real. During the last number she even imagined she was doing it for real, that the seats in the auditorium were filled with people. And then they all started fanning their programs and her knees shook and if she'd stopped for even a moment, if there'd been a rest in the song just then, she wouldn't have been able to pick it up again. If she'd stopped to think about it, she would have forgotten it all. All of them, fanning and fanning.

She doesn't tell Nate anything. When he asks, *Why not?* she lets it go unanswered. She wants a different question. He asks, Will she go with him to The Mad Hatter? And because she's already said no so many times, and this is clearly an easier thing to do, she tells him yes.

They go and it's a jumping place tonight. Several of the cast are there and it's an electric mood they're in. The pharmacist who plays the old-timer narrator buys a round and that's how Clare comes to have two beers instead of her usual one. Besides those two, she's seen Nate pouring from his bottle into her glass a couple of times, an unspecified amount, some extra she can't measure.

Under the table there's funny stuff going on. Bumping and chance meetings of knees and feet. This has happened here before. These tables are narrow. It's happened before that Nate, with his long legs, has stepped on her toe or rubbed against her leg under the table. She's moved aside those times, given him some extra space. Tonight there are four people around the table and she is sitting next to Nate. She becomes sure the touching is not accidental when he lays a hand on the inside of her thigh. He does this with complete familiarity, with no registration of anything strange in his face. Clare takes care of her own face, which is an effort, and works on deciding what to do about this. The next move is clearly hers.

She wonders how she could have gotten this far into her life without discovering how potent these actions are that we make romancing undercover. All those glances, those touches that make our cheeks warm and our legs walk funny out in the real world. Put them under a table, among extraneous others who shouldn't see them, and just watch what happens. See if your heart isn't crashing in your throat, and your legs squeezing the hand, and your bleary mind trying to figure out whether that's to keep it from moving higher or to keep it from leaving. Clare supposes all the world knows this already. But for her, the last woman on earth to find out, it's new.

She risks a look at Nate. She meets his eyes, already on her. He's been watching her. She realizes that and feels found out again, again the last to know. She glances away. He squeezes her leg and it draws her eyes right back to him. He looks at her and she lets him. His above-the-table hand lifts his bottle and pours beer into her glass. She thinks she won't drink it. She feels his other hand there at the edge of her shorts and loosens her legs the slightest bit. His hand slides easily under the fabric, like he's done this a hundred times before, like he belongs there, like she's his. It's that—feeling his—more than any other thought that draws her back. She's not. She's not his and he's not hers. She ought to remember that. She'd better remember that.

Clare gets up. She stands, which wobbles the table. Nate's hand slides off of her. She sees him draw it into a fist and rest it against the edge of the table. The conversation, which has been nothing more than noise to Clare's ears for several minutes, suddenly stops. Nate has to get up from the booth to let her out. He touches her arm as she squeezes past. "Clare, wait," he says. "Wait. I'll come with you."

"No, don't," she whispers.

He pauses, takes a quick glance around the surrounding tables.

"Okay. I get it." He's whispering now too. "I'll meet you at your car in ten minutes."

"No," she says, more urgently. She feels her forehead wrinkling into a frown.

She looks at Nate and he's trying and failing to remove his smile. "Please?" he says, close to her ear.

"I won't be there," Clare says. She pushes past him and heads for the door.

❦

The thing that makes her come back, makes her drive by the parking lot after she's left it, is wanting to know if he came. She isn't going to meet him. She isn't. But she wants to know: did he actually come? Did he leave The Mad Hatter and come to meet her?

She circles past, ten minutes later, like he said. He's there at his car, which was parked near hers, sitting on the bumper, arms folded over his chest. Clare feels her face flush. Her fingers go numb against the steering wheel, and when she flexes them back to life they feel too full, turgid and ready to burst. She looks at him, thinks, That's silly. Obviously, she's not there. She's left. Her car is gone. What's he doing? She's thinking this as she's driving past, as she registers the fact of his wave. There, on his bumper, he's waving to her. He's seen her. He's waving.

She goes on by, looking straight ahead, stops at the red light, and sees in her rearview mirror that he's still there on the bumper. Just sitting there. She turns right on red, follows the street down a block and turns again. She keeps coming without really deciding to, comes all the way back around until she's coming past again. Coming past that silly fool on the bumper, the one who's waving again. The one waiting for her—what else?

Once more. That's all, but once more. She comes around. He waves again. He must know by now she isn't going to stop, Clare thinks. She isn't. No. The light turns red again. She's forced to wait because she's not turning. She's going straight. She is.

Nate is on his feet. In her rearview mirror Clare can see him. It turns her face and fingers hot and full again.

He's walking toward her car. He's running. She thinks she can hear his feet pounding the sidewalk, but her windows are up and she tells herself that this couldn't be. She reaches back and presses down the lock by her left shoulder. All of the doors in the car lock with one deafening click and then the light turns green. She goes on through the intersection. She doesn't look back at him and doesn't check her mirror. She doesn't want to see this. This she just doesn't know what to do with.

33

Paul tells Clare as they're getting into bed that he's going to Phoenix the next day. He has a few details to finalize on Thursday and then, on Friday, he'll present the proposal to the dairy company. He'll stay overnight.

It's dangerous news, and she wants to tell him so. Tomorrow she'll take Jeanine to the doctor to talk about birth control. The show is Saturday night. The trip to Minnesota is next week. And most urgently, what she thought was a harmless flirtation with Nate is becoming something that scares her. She wants to tell Paul: don't go. Don't go now.

It's hard to believe she once went to Paul and issued a warning about Nate. Told him: he wants me. Nate wants me to be his lover. When did she become so covert? Not only is it surprising, it's despicable to her. She's always been a compulsive truth-teller. She's going to start lying now?

It's a revelation. It's news that leaves Clare with nothing to say but *okay*. Okay, she says, holding Paul in the bed, you go. You'll be back in time for the show. And would he like to go up onto the foothills afterwards and watch the fireworks? Later they could come home and play around on the air mattress in the pool. They still haven't gotten to that yet. These busy lives of theirs.

Playing around in the pool is not a thing you can bear to schedule. You just want to think of it, feel the inclination, and then do it. Do people actually make appointments for sex? People who aren't likely to be in the same bed at the same time unless they synchronize schedules. Lovers meeting over the noon hour — how do they work out the details? *I have thirty minutes on Tuesday — is that long enough? Or would you rather wait until Wednesday and go for an hour?* What do they write in their daytimers? A name? XXX? *I'll X out two hours for us next Friday. That'll allow for traffic.* They say these things to each other?

Just considering the preliminaries is exhausting to Clare. How would she ever get beyond them? She wants to turn to Paul right this minute, look him straight in the eye and say something simple like, Let's plan a picnic. Food in a basket. Let's have cold chicken and coleslaw. Beer in a Playmate cooler. An apple pie. Let's just get in the car when we feel like it and go. Let's have licorice. Do you want licorice? You and I. Jeanine and oh. Oh, Jeffrey. Jeanine would want to invite Jeffrey of course. If they had such a picnic, this simple picnic, were they going to invite Jeffrey?

In the morning Paul is getting his files and a folded shirt into his briefcase. He brings out an envelope and hands it to Clare. "The plane tickets," he says. "I picked them up yesterday."

Clare takes the envelope, opens it. Inside are three packets. They're printed with their names. She sees hers on the middle one: Clare Nichols. She opens it and there are her ticket with its red carbons and a folded itinerary on the travel agency's stationery. In case she didn't know, it tells her where she's going: Minneapolis. It tells her she'll go on Sunday and she'll stay ten days. It says it there in red and it looks official. She will travel in coach and eat lunch. There's no hint about what will happen once she gets there. Of course not.

"Almost D-Day," Paul says, snapping his briefcase shut.

"D-Day? What's that mean? We have a nifty label for it now do we?"

"No. Jesus, Clare. It's just an expression. D-Day."

"It's from a war." Clare folds her arms and sits on the edge of the dresser where Paul's set the briefcase. She puts herself between it and Paul. "You think of it as a war?"

"No. Of course not." She's directly in his path and she's settling in to stay a while. He moves to go around her and she stops him with her leg. "Don't do this, Clare. I have to go. I didn't mean anything in particular. It was thoughtless, I'm sorry, and I'm late." She stops him again and this time he sighs. "It was nothing," he says. He looks at her with his eyes only half open, the weary look, the one asking for a break.

"You have things to do, places to go, people to see," she says.

"Well," he says. He's looking for something better to say, but finally just says it: "Yeah."

"Yeah. And besides you just said it without thinking. You didn't mean anything."

"Right." He goes for the briefcase again.

Clare stands up, blocks his way. "Is this something you do often?"

"What's that?"

"Tell me things you don't mean, things you haven't even thought about?"

"Clare," he says. He puts his hands to her arms, which are tight against her body. He's going to move her? Move her over like a child? She moves. "I don't want to leave for two days with you mad like this," Paul says.

"So, what'll you do? Stay?"

"I can't stay."

"So I should stop being mad so you can go and not worry?"

He has the briefcase now. He's moved toward the door. His keys are in his hand. All the old keys and the new house key, too, Clare imagines. A whole life, jingling in his hand. "If you want to fight, do me the justice of a real fight," he says. "I won't stand here and quarrel with you."

"All right," Clare says hotly. "Let's fight then. A fight would be good. We never fight, Paul. Have you noticed?"

"This isn't a fight. This is a quarrel."

"And you don't do quarrels."

Paul says nothing. He walks to the door. He hesitates a moment, like he's forgotten something, or like there's something more to say.

"You should put your clean shirt on a hanger when you get to the hotel. It'll be wrinkled tomorrow if you don't." Clare comes over to him as she says this and Paul nods to show he's heard. Then he bends to kiss her, briefly, on the lips. "It was a fight," she says then as he's turning to go out the door.

"A quarrel," he says, leaving. "I'll call tonight. It was a quarrel."

"It was a fight," Clare shouts after him. "I was there. It was a fight."

Paul shakes his head as he lifts the briefcase into the back of the Jeep and gets in.

Clare's standing at the open door. She watches as he pulls out. The garage door is coming down between them as she sees his mouth moving behind the windshield. Either he's throwing a kiss into the air—she thinks that first—or he's mouthing the word *quarrel*.

The garage door comes down and Clare goes inside. In front of the bathroom mirror she says the word *quarrel*. She watches her mouth open around the *qu* and feels her tongue lift for the *l*. She says it again and then she smacks a kiss into the mirror. *Quarrel*. Smack. Smack. *Quarrel*. They look almost the same. *Quarrel*: it looks almost like a kiss.

34

Clare thinks she has a solution to the problem of Maureen's hoarse voice. She doesn't expect the response she gets from Nate when she suggests it to him before rehearsal that evening.

"It won't work, Clare." She's met up with him at the vending machines in the hallway of the Arts Center. He's buying a Coke and chips. "It might sound easy, but it'd be a major shake-up. You can't just split a character, give the spoken lines to one actress and the singing to another. How could that work?" He's digging in his pocket for more change. "You wouldn't have a quarter would you?" he asks.

Clare opens her purse, finds one and gives it to him. He puts it into the machine and gets a second bag of chips. "Just a little alteration of the script," she says. "With a few adjustments, Maureen can keep her lines and Sharon can do the solos. Is that your dinner?"

"It would screw up the choreography completely. There are only two rehearsals to go. Just sing it, Clare." He pushes a bag of chips toward her chest as he says this. It touches her lightly and makes a crinkling sound. She looks at it in his hand. They're sour cream and onion. "You know the part better than anyone, lines and music. You probably could have done it better than Maureen in the first place. Christ, you wrote it. Why won't you sing it?"

Clare's forgotten for a moment to listen to what he's saying. She's been distracted by the visuals of it. His hands, the way he's throwing them around with the Coke can and the bags of chips in them. His face, the undisguised intensity in it. His eyes. His eyes. She thinks of him waving to her last night from the bumper of his car. Then she thinks of him behind her on his bike the time he rode her home. She thinks of him at her car window, beside her in the auditorium, at the table at The Mad Hatter. On the stage, dancing, when he didn't know she was there in the darkness, watching. She thinks of the first time he kissed her — the last night of *Carousel* — of him saying "I want the rest of you, too." If he said that again with the intensity she's seeing now, with those hands, those eyes, how would she say no?

No is the necessary thing. He's too young; Susanna is too fresh in his mind. She herself is too married. But the thing that's stirring in her, that's demanding to be said, is yes. Whatever it is he's asking—she tunes in again, tries to find this out—she wants to tell him yes.

What he wants is for her to sing. Yes. This is easy. Of all the things he could have asked, this is easy. She can do this. Yes.

"All right, Nate," she says. "All right. I'll do it."

He lets out a whoop, which attracts the attention of the cast members who've gathered in the hall. They're looking their way when Nate plants a kiss squarely on her mouth.

"I'm going to take Maureen's part," Clare explains when her mouth is available. "He's . . ." She looks at Nate, hesitates for the word. "He's relieved," she says finally.

Nate laughs at this, lays a hand flat across her bottom and then gives it a squeeze that makes her heart jump. This she doesn't attempt to explain to the citizenry. This, a moment later, she isn't sure she can explain to herself. They're taking a break during rehearsal when she finally has to ask him. "Was that you squeezing my rear a while ago?"

"Someone's squeezing your rear?"

"You did."

"Why'd I do that?"

"You tell me."

"I think you asked me to."

"I did not!"

"You didn't?"

"No!"

"Sorry. My mistake. It won't happen again."

"Never ever?"

"Clare, you're sending mixed signals."

"Sorry. It won't happen again."

"Which now?"

The costume designer, Brenda, has come up to Clare with a tape measure. "If you can just slip on those two dresses when you get done tonight, I'll be able to get them fitted for you by the dress rehearsal tomorrow. Here. Let me just check the length." Brenda holds one end of the tape measure to the back of Clare's waist, stretches the other toward the floor. As she stoops to take the measurement, the top end slips out of her hand.

"Let me," Nate says. He takes the tape and holds it in place at Clare's waist. Brenda marks down a number on a piece of paper and next places the end of the tape at the side seam, under Clare's arm. Nate holds it there, too. It's a job that could have been done with one finger but Nate uses his whole hand. It's a job that takes Brenda ten seconds, but Nate keeps his hand there longer. This is no squeeze. It's barely a caress. But it makes no difference what she calls it. It's a touch, his touch, and it sends a pulse through her and puts her body on alert. She takes note during those ten seconds of all the small progressions, feels them sharp and new.

She looks down at the floor, at Brenda's curved back, at her fingers moving with pencil and paper, and then she looks at Nate. He's already looking at her, first at the draw again. Again she arrives a moment late and out of breath. He's looking. He sees. He feels the pulse there beside her breast. His eyes.

She does the simplest thing. She closes her eyes. Closes her mouth. Closes her ears to the voice inside her, the one urging her: Yes.

❦

By the end of rehearsal, Clare's feeling lightheaded. Whether the cause is physical or emotional she can't be sure. She's been under the heat of the lights and Nate's eyes for three hours. She's done a fine job with Maureen's part. This public performance, her first in years, is going to be okay. Better than okay. Several people tonight have told her so.

She sees Jeffrey at the back of the auditorium and Jeanine coming down the steps from the stage, toward him, and something tightens in her chest. She hopes she's made all the necessary things clear to Jeanine. She hopes Jeanine believed enough of it to exercise good judgment in this eternity before her doctor appointment. Jeffrey has his arm around Jeanine's waist and as they walk off he squeezes her to him and she tips her head toward his and they kiss.

After all the small details have been tended to and the cast has begun to leave, Clare goes into the dressing room to be fitted with her costumes. A few tucks here and there will do the job. The length, it turns out, will be okay just as it is. Brenda zips the dresses into a plastic garment bag and takes them with her to work on at home.

Clare puts her own clothes back on and, when she opens the dressing room door to leave, gives a start. Nate is there, just outside the door, standing on one foot, hands in the back pockets of his jeans. Her throat is too dry to speak. The realization that he's here, he's been here—how long?—possibly while she stood on the other side of the door in nothing but her underwear turns her cold. Then hot. Was he there when Brenda opened the door to leave? Tending to this rush of business inside her keeps her quiet a minute. She has to prompt herself: Say something. Anything.

"What are you doing here?" she says, and immediately she regrets it. She's asked him straight out and now he's going to say straight out: I've come to ravish you. Here, in this dressing room where no one is. Here where there's a lock on the door because people take off their clothes here. Here where there's a couch that's seven feet long. Seven feet not so four can sit but so two can lie down.

Clare's amazed to discover what's going on in her head at this moment. She would have hoped she'd be considering more noble things than she is—like Paul's enduring faith in her, the precious and precarious nature of marital fidelity, how recently Nate's been hurt in love—but no. She's thinking she needs nicer underwear. She's thinking she needs to lose ten pounds. She's thinking of the silvery white stretch marks her pregnancies have left on her belly, of how strange and ugly they'd look to a childless man. She's thinking how she doesn't know the first thing about him as a lover and that it may be embarrassing to find out. She's thinking that probably a lot of the right things we do are done for all the wrong reasons.

"You were terrific. Just like I knew you would be," Nate says then. "The music is so good. I was just wondering if you were coming for a beer. Do you need to get home right away?"

Clare looks at him and laughs, and then she recognizes the need to stop that quickly before he thinks she's laughing at him. "No, I don't need to hurry home. Paul won't even be home tonight. He's gone to Phoenix." But why say so? He's right—she is sending mixed signals. Why is she?

"Well good. Come on then," he says. He waits for her to go ahead of him and then comes alongside her in the hall, hangs his arm around her shoulder and smiles. They walk like that until they leave the building. In the street they walk side by side. The whole way to The Mad Hatter they don't talk at all. Sometimes they look at each other and when they do they smile.

☙

It's with some deliberation that Clare does all the right things at The Mad Hatter. She has one beer. She sits across from Nate rather than beside him. She pretends it was accidental when he taps his foot on her toes. At her car afterwards she kisses him just once, with more finality than promise. After that he kisses her and that difference — she kissing him, he kissing her — matters. His kisses are full of questions. His tongue is in her mouth and his hands under her blouse when she stops him, and it makes her feel fifteen. This is familiar. These are those grand old rules, the ones your mother in some halting way conveys to you sometime soon after boys start calling on the phone. The ones she and Paul respected for quite a while actually. The very rhymes that sounded so old and out-dated when she brought them out for Jeanine the other night. Amusing artifacts. Does anyone play by these rules anymore? Above the waist, below the waist, shirts and skins? And just what do the rules have to say about coming back twenty-five years later? Just how should a nice but not dead forty-year-old married woman behave with her thirty-year-old, perhaps still on the rebound prospective lover? Was this all written down somewhere? Would she have to ask her mother?

"Will you come home with me?" Nate says. His mouth is warm and searching against her neck.

She pretends for just an instant that she'll say yes — a brief, sweet thought — and then she tells him the other thing: No. No, she can't. No, Jeanine will wonder. Or she won't. She'll know. No, Paul will be calling. No, she's too nice. No, she's too afraid. At any rate, no.

Clare does it again: the right thing. She gets into her car. She locks the doors. She fastens her seatbelt. She keeps her windows up. She waves goodbye. She goes.

35

Jeanine isn't at home. Paul calls and Clare tells him she's going to sing. "That's great, Clare," he says.

When the kids were little and they'd come to her with a crayon drawing or a chunk of Playdough with a thumbprint in the middle, and she was busy with some passing thing, that was what she'd say. *That's great, Michael. That's great, Jeanine.* If the news was of the bad sort—a broken balloon, a block tower tumbled down—the response was *That's too bad.* One or the other would suffice at those moments when she couldn't think. When it wasn't in her to bend down and look into their faces and say something they couldn't guess, she'd say these easy things.

Once she was caught at it, at being in neutral, merely treading water. Once Michael came into the kitchen to tell her the toad he'd been keeping in the window well with a paper plate of grass and a medicine cup of water was gone, disappeared. When she'd absently said, *That's too bad*, he'd swatted her. Slapped his whole arm across her rear and pushed at her hard enough to throw himself off balance and against the refrigerator. He hit it hard and then fell onto his bottom. A magnet and a recipe card fell

238

off the refrigerator. The magnet plunked him right on the forehead and the recipe card floated down into his lap. It was her mother's recipe for Ice Water Cake. He took it between his teeth, ripped it, and threw it at her, and then he shouted, "You're not listening to me!" The truth of it clutched her throat like a hand. She sat right down next to him on the floor. She had a carrot in her hand. "You're right," she said. "I wasn't. Please. Say it again." He gave her a scowl first, and then a benign, magnanimous smile. He said it again and this is how she can remember it at all because she truly hadn't heard the first time. She wouldn't know now what the news had been if he hadn't repeated it for her. She listened and then she put the carrot in the sink and they went to look for the toad, which they never found. They found a toad, but not *the* toad, not the one. Michael was sure of that. He told her so in a voice meant for bearing up under trouble and she heard him. "It's too bad," she said, and it was all right to say so because it was true. They'd looked for the toad and hadn't found him and it was too bad.

There are few ways to swat or push someone over the phone and all of them are childish anyway. Clare tells Paul briefly about rehearsal. He tells her briefly about his day. She decides not to mention that Jeanine isn't home yet. They hang up.

Jeanine arrives before midnight, which is conscientious if her curfew is twelve, but Clare can't remember what it is now, tonight, this night, this time. They've gone around so many times on this she can't be sure. She ought to give Jeanine the benefit of the doubt. She's arrived before midnight rather than after. That must mean something. But she's been with Jeffrey, she's had fun no doubt, doing one thing or another, and it all makes Clare mad. She's mad, not so mad she can't see the danger in what she's doing, but mad enough to do it anyway. "Well I just hope you used your head," she says to her daughter. "I just hope you used your head as much as the rest of you."

It's a stunningly hurtful thing to have said. Clare can't quite believe she's said it, and from the look on Jeanine's face, neither can she. They look at each other for a moment, standing on opposite sides of the couch, and then Jeanine tosses her hair in that way daughters do, that way that just ages their mothers on the spot. Clare stands there and takes her punishment. She stands there, growing old. Jeanine turns stiffly toward the stairs, walks away, and still Clare can't leave it alone. She's made love to him, she's thinking. She's made love to Jeffrey tonight and now she's going upstairs to think about it, to put it all away in her thoughts, to anticipate the next time. She's at the beginning. She's at the very beginning.

☙

Clare goes into the bedroom and gets into her nightgown. She comes back out to the family room and sits on the couch. For a while she can hear Jeanine's feet above her, stamping with angry force. The sounds move from bedroom to bathroom and back and then it's quiet upstairs.

Hearing her, but not seeing her, Clare is reminded of Nate's dancing that day on the stage, of how she strained to make out his form in the dark, how she assembled a vision of him from his brief crossings in the light, how she guessed at what was in his heart just from listening to the sounds of his feet. She felt she knew him — knew him intimately — there in the dark. She had stumbled on him really. It was an accident that she was there at all as he danced, and it had allowed her to see him as she had never seen him before.

So much of life depends on these accidents of opportunity. If Maureen hadn't gotten sick Clare wouldn't have had to sing. Wouldn't have been able to sing. She wonders how all this may have been different with Jeanine and Jeffrey if they'd had less opportunity to be alone together. If Jeanine had gone to the lake this summer. If Clare had been home more. If Clare had been thinking more worthy thoughts herself. Maybe this had to do with a psychic charge in the atmosphere. Who could say?

How would things have been different for her and Paul if there'd been no lake cabin, empty and closed up all winter, if she'd never had the chance to copy her father's key, if Paul hadn't had the convertible to drive them to the lake? These were the opportunities that finally crunched the rules for them. They had their car, they had their key, and so they had their times alone together in the dark, unheated bedroom that had once been purple. Had she said calculated sex was unromantic? The days leading up to a rendezvous, once they'd made the plan, were luscious. Those drives to the cabin were fifty miles of heaven. Messing up their footprints in the snow on the way out was just plain fun. It was the kind of fun she could do with now. The sort of thing she thought she was buying at the hardware store the other day.

There's a sound that Clare, after a false glance toward the stairs, realizes is at the front door. What now? It's almost twelve-thirty.

She goes to the door, spreads apart the slats of the blind at the side window and sees Nate's bent elbow, his hand slid into his back pocket. He's shifting from foot to foot. It's not even surprising to see him there. It's as though she'd entertained the possibility he might come and then, inevitably, he did, though truly she hasn't thought it consciously at all. She unlocks the door, opens it six inches, stands behind it. "So — you've come," she says.

Whatever Nate was expecting, it clearly wasn't this. "Can I come in?" he asks.

"Why?" Clare says. She already knows she's going to let him in, but she waves this last flag of opposition at him anyway. She sees his tongue move into his cheek. His eyes do a quick sweep of the door.

"Can I just come in and talk to you?" he says, an urgent whisper.

Clare steps aside, opens the door enough for him to come through. When he has, she closes it, turns the lock again. She turns to him, leads the way into the family room. "Have a chair," she says. He's being circumspect about it but he's nevertheless taking in the sight of her in her nightgown. "Excuse me a minute," she says and goes into the bedroom to put on her bathrobe.

When she comes back, he's sitting on the very edge of the couch with his knees too bent and his head too far forward. "Beer?" she says.

"Sure. Thanks."

She gets one from the refrigerator, twists off the top, and brings it to him. "Aren't you going to have one?" he asks.

"No. I'm going to bed in a minute."

His eyes leave her face quickly. He takes a drink of the beer. "You have a nice place," he says then, glancing deliberately around the room. "Nice place."

"Thank you. We like it." Clare settles on the other end of the couch, draws her legs up under her and smoothes her robe over her knees.

"You and Paul."

"And Jeanine."

"Right. Jeanine. Where is she, Jeanine?"

"It's twelve-thirty, Nate. She's in bed."

"Oh, right. Where you're going any minute now."

Clare looks at him. This assortment of words is sounding odd.

"You said that," Nate explains. "About going to bed."

"Oh," Clare says. Then, because it's silent too long, she says, "It's okay. Drink your beer. What was it you wanted?"

Nate puts his head back against the couch, looks up to the ceiling. When he looks at her again his tongue is back in his cheek. "Is this going to be one of those conversations where everything you say means a couple of things?"

"I hope not," Clare says. "I'm too tired to keep up with something like that."

"You sang really well tonight. Really. It's going to be terrific."

"Thanks. It was more fun than I thought it would be. It was actually fun."

"You were nervous about it?"

"I haven't sung publicly for a long time. A real long time."

"Well, it's about time then." He puts the beer bottle on the coffee table and slides over to where she is on the couch.

Clare straightens, slides her legs out from under her and puts her feet on the floor. "What does that mean exactly?"

"What do you want it to mean?" Nate says, bringing his face within inches of hers. His arm is around her and tightening.

The trouble with coming back to this stuff halfway through your life is that the territory looks familiar to you every now and then. At this moment or that one something happens or something is said that is so clearly recognizable that you feel yourself doing the double take. Right now, right here in her family room, Clare can clearly see that she's sitting on the couch in her nightgown and that Nate is inches away, putting moves on her. He's putting moves on her.

"You're putting moves on me," she says. He's so close she can't see his whole face at once.

He pulls back a little, smiles. "Well, yes," he says. "But did you have to say so?"

Clare pulls away. She stands up and she tightens the belt on her robe. "Is that why you came here?"

Nate gets up now, too. He walks a little pattern as he talks. "Well, no. I came here to take you away to the

South Seas so I could listen to you sing all day and make love to you all night, but once I got here and came in and all, that just seemed too ridiculous, so yeah, I thought I could settle for this. One night in America. You don't have to sing if you don't want."

Clare looks at him. She looks right into his eyes and then she takes his arms, facing him. She moves him right back over to the couch and says, "Sit down." She says it again: "Sit down." This time he does.

She sits, too, at a safe distance. She picks up his beer, half full, and has a swallow herself. She hands it to him and he has one, too. He hands it back to her and she sets it on the table. "Tell me about Susanna," she says.

"What?" Nate says.

"Tell me about Susanna."

He looks at her hard, then lays his head back and sighs. He sits up, takes another drink, and looks at her again. "I think she was going to kill me with a grapefruit knife once."

"Why? What had you done?"

"I spent the night with a woman named Kristine."

"Doing the implied things."

"It was before Susanna and I were living together."

"That's rotten."

"She should have killed me?"

"How long did you live together?"

"Seven years. Would Paul kill you with a grapefruit knife if you slept with me?"

"No. He'd kill you. He'd use a butcher knife."

"Is he bigger than me?"

Clare raises an eyebrow and lets the smile come. "No. But he'd be madder than you."

Susanna looked, Nate tells her, a little like Julia Roberts only with lighter hair. Susanna's was reddish blonde, always tied up in some sort of ponytail or knot on her head and always falling down. On anyone else it would have looked a mess. On her, to him, it looked perfectly her and beautiful. She was gentle — usually — and meticulous about ordinary things. On the subject of grapefruit knives, not only was she capable of worrying him about what part of his anatomy she might choose to inflict a wound upon, but she could section a half grapefruit so perfectly you could eat it with no speck of rind or membrane coming into your mouth. She had the softest skin of any woman on earth.

She was a physical therapist. She'd been his. He'd taken a reckless excursion down a ski slope called Fools Only. The first hundred yards or so he navigated on skis. The rest he did on a sled bed. The first thing he could remember Susanna saying to him was the admonition that dancers shouldn't ski. She took care of him. She started with his knee and then diversified. She loved the poetry of Robert Bly and the Colobus monkeys at the zoo and she owned a waffle iron which she really used on Sundays. He'd tried once to get her a monkey like the ones at the zoo, but ended up taking her to St. Croix instead. She sunburned easily. She made the waffles with strawberries or blueberries and sometimes with a creamy egg custard which he liked best. She had the softest skin . . .

"Right. Right. I got that," Clare tells him.

"You're wondering why she left me," Nate says. "You'd like to know that, wouldn't you?"

Yes. "Why did she leave you?"

"Was I going to tell you that? What are you doing to me, Clare?" He takes a drink of that old, warm beer.

"Isn't that warm? Do you want another?"

"No, thanks. I'm fine." He puts the bottle back on the table. "What happened is she found out what a jerk I am. It's not something I want you to know, but I am."

"How do you know this?"

"What?"

"That you're a jerk."

Nate gets up and walks over to the window. He looks out, then back at her. "I've had four months to think it over," he says. "It's the conclusion I've come to."

"Was it Kristine?" She feels she's prying. It's not a question she should ask. But he's right: she wants to know. And there's something more. She feels he wants to tell her. She feels him waiting for a question just such as this. For her to take something of his—not at all her business—and make it hers. Now she sees: this is what he's been needing.

Nate comes back and sits by her on the couch. He takes her in his arms and it feels absolutely right. All of it—his being here, his holding her, his kissing her (because that's the next thing)—it feels completely natural. It's the most unexpected thing to have it feel this way, and not something Clare would want to try to explain.

"I want to make love to you, Clare," Nate says.

She looks away. She isn't sure what message her eyes are giving and she doesn't want him to know before she does.

"I see it that way too," Clare says, and not only does it sound ridiculous, she doesn't even know what it means. That she knows he does? That she wants to, too? She pulls away from him and slides over on the couch.

"It wasn't Kristine," Nate says. "That was way before. Years. I don't even know where she is now. And it wasn't anybody else. For me or Susanna. It wasn't that."

"What then?"

Nate leans back against the couch. He runs his hand through his hair and gives a sigh. "It's a long story, Clare. A long, ugly story. I didn't behave well and I'd rather not talk about it."

Clare says nothing to this. She looks at him, but doesn't say anything.

Nate looks away. He picks up the beer again and takes a sip. Clare gets up and goes to the refrigerator. She takes out a cold beer and opens it. She brings it to him. She watches him take a drink and then goes back to the refrigerator and gets one for herself. They sit on opposite ends of the couch and take sips from the beer and don't talk. Twice Clare steals a look at him and he's not looking at her. When he starts to tell her, he's still looking somewhere else.

"She wanted to get married. Not such an unusual thing. She was pregnant, which maybe isn't so unusual either, and she wanted to get married. I wasn't ready for it — isn't that what guys who've acted like assholes say? I didn't even want to think about it. I wanted her to have an abortion so we could just go on like we were. I didn't even want to think about any other way. I told you, I was just a complete jerk."

"What happened?"

He looks at her finally, studies her in fact, and then he takes another drink. "It went on like that for a few weeks. Her trying to talk to me, trying to make me think, which I was averse to in those days. Me being selfish and immature. Like that, I'd say. Pretty much like that. And a baby growing in her. Just going about his business as if everything was a go on the outside. I behaved so badly, Clare." Nate looks over at her and that sinking feeling starts again and she thinks, He's tricking me. Now he's appealing to my sympathies. It's a classic melodrama we're playing out here, isn't it, and in the next scene we fall into each other's arms, drown our sadness with sex, and then we part, also sadly, and for the rest of our sad, sad lives we remember this night as a flash of light in the darkness. Curtain. Applause.

"Do you want to go to the South Seas with me now?" Nate says. He smiles, but with none of his usual charm. The smile is flat and sad, and she thinks, Clare, you pathetic excuse for a human being. Here's someone trusting you with a piece of his life. It's your heart he needs now, or haven't you got one anymore?

"She left while I was at work and I only talked to her once afterwards, on the phone. She went home to Ohio. The really sad thing is that she had the abortion anyway. She did the thing she didn't want to do and I wasn't there for her. That's the thing I regret the most. I'm sorry she left, but I deserved that. I'm even sorry about the baby. But the thing I can't stand . . ." Clare doesn't look at him. She looks at the couch. She memorizes its weave, its texture, how it looks and how it feels under the palm of her hand. She doesn't look at him. She hears him take a breath like a long inverted sigh. "So I *am* a jerk," he says. "Wouldn't you say? Aren't I right?"

"No," she says without hesitation. She moves over next to him. "If you were a jerk you wouldn't know about it. You've had a hard time. I'm sorry." She puts a hand on his leg and he takes it. He pulls her toward him and slides his arm behind her shoulders. He holds her against him and lets his face rest against the top of her head.

"I think about her every day," he says. "I still do. I think about the baby, too. I think of him as a boy. I feel like I know him and he isn't even alive. That's pretty crazy, isn't it."

"I don't think so," Clare says. She stops and looks at him and then she goes ahead. "I do that, too. I had a son who would be sixteen now and I imagine him sixteen sometimes. I've imagined him every age. I've imagined him seventy, which is really nuts because I probably wouldn't have lived to see him seventy regardless."

Nate has straightened and his hand holding hers has gone limp. "A son?" he says. "What happened to him?"

It's the question she's needed and now that it's here her throat is full of a hundred unidentified emotions and there's hardly room to put the words through. "He died," she says. "He died when he was five."

"Oh. Clare, I'm really sorry." He holds her tighter for a few seconds, then again, a few seconds more. "I'm so sorry," he says again.

"It was an accident. No one was to blame. An accident," she says. "He drowned in the lake in Minnesota where my parents live. A boating accident. He was out in the boat with my father and a storm came up. A tornado touched down on the other side of the lake. Before they could get back, the boat capsized and Michael drowned. My father did everything he could. It was an accident."

"His name was Michael?"

"Michael." Blond and blue-eyed and five years old. "His name is Michael."

"That's where you're going after the show—Minnesota."

"Yes. My parents still have the cabin there. We're going for their fiftieth wedding anniversary. . . . We haven't been there in nine years."

"Is this going to be a rough visit?"

"Maybe. Probably. I don't know." Clare gets up from the couch. She takes Nate's hand and pulls him up, too. "Come here. Come here, I want to show you something." She takes him into the Singing Room. She gets down on her knees and slides the finished collage out from under the piano. She sits down there next to it and so does Nate. "This is Michael," she says, and she points him out in several pictures on the collage. Michael on his birthdays, Michael as a Fifties greaser, Michael standing on the dock at the lake with a fishing rod in his hand. "This is my father," she says. "My mother." She points them out in the large photo of them on their wedding day at the center of the collage.

"And this is you and Paul on your wedding day," Nate says and he's right.

"I can't believe I'm doing this to you. It's like making you watch home movies."

"Is this you as a little girl?" he asks. It's the picture of Jeanine dancing with Sam at Stace's wedding.

"It's Jeanine. And that's my brother. His name is Sam."

"A lot of weddings in this family. You all must have a lot more confidence in love than my family does."

It's such a strange thing to hear from Nate that Clare has no response. She sits there by the piano and just looks at him for a moment. And even while she's considering this—love and marriage in her family—she lets him pull her down to him and she lies with him there under the piano. He lies on top of her and she feels the full weight of him along the whole length of her body and she allows herself to complete this thought: she wants him. She very much wants him inside her.

It's Nate who hesitates. "I never knew this about you," he says. He moves off of her and touches his hand to the side of her face. "You're so beautiful, Clare." He kisses her mouth and then the side of her neck. He opens her robe and the top of her nightgown and lays one kiss between her breasts. It's the gentlest of the three. Then he buttons her gown and bumps his head on his way out from under the piano. It's Clare who says, "Oh!" and then she stands up, too, and puts her arms around him tightly. Their bodies mold again but they don't kiss. That's just what they're doing—holding each other and looking at each other—when Jeanine comes down the stairs and says to Clare, "Oh, that's just great, Mother. That's just great."

Nate has more presence of mind than Clare does and

he breaks the embrace and moves toward the door. Every response Clare has is delayed. It takes her several awkward, foggy moments to realize the scene: herself in her nightgown in Nate's arms, her daughter in clothes at the bottom of the stairway, then Nate opening the front door and Jeffrey sitting there on the porch eating a chocolate bar. It comes to her eventually, though, the question, and she poses it: *What are you doing here?* and it sets everyone in motion. Nate and Jeffrey leave a pace apart down the driveway. Jeanine shrieks and tosses her hair and stamps back up the stairs. And Clare stands in the Singing Room feeling the night turn itself back three hours. She would have thought it was midnight except for the sound of the mantel clock striking the hour, which is three.

36

In the morning Clare is awake early. She wakes and feels Paul gone and then remembers he's not there. She takes his pillow and holds it to her and the day starts to focus. Jeanine's doctor appointment this afternoon. Dress rehearsal tonight. She recalls the two lines she flubbed last night and then the rest of last night comes back in a rush that makes her sit up quickly, Paul's pillow flipped on end next to her.

Last night Nate was here. He kissed her. He kissed her a lot. It's soft skin he loves. He'd been afraid to marry Susanna. He knew now about Michael. He lay on top of her under the piano. He opened her nightgown and kissed her there. He buttoned it up again. Jeanine had seen them holding each other. She'd assumed things that weren't true. She was about to leave the house in the middle of the night to meet Jeffrey. He was waiting for her on the porch. He was eating a chocolate bar. Hershey's.

Clare's heart is pounding now and she swings her legs out of bed and heads directly to the shower. She turns it on hot and stays in a long time. If Jeanine is going to sing in the shower this morning it'll have to be something short or something she can sing under cold water. Clare washes her hair twice and all the facts are settled in: the kisses, the piano, the skin, the Hershey bar. She gets out of the shower and gets dressed and then it's seven o'clock and the whole day stretches ahead.

❦

Jeanine sleeps until eleven. Actually Clare wakes her then so they can make the appointment at twelve-thirty. Letting her sleep that late feels indulgent and exactly wrong but it's something Clare does to give herself time to think this out. Time for the hot water to replenish. Time for something, anything. Any excuse. She's tired.

When she made this appointment for Jeanine she didn't intend to convey a permission. She didn't mean to imply that it would be okay to stay out late, or to sneak out of the house in the middle of the night. Where had this communiqué gone wrong? What exactly had she intended by taking Jeanine to a doctor for the purpose of acquiring birth control pills? Did she think Jeanine would simply carry them in her purse? Perhaps swallow one every now and then, but not because she needed to?

Swallowing a pill daily seems suddenly a large act. It is deliberate and premeditated. It assumes some need to do so. Every morning over orange juice or every night over milk Clare will be prompted to consider that Jeanine and Jeffrey are having sex somewhat as regularly as the disappearance day by day of the tiny white pills in the round plastic dispenser.

It's not what she bargained for. And there aren't only

the whens but the wheres. Has Jeanine assumed it will now be all right to take Jeffrey into her bedroom whenever she's moved? Perhaps they'll want the family room couch between ten and midnight on Fridays? The air mattress in the pool? A loan for a hotel room every other weekend?

And the whos. If Jeanine and Jeffrey quarrel over which hotel to visit and break up, what does Jeanine do at the next orange juice or milk? Stop? Go on? When the next boyfriend comes along—or how about the next casual acquaintance?—what is she—ready? safe? wise? loose?

Let's not even consider the whats. Let's cut straight to the whys. Why to keep this appointment today. Why not to. Clare has her hand already on the telephone, ready to cancel, when Jeanine comes into the kitchen and pours a glass of orange juice. Clare can just barely take it. Even orange juice won't just be orange juice anymore.

"Where were you going last night?" Clare asks.

Jeanine looks at her over the glass tipped to her mouth. She sets it down on the counter. "What should I tell you, Mother? That I was going to return a library book? Where do you think I was going?"

"It looked like you were going to meet Jeffrey."

"I was."

"That's not allowed." It sounds ridiculous, even to Clare. Jeanine wears the somewhat horrified tolerance one has for people who are doing crazy stuff and can't help themselves.

Clare tries again. "I mean, don't get the idea that's how it's going to be. That these pills are a complete license. I think actually they're the wrong thing. I think I was wrong about this. I think you ought to just . . ."

"Say no?" Jeanine offers.

"Are you and Jeffrey actually saying yes? I mean yes altogether and the whole thing?"

"Are you and Nate?"

Now this is a spin. This . . . "That . . . is none of your business," Clare says. She wonders: how hotly, how defensively? Jeanine doesn't soften her gaze at all and it's Clare who looks away first.

"But Jeffrey and I are your business."

"Yes!"

Jeanine's eyes make a complete scan through the kitchen. They tear up suddenly, which takes Clare off guard. She looks again to be sure but Jeanine has already blinked the tears away. "I want to keep the appointment," she says.

Clare feels her distant, detached from her, and she thinks: she's changed. It's changed her already. She's weeping at unexpected moments and she was never this cheeky. It's with a good deal of resignation that Clare says, "All right then. Go get dressed. Let's go."

❦

At the doctor's office they sit with an empty chair between them. Everyone else in the waiting room is more happy than they are. The fish in the aquarium are brighter than they've ever been and not one of the small children playing on the floor has a crusty nose. These are healthy, happy children, Clare thinks. What are they doing here?

When Jeanine's name is called it sounds foreign. Clare is on her feet, ready to go in, before Jeanine tells her she wants to go alone.

Clare sits down. She looks up at Jeanine and it's the back of her she sees, passing through the waiting room doorway. Clare sits and she waits. It's a chauffeur she is then. None of her business. Well, that's fine. Let her go. How much can a mother bear to know about these things anyway? How much?

Clare waits and she thinks of Nate. She imagines him standing, like he told her last night, across the kitchen from Susanna. Susanna, sectioning a grapefruit, seeing him come in, knowing where he's been, all night with Kristine. Clare imagines that half grapefruit, perfectly sectioned, moving through air—she threw it at him—the thwack of it meeting his body, the burning of the juice on his skin. She can see their mouths moving with the angry words and Susanna does look, as Nate said last night, like a goddess enraged. Flaming and beautiful. Clare gives Nate his timeless thought: how soft the skin is on Susanna's bottom, how it fills his hands fuller than full. And then the next thing: Susanna pummeling his body with grapefruit, the ones in the basket, ones she hasn't set the knife to. Nate forced to defend himself, to turn and dodge and say things like, *Susanna, Susanna please*, and to stay alert to the knife. The thought of the knife, the possibility of it, keeping a cold spot of fear on his tongue, and his heart pounding in readiness. Any minute he could lose something essential.

Clare waits. She is sure now that she has never seen fish as bright as these in the aquarium. He opened her nightgown. He kissed her between her breasts. He closed it up again. She is sure she has never seen such happy children as these playing on the floor. It's something far down inside them and invisible. The disease, the thing they must see the doctor about. It's deep inside. No one can see it. To anyone they are happy, the happiest children in the world. He closed it up again, her nightgown. He kissed her and then he stopped kissing her.

❧

On the way home, Clare and Jeanine are two women on a bus, two women passing in a supermarket, two women in a line at the post office. They are polite and do not engage in that awful thing — quarreling — but they each have their own business. In the driveway Clare says, "You know of course that they aren't effective immediately," and then, "It's none of your business, but no, Nate and I absolutely aren't." They go in and Jeanine goes upstairs and pretty soon there's music slow and blue and then the phone rings once and Jeanine has already picked it up before Clare can even get to the kitchen and so she understands Jeanine was expecting this call. She understands it's Jeffrey.

Clare takes her keys and goes back out to the car. She starts it and pushes a tape into the tape player. She sits and just listens for a few minutes while David Sanborn plays his saxophone. Then she ejects the tape and turns it over in her hand. She reads song titles, the most naked of indicators: *Breaking Point, A Change of Heart, Summer, The Dream*.

She puts the tape back into the player. The music comes into her like water: painful and suffocating and demanding a response. She puts the car in reverse. She drives the distance to the Arts Center with knees trembling and hands locked to the wheel. She arrives and parks and goes in. It's three hours until rehearsal. She goes first to the auditorium, turns on a light, calls his name. She runs up the ramp to the stage, glances down into the orchestra pit, pulls aside the curtain and stumbles through the darkness backstage, calling him. She moves to the hallway, rushes down it, throwing open doors, calls him.

At last he comes. Through the door of the green room he emerges, hands open, face paled. He's here.

"What is it?" Nate says, and lets her into his arms. "Clare, what is it?"

☙

They sit on the couch in the green room and she tells him. Blond and blue-eyed and five years old. Michael. He should have been wearing a life preserver. If he'd been wearing a life preserver he might be alive now. He'd be sixteen and later seventy. Someone should have insisted on the life preserver. Her father should have seen to it he wore a life preserver. Her father should have seen a storm was coming. He should have turned back sooner. He should have been able to recognize a tornado cloud. He should have gone to shore where they were instead of trying to make it home. He should have kept calm and kept the boat upright. He should have held on to him when the boat tipped. He should have grabbed him as soon as they were in the water. Michael. He should have dived under and found him right away. Michael. He should have looked longer. Michael. He should have found him. Michael. He should have found him.

Nate has her. Clare can feel his heart pounding against her face and his arms around her are trembling. He's breathing fast and so is she.

"They found him within two hours. All that time I had hope. The wildest mother sort of hope. He'd swum ashore somewhere and was safe. We hadn't heard because he'd collapsed in exhaustion without saying his name. Or he was still in the water but would be revived by a miracle of science. He would be the first child ever to survive after so long underwater. Or it wasn't him. My father had thought it was Michael he was taking out in the boat, but in fact it wasn't. Someone else had lost their child, but it wasn't Michael."

Nate holds her. Just holds her.

"But it was. Of course, it was. When they brought him and I held him, it was him. So then I had to think of what it was that had happened to him. He'd been knocked unconscious. He'd been bitten by a mosquito and would sleep a long time. He was in a coma but he'd wake up eventually."

He holds her.

"But that wasn't true either. There wasn't a mark on him, but it was Michael and he was drowned. He was dead is what I mean."

Nate puts his face to her hair and sighs loudly. Then he takes in a long, deep breath. They sit there together a few minutes more without talking. They take the time necessary to be breathing normally again, for their hearts to slow to a reasonable pace. Clare knows it's time to leave when she begins to want to kiss him. She's conscious of him next to her. She can feel the heat of him. She wants to press her body to his and look directly into his eyes and kiss him.

Clare touches her hand to his cheek. He looks at her. He doesn't touch her or say anything to her. She gets up from the couch. She leaves.

37

A t dress rehearsal that evening Clare's costumes fit just right and she gets the lines the way they're supposed to be. Frankie throws his bricks in flawless rhythm, Jeanine sublimates the funk she's been in all day, and the major historical events of Mirage, Arizona, tick across the stage with hardly a hitch. When the curtain comes down there's an explosion of whoops and chatter on the stage. There's hugging and back-slapping and Clare is congratulated repeatedly. Nate gives her a brief public hug and then is swept aside by well-wishers and cast members with questions. Jeanine goes off toward the dressing room without a word to Clare and the next person to squeeze an arm around Clare's waist is Paul. She looks at him, they both step aside to let a tuba and its player pass and then she looks at him again. "Paul."

"Surprise," he says. He's still in his suit and tie and wearing the shirt she watched him pack into his briefcase yesterday morning.

"Did you see the show?" Clare asks. "When did you get here?"

"Oh, not until about 1985. I heard you sing at the end. It sounded good, really good."

"How was Phoenix?"

"Good. Got it done. That's done. Where's Jeanine?"

Clare glances around the auditorium. It's clearing out and there's no sign of her. "She may still be in the dressing room. Or she may have left. She usually gets a ride with Jeffrey, you know."

"How'd that go today? The appointment."

"Oh, you know. I'll tell you at home."

"Okay. You ready to go?"

"I have to get this dress off. And I have my car. Should I meet you at home?"

"I'll wait. I'll take a look around. See if I see Jeanine."

"Okay then."

"Okay."

Clare goes off to change and meets up with Nate in the hallway. "Coming for a beer?" he says.

"Not tonight," she says. "Paul's here. He's waiting for me."

"He's here? I'd like to meet him. Could I meet him?"

"Well, sure. That's nice. Come on. He's just out here." She's unbuttoned the cuffs of her dress, but she goes with Nate back out into the auditorium. She calls to Paul and he comes over to them. "Paul, this is Nate. Nate, Paul."

They shake hands and exchange the stock greetings and then they gravitate to what they have in common, and that's Clare. "I don't know what we would've done without her," Nate says.

"I'm glad she's doing it," Paul says.

Nate asks if Paul will be at the performance tomorrow night. He says he will, that he's looking forward to seeing the whole show, and then they shake hands again, and Nate takes a step backward and excuses himself.

Clare watches him for just a moment, the back of him, walking away, and then she says to Paul. "I'll change. It'll be just a minute. Will you wait?"

"I'll be here," he says.

She goes and changes clothes and takes the chance to tell Nate the show was great, he's done a super job. He thanks her with the same sort of voice he used speaking to Paul. He tells her again she was great, too, and it sounds just like what he said to the cast after rehearsal tonight: you're great, it was great. The modulations of intimacy are absent from his voice. She tries to see from his eyes if this is something she's imagining, but he's taken his eyes back to himself, too. He takes a step backward and waves as he says goodbye.

When Clare comes back into the auditorium, Paul's waiting. He's right there, as he said he would be, waiting.

❦

At home Clare gives Paul a factual version of the trip to see the doctor. They went. Jeanine went in alone. In forty minutes, she came back. She had pills and a pamphlet. Clare wrote a check. They went home. Without the other things—her doubts, her thoughts of Nate, the fish, the children waiting—it seems it went all right. In fact, that's what he says: I'm glad it went all right.

Clare begins to tell him, *No it didn't. No, I think this was the wrong thing. I wish I'd never taken her. And do you think they'll want to use Jeanine's bedroom?* But it's all too elusive. It feels impossible right now to make any of this clear to him. And so she says instead, *Yes, me too. I'm glad it went all right.*

When they get into bed, Paul holds her as always. His arms are loose around her and his chin is resting on her shoulder and he's far, far away. She's right up against him and it's not close enough.

She told Nate too much today. She started and said too many things. It was too much to hear and he pulled away from it. That was what she'd seen in him tonight, what had changed his voice and his eyes. With Jeanine she'd said the wrong things. Hurtful—and was it jealous?—things. And now Jeanine was far away, too. To Paul she said too little. She made him a flat, stick-figure picture and now she's running her hand along his back and all she feels is skin.

She's apart from them all. Everybody's wearing plastic gloves. They're speaking through cans tied to a hundred yards of tangled string.

"Paul," she whispers. "Paul?"

"Mmm," he says, from somewhere near sleep.

"Will you tell me about Michael?"

38

Sally Brandt is over in the morning. She's heard that Clare is singing in the show and offers her encouragement. She brings a copy of the centennial commemorative book, fresh from the printer. "Here," she says, flipping through the pages. "Here's you."

She's opened the book to a story about the first hospital in Mirage. Beside a photo of the building under construction there's one of Dr. William Bradford and his wife Lucy, Clare's character in the show. Lucy Bradford, who helped spearhead the effort to found the hospital, who later instituted the hospital auxiliary, as well as other community projects. The photo has the caption, "Dr. and Mrs. William Bradford circa 1950." Lucy is brunette with bobbed hair and thin arms with pointed elbows. Her face is intense, or maybe she was just looking into the sun.

"I'd like to read about her," Clare says. "Can I hold on to this?"

"Keep it," Sally says. "It's yours. Are you coming to the parade?"

The centennial parade is this afternoon. The Encore band will be marching, without Paul. It would have been sweet to see him play his saxophone again, like those days when she used to watch him from the percussion section. But he's been so busy, and it's not a thing you can just pick up after twenty-five years and do without some practice.

"No," Clare tells Sally. "No, I guess not. The cast is having pictures taken before the show. I guess I'll be heading over there."

"Okay, then," Sally says. "See you at the barbecue." The Kiwanis Club is putting on a barbecue at the college before the show tonight.

"Okay," Clare says.

❧

The cast is to gather at the Arts Center at four o'clock for pictures. By four-thirty they are into costume and the photographer is directing them through still-life snaps of the scenes they'll be playing out later. It's like the fast-forward rush that happens before weddings, Clare's thinking. The bride and groom up on the altar, pretending their way through the ceremony, as the photographer coaches them into intimate looks and fetching turns of the shoulder and the camera records it all before it's even happened.

They move through posture after posture, scene after scene, and then the photographer directs them outside for group shots of the whole cast. They gather in front of the building, facing the center of the campus where there's a fountain. A kiddy tricycle parade is just getting over on the central mall and parents are corralling small children riding vehicles decked out with crepe paper and balloons. A boy with a horn on his handlebars is giving his mother a chase. Around the central fountain, tables and charcoal grills are set up for the evening barbecue.

Between shots that involve her, Clare reads about Lucy Bradford. It occurs to her as she reads what Sally's compiled in the centennial book that someone will probably make some sort of booklet about the centennial celebration itself, that that is where all these pictures they're taking right now are likely to end up. When Nate comments on how quiet she is, Clare tells him she's saving her voice for the real thing.

❧

After the pictures, Clare goes home and gets Paul and they meet the Brandts at the barbecue. Jeanine gets into the serving line with Jeffrey, Mark, and Stephanie, and later Clare sees them at another table racing to be the first to eat a cob of corn. Mark's the apparent winner, jumping up and raising the cob, nibbled clean, high over his head.

There's also barbecued chicken and ribs, three different salads and something like apple pie made for a crowd in sheet cake pans. Clare has no appetite. Paul teases her about being nervous, Sally calls her Lucy all through dinner, and then they all help Frankie Lawson search the trash can for his orthodontic appliance which, by the time they have to go get ready for the show, they haven't found.

"My dad is going to kill me," Frankie's saying in the lobby of the Arts Center.

"Oh, he won't," Clare tells him. "It was an accident. And maybe someone's found it by now."

"But I've done this three times before," Frankie says. There's a slight lisp in his speech that Clare hasn't noticed before.

❦

Maureen is backstage before curtain time, saying hello. "Oh, listen to you," Clare says. "You could have done your part after all."

"No way. I'm hoarse after three sentences," Maureen says. "And I absolutely can't sing without coughing. I came to watch for as long as he'll be good." She holds her baby on her hip. He's pulling at her earrings.

"Paul's out there with Sally and Les. About the fourth or fifth row on the left."

"Maybe I'll go sit with them then. Good luck, Clare. You look better in the dress than I did, I have to say that. Will I ever get my shape back?"

"It's your name in the program. I'll try not to embarrass you."

"You won't," she says, coughing.

39

Nate is like a little boy backstage, wisecracking and teasing between scenes, apparently so completely confident the show's going to go well that he feels no need to worry about it. He's having fun, which is hard for Clare to take in her state.

"My voice was shaking on the opening. Could you hear it, Nate?" she asks.

He's helping the stagehands get Frankie's wagon of bricks turned around. "Yeah, I heard it. It was awful. Try to fix it, will you?"

"You're no help," she says. Frankie pushes past her. One of his red suspenders has dropped to his elbow and Clare pulls it up for him. "I don't want to hear another thing from you until this is over," she shouts across to Nate. "I don't even want to see you."

"Clare, loosen up. It's going swell." He draws out the *swell* and makes mooning eyes at her.

"Quit. Quit already."

"Loosen up," he says, coming back over to her. "That's from your director. Your voice will shake less."

"You really did hear it then."

"I didn't notice a thing wrong," Nate says. He draws a line across his heart. "Honest."

☙

Just before Clare's due to go on as Lucy Bradford, when the soldiers march home from World War II and the plywood cars move across the stage, there's a surprise for her. There, on the running board of a black Ford, is a cut-out of a little girl. Clare recognizes her immediately as Rosemary, the baby the woman in the nursing home wrote to Sally about, the miracle survivor of a thirty-mile trip into Phoenix with her harried father at the wheel.

Clare's heart is beating fast already in anticipation of her cue, but the sight of Rosemary prompts a new surge and then a kind of calm breaks over her and she feels absolutely steady when she goes on stage. She looks out to where she knows Paul is, though she can't make out his face with the glare from the footlights, and smiles. When Mrs. Daley skips a line, Clare catches it and jumps ahead to her next one with hardly a ripple. She comes off stage feeling exhilarated and hot in the face and goes immediately over to where the cars are propped against the wall and takes a closer look.

Rosemary's been sketched and painted on white cardboard and attached to the car with two wide strips of double-stick tape. He's given her blonde hair which is blowing back from her face, and blue eyes which are squinting, and a small puckered mouth formed into a kind of half-smiling endurance. She's wearing a pink, short-sleeved shirt and an authentic-looking diaper. Her hands are curved and have a slit cut into them so she can grip the handle of the car door.

"Where's Nate?" Clare asks the group assembling in the wings for the next scene. No one has an answer before they move on stage. Those coming off brush by her and then she hears Jeanine's voice. "Where's Brenda anyway?" Jeanine says peevishly, reaching one arm up over her shoulder. "This zipper is stuck." Clare goes over to her. She works loose a piece of fabric caught in the zipper and then pulls it up. She gives Jeanine's shoulders a squeeze. Jeanine pulls away from Clare's touch and goes to wait for her cue.

It's time for the final number and then the curtain call before Clare sees Nate again. She's already on stage with the rest of the cast, and Nate comes out from the side curtain, running on stage elated and breathless. He's changed into slacks and a pressed shirt and he's wearing a tie. Shoes even, though they're his Reeboks. He takes his bow and then sweeps an arm toward the orchestra and they stand. He comes next to Clare, takes her hand and brings her arm up into the air and the clapping intensifies.

Clare's not expected this. She wonders if she's being recognized as Lucy Bradford, or as the co-director, or as the composer of the show's music. Moisture breaks out on her back and she can feel her pulse down into her fingertips. Nate must be able to feel her hand throbbing in his palm. The blood rushes into her face when she lowers her head in a bow.

A little girl in a pink frilly dress comes carefully across the stage with red roses laid across her extended arms.

Nate picks her up when she gets to them and she presents the roses to Clare. He gives the girl a kiss as he sets her down and she runs off, slipping once on her patent leather shoes. The audience applauds again and they all take a final bow, Nate's arm tight around Clare's waist as they lean forward and then straighten. The roses are fragrant and there's a thorn pressing into her arm. Her head pulses with light, applause, and thrill. Her skin is burning with pleasure.

☙

Afterward the stage is a crawling mass of people. Nate's arm slips off her waist and then there are heads and shoulders and raised arms between them before Clare can say anything about Rosemary. There are voices coming into her ears, pats onto her back, and kisses onto her cheeks. A few feet away, Frankie has both arms above his head, waving and crossing them like a call for help, and he hollers to her, "Hey, look. Mr. Brandt found my retainer." Someone pushes by next to her and the roses slip in her arms. She feels a scratch.

She can see Nate on the ramp leading up to the stage, surrounded. Ty Greggory is there, too. She makes her way over to them and inquires about Ty's health, and then Paul is there next to her, an arm around her shoulders, a kiss on her cheek. Clare introduces him to Ty.

"You have a talented wife, Paul," Ty says. "The music she wrote for the show is wonderful."

Paul hangs on the words for a moment, then looks at

Clare. His glance feels new and appraising. She looks at him and confirms with her eyes what Ty is saying. Paul holds her a little tighter. There's a moment's silence that is just about to become awkward when Paul speaks. "Thank you," he says to Ty. "You're right. She's really something." He looks at Nate and then at Clare again, a little uncertain. His arm pulls tight and stays right there around her.

Clare shivers the way you can even in a warm room. She looks again at Paul and then sees Les and Sally coming up onto the stage. They congratulate her and close behind is Maureen, who comes to tell her she hopes a few of the people mistook Clare for her.

Clare accepts their compliments and then she glances out into the auditorium and locates Jeanine. She's talking with a boy Clare doesn't know. Jeffrey and Mark and Stephanie are standing nearby. Stephanie's taking apart her flute and fitting it into its case.

The doors to the outside have been opened and a warm breeze moves through the auditorium. The word is circulating: dancing and fireworks on the plaza downtown. The crowd begins to thin.

"Are we going dancing?" Paul asks.

"Of course we're going dancing," Sally says.

"We are?" says Les, something less than enthusiastic.

"I've got to get this costume off," Clare says. "And, you know, I think I'm going to stop at home first. What I'd really like is a shower and something to eat."

"Now her appetite's back," Sally says.

"You go on, Paul. Go with Sally and Les and I'll catch up with you downtown a little later."

Paul looks to Les, who nods, and says, "Okay then."

❦

Clare makes her stop in the dressing room quick and then goes to look for Nate. She finds him backstage, straightening things up. He's changed back into jeans and a T-shirt and is barefoot. He seems deep in thought and startles a little when she speaks.

"I really loved that," Clare says.

"Oh," he says as he looks up, as he gathers together what's happening. "What? The show?"

"Rosemary. Rosemary on the running board. I just loved that. You were so dear to think of it."

"Rosemary? Was that her name?"

"The baby who survived the trip into Phoenix."

"Yeah. Well, you told me she ought to be there. It was your idea, wasn't it?"

"Well, you know. The kind of idea you never do anything about. And you did." She goes over to him, takes his hands, swings his arms out and in. "Are you going dancing?"

"No," he says. "I'm not much in the mood. I'm going home, I guess. Come here."

He takes her hand and walks over to the cars propped against the wall. He finds the one with Rosemary on it and Clare helps him pull it out and set it apart from the others. The tape makes a ripping sound as he pulls Rosemary off the car. He takes the strips of tape off the back of her and wads them up into a ball. "Here," he says. "You keep her. Souvenir of the show. Of a fine partnership. It was good." He holds the cardboard figure out to Clare.

She takes it hesitantly. "Sounds like a goodbye to me."

"I'm thinking of going to Ohio. I'm thinking of trying to find her."

"Susanna."

"Yeah."

"Good. If that's what you want, you should."

"There's almost two months before school starts."

"So you'll be back?"

"I don't know. I just don't know. When do you leave for Minnesota?"

"Tomorrow."

"I hope it all goes okay for you. Are you going dancing?"

"Everybody's gone on ahead. I said I'd meet them. I'm going home first."

"Good."

"Yeah."

"It was really good doing the show with you, Clare. It really was a fine partnership. I mean that."

"I thought so, too. It meant a lot to me to use my music and I'm even glad I sang it. In fact, I'm especially glad I sang it."

He leans toward her and kisses her lightly. "Just throw that in the trash if you don't want it," he says.

"No," Clare says. "I want her. I'm going to keep her. Will you let me know what happens? If you go to Ohio and all? I'd like to know."

"Sure. Sure, okay. Good luck with your trip and all."

"Thanks." She takes his hands again and kisses him in the exact, careful way he kissed her. She keeps his hands a moment and looks at him. "It's a good feeling I have for you, Nate. I think it's going to stay with me."

He looks away, but squeezes her hands. "I hope it does," he says. "And Clare?" He looks at her now. "I feel it, too."

She kisses him again and then she's off, Rosemary in her arms.

40

At home, Clare has a shower. Before she dresses, she looks at her reflection in the shower-steamed mirror. She poses: first position, second, third. Then three more, of her own invention. One: stomach muscles tightened, breasts lifted in her hands, high on her chest. Two: stomach relaxed, hands down, breasts lowered and loose. Three: stomach flaccid, shoulders rolled forward, breasts sagging still lower.

She dips into a *plié*, turns her head upside down and musses her hair. Then she stands, rubs her chest until it is flushed, raises her arms up over her head, and looks piercingly into the mirror. Her memory sounds a sharp breath, a door slamming, sobs.

Plié.

She lowers her arms, rolls her hip to the side, puts a hand to it, and tosses her hair that way Jeanine does. In twenty years, this could be the image her memory echoes back when she calls down the life line: Jeanine, Jeanine.

Plié.

She looks into the mirror. She covers her face with her hands, then runs them down over her neck and the front of her body. At her stomach she stops to stroke her fingertips over the silver-white stretch lines. This body isn't young and some of its history is clearly visible, but her skin, she notes with some unexpected new loss, is still as soft as any woman's on earth.

※

Clare gets dressed, has an egg salad sandwich and wonders what to do with Rosemary. Her story is amazing and maybe one she'll tell Paul someday. But the fact that Nate has spent time recreating her in cardboard and paint and that Clare has the desire to take her home and keep her seems something of a revelation. It divulges something about their relationship and announces a secret that's been theirs only. A secret, she realizes with some surprise, she doesn't want to have to share with Paul.

She slides Rosemary behind the dresser in their bedroom. There are two suitcases set out on the floor, partially packed. The collage is wrapped in brown paper and tied with string and set against the wall. Clare picks up a pair of her shoes and tucks them into the suitcase that holds her clothes. Then, standing in front of the dresser mirror—she can see her hands moving in the reflection— she opens the middle drawer, takes out a blue sweater, and tosses it into the suitcase. Now there's only one sweater left in the drawer and her father's letters are visible. The newspaper clipping is there, too, the story about the woman Faith who lost her son Michael when he fell out of the car and was run over. Clare unfolds it and looks at the photo of this Michael's shoes standing at attention on the pavement. She puts it back into the drawer.

There are a lot of letters. At first he wrote sporadically, a few attempts over the first couple of years they were in Arizona. Clare read them but didn't answer them and then for nearly a year, after their one visit to the lake, no letters came at all. This was worse than having them come, which was awful in its own way. Pages of routine news, commentary on the weather, the local wheat harvest, the pollen count. All the sorts of things that fill letters when there is really nothing that needs to be said. The things you can't bear to hear when there is something else that matters.

When the letters started again, it was a relief in some ways. At least they were coming, but on the other hand, they were coming. Clare didn't read them. She didn't even open them. She made a place for them — the drawer — so they'd have somewhere to immediately be and stay, out of sight. She didn't read them and her father wrote them with new tenacity. They arrived by the tenth of the month, every month. She imagined him paying this debt along with his other bills. The telephone, the water and electric, the cable TV, and Clare.

Clare takes a nail file from the top of the dresser, slides it into an envelope postmarked July 8, 1986. She tears it open and tosses it back into the drawer. She picks up another, tears it open, throws it back. The letters have been stacked somewhat neatly in the drawer, each new one on top of the one just before it. Now she pulls out any, at random, tears them open and throws them back. After a few moments, so many have been opened that she begins to get open ones when she reaches into the drawer.

The more she opens, the longer it takes each time to find one that's still sealed. But she opens them all and then she unfolds the newspaper clipping, too. She takes the sweater to the closet and finds a place for it on the shelf. She closes the drawer, shoves it with her foot, and it slams. She goes to dry her hair. Paul calls on the phone and she tells him she's coming. That she's packing up a few things for the trip, but she's coming. Then she's back in the bedroom.

She opens the drawer. She sets the newspaper clipping on the bed. Then she does the same to the letters. She takes each one out and sets it on its envelope on the bed. She lays them out, one by one, and as they accumulate, she begins to arrange them in chronological order. She starts at Paul's pillow with the oldest ones, works a row down his side of the bed, across the foot, the letters getting more recent, and then up her side. There are more letters than this, so she sets them three deep by her pillow.

Finally the drawer is empty except for a dull, flat stone. Clare picks it up and rubs it between her fingers. There had to have been something special about this stone once. Michael had it in his pocket when he died. It must have been shiny or it was warm or it was just the right shape for skipping across the water. Something drew Michael to it, moved him to pick it up and put it into his pocket for safekeeping.

When they gave her his clothes they were still damp. They smelled only of lake water, that green, fish smell. The scent of Michael—Johnson's shampoo and apple juice—was already gone. The clothes were folded and placed in a plastic bag with a drawstring top. A pair of blue shorts with a row of jumping dolphins around the left hem. A white T-shirt with a blue stripe around the neck and a blue dolphin on the breast pocket. The dolphin was wearing sunglasses. Two white socks, turned inside out in little wads, and his underwear. Two sneakers, sodden and heavy. They'd pulled them off of him without untying the laces or someone unknown had done her the small kindness of re-tying them. This was everything he was wearing. In the pocket of the shorts was the dull, flat stone, cold and hopeless.

41

Dear Clare,
Despite all these attempts, I still cannot express to you the full extent of my regret and grief at what has happened. Though the Lord knows I've tortured myself enough looking for the ways in which I might have prevented Michael's death, I've now made my peace with the fact that I've lost my precious grandson, and whether I was at fault in his death or not, nothing will bring him back. What continues to break my heart is my failure to make my peace with you, because you, Clare, can be brought back to me, and until this possibility is obliterated by my death, I will not rest from its pursuit. Your loss has been enormous. My regret over your pain is almost unendurable. The moments I spent struggling to grab hold of Michael in the water seemed to last an eternity, but this struggle to pull you back to me is the greater pain. My hope is that you can understand, having lost a child yourself, what it is I'm suffering, and will see fit to forgive me.

❧

Dear Clare,

The last thing I saw of Michael was the top of his head. The last thing I touched was his hand. The last thing I heard was his voice. He called me twice. Grandpa, Grandpa. Two times.

❦

Dear Clare,

I didn't think I could bear it when they brought him into the hospital and I saw you holding him. I misjudged. Forgive me. It's carved out the bottom of my soul. I couldn't find him. Forgive me, Clare, please.

❦

Dear Clare,

I couldn't find him. Can you find it in your heart to forgive me? I could hear him and I couldn't see him or touch him.

Dear Clare,

Dear Clare,

Clare

oh Clare

oh Clare

❦

They're all laid open now, and she's been so wrong. Clare sees what she's done and she's been weeping since Paul's side of the bed. It's been Clare this time, not her father, who has pretended not to hear. She's covered her ears. She's made herself deaf. She's been more like her father than he himself has been.

42

Clare finds his address on the cast list and writes it down with a shaking hand on the back of her program from the show. She leaves the letters as they are, takes her purse, and gets into the car. David Sanborn begins playing as soon as she turns the key, and Clare ejects the tape from the player. She can see fireworks in the sky as she drives—red and green bursts and the silver sparkling ones—and their light is refracted into rippling pools of color by the tears standing in her eyes.

She finds his apartment building easily, less than a mile from her house, on the road to Roadrunner Park. She parks and goes inside. There is a security system and she sees she will have to ring for him to let her in. She checks her watch. It's almost midnight. The strangeness of that time and this place make her pause with her finger at the buzzer.

It's midnight and Jeanine wasn't home yet. Of course. She's downtown dancing with Jeffrey or that other boy she saw after the show. Who was he? Jeanine's downtown, where Paul is, waiting for her. Paul, whom she left no note for at home. She left him a hundred letters on the bed. These things will have to be explained. She will have to explain to Paul. Sally and Les. Right now she is being missed, perhaps worried about.

Clare presses the buzzer. It occurs to her suddenly that she'll have to say something to Nate. If he's here, if he answers, she'll have to identify herself.

"Hello?" she hears.

"Nate, it's Clare." She hesitates. "Clare Nichols."

"Oh," he says. "Well, come on up. 302."

The door buzzes and Clare opens it. The two flights of stairs feel like twenty and her legs are trembling by the time she finds Nate's door. The hallway is narrow and smells of cigarettes and celery. She knocks softly. She hears his feet approaching the door. He opens it. He's dressed but his hair is uncombed.

"Were you sleeping?" Clare asks.

"Oh, not that well. Come on in."

She sees his bicycle there against the wall behind the door. He walks ahead of her into the living room and turns on a lamp. The room is small and sparsely furnished. There is one chair, with a floor lamp behind it and a table beside, piled with newspapers. There are more newspapers and an empty plate on the floor.

They sit on the other piece of furniture, something like a futon. It's soft and low to the floor and has no back. The cushion is warm against Clare's bare leg and she realizes that Nate was napping here, or maybe this is where he sleeps. The apartment is small — she can see right into the kitchen from where she sits — but no, he must have a bed. Probably there's a bedroom in the back with a king-size bed and satin sheets. A Roman tub. Mirrors. Isn't that the way single men live?

"Do you want something to drink?" Nate says.

"No thanks," Clare says, though her throat is dry and aching.

Nate walks over to the window and opens the drapes. "You can see the fireworks from downtown." The window is actually a patio door that opens out onto a small balcony with wrought iron rails. He opens the door and turns to her. She comes and they go out onto the balcony. The night is still warm and there's a breeze. Clare goes to the railing and puts her hands on it. Nate comes beside her, leans against the rail, facing her. He looks out toward downtown. "Have you been dancing?"

"No, I haven't gone yet."

"I think the party's going to be over before you get there."

"I'm not going. I've decided. I'm not going."

"Isn't Paul waiting for you?"

"Paul?"

"Clare," Nate says, taking hold of her eyes. "What's going on?"

She presses her lips together and grips the rail a little tighter. "My father writes me letters. He writes me a letter every month."

Nate looks at her hard, then looks away. "He sounds very devoted."

"He's done this for years and I haven't read any of them. How does that sound?" Her voice is strained, her throat too narrow a passageway for these words.

"Well, I suppose you have some reason for that," Nate says. Carefully, evenly.

"I didn't want to. I thought I knew what they said and I didn't want to read them. I couldn't be bothered."

Nate doesn't say anything. He leans against the railing and looks at the ground.

"I read them tonight. Tonight after the show. I went home and opened them all up and read them."

Nate looks up cautiously. "What did they say?"

"He thinks I blame him for Michael's death. He thinks he's lost me like I lost Michael."

"Has he?"

Clare takes a sharp breath. "Well, yes. Yes, I suppose he has." Her tears come. "How could I have done this?"

Nate takes her in his arms and she presses against his shoulder. He lifts her face and looks at her and then he kisses her long and deep. "Come here," he says then. "Come on in here."

He takes her arm and they go inside. They sit on the futon and she cries for a minute or so, softly. He sits next to her and waits. She wipes her eyes with the back of her hand and then she looks at him. She looks at him so intently that he looks away and then she brings her arms up around his neck and pulls him to her. She kisses him twice. During the third kiss she lies back and brings him along so he's lying on top of her. She brings her hands up under his shirt and runs them along his back. Under her fingers his muscles are taut with the embrace. He kisses her once more before he says, "Clare. Wait a minute. Come here." He lifts himself off of her and pulls her up to sitting beside him. "Listen to me."

She looks at his face. There's stubble on his chin and

his hair is wild and his eyes — they're full of her things. His voice — it's full of her song. She thought her heart was extended full width and now it turns itself out another fold. The pain and the joy of the stretch set it beating more urgently than ever. She kisses him again.

"Clare," he says. No one's ever said her name this way. He touches her face. "Listen to me." He shifts next to her, faces her. "Look, two months ago, two weeks ago, shit, two nights ago, I would have sold my soul for this."

She looks at him, hears it, hears what he's about to say. "But? What? I'm too late? I've arrived after the deadline?"

He looks away. "I just feel different now. I didn't know you. Not really."

"I see. You like me better as an anonymous character, is that it? Fortyish woman has last taste of youth with younger man? He fills her with dancing. She fills him with . . . what? Pleasure? Aren't I following the script, Nate? They bring their bodies together — willfully, no accident, this — because love conquers all and if not love, well then sex is close enough. It conquers all and by God, there are things to conquer. Here's your chance, Nate. Here I am. Conquer me."

Nate's face darkens. "Aw, Clare. Stop it." He gets up and runs his hand through his hair. "Just stop it." He shouts it. He has his back to her and she's suddenly in an unknown place in the middle of the night and afraid. Then he turns to her. "Can't you see it's a wonderful thing I'm trying to say to you?"

He walks away, into the kitchen, and she sits there a moment longer, cold and flooded with an emotion that feels like a physical illness. She gets up and goes to him. He's at the sink, shoulders hunched forward, like he may lean over it and be sick himself. She touches his arm and he turns to her, which fills her with a simple gratitude. His face is pale and his eyes red.

"I'm sorry," she says. "I'm just a mess tonight. I'm not saying the right things."

He sighs deeply. "No, it's me who's sorry. I can see that. I can see you're upset. I shouldn't have flown at you. I don't know. Maybe I do have weird ideas about all this. You wouldn't be the first to say so."

It wounds her to hear him say this and she regrets her words all over again. She can't bear to think of hurting him. It brings the tears back into her eyes. She comes to him and puts her arms around his waist. He lets her and she loves him for that, too.

"It's not you," she says. "It's me. I'm sorry, Nate. You've stepped into the middle of something here and I'm sorry to have done that to you."

"No, I've pushed my way in. That's what I mean. I see now, that's true. I've pretty much made a career of thinking of myself first. But if I care for you, and Clare, I do, why would I want to make you miserable by coming between you and Paul? You love him, don't you?"

She's face to face with him. Her arms are around him and she tells him, "Yes. Yes, I do."

"So why are you here?" Nate says.

It flares inside her again and she throws her arms down. "So *I'm* the wicked one, am I?" She walks away, into the living room, and it's not far enough away from him. "It's a damn small place you've got here."

"Thanks," he says. "Thanks a lot."

"Sarcasm doesn't suit you."

"No. You neither." He's right beside her now. He takes her roughly by the arm, turns her to him, and he kisses her. Then he looks at her and says, "Does that feel right to you?"

He's ready for her slap and grabs her hand mid-air. She struggles against him for a moment and then she lets it go and says something so quietly Nate has to say, "What?"

She says it again. "He could have put a life preserver on him. He was right there. He could have done that."

Nate's breath catches. "Don't. Don't now, Clare."

"If he'd done that, Michael would be alive now."

"Don't, Clare. Please."

She looks at him. She waits, but then she goes on. "I'd like to look right at Paul and say, 'Why didn't you put the life preserver on Michael? Why didn't you?'"

Nate stares at her a moment and then he takes her arm. "Come on," he says. "Come on." He picks up her purse and opens it, takes out a set of keys. "Are these your car keys?" he says. She nods. "Come on," he says again, and moves her toward the door.

They walk to Clare's car and he opens the passenger door and closes it after Clare gets in. He gets in on the driver's side, pushes the seat back, and starts the car. It's clear to her within a minute where they're going, and she just lets him drive. He drives her home and doesn't say anything to her the whole time. All she says to him is, "I can drive, you know." He parks the car in the driveway, comes around to Clare's side and opens the door. He walks with her to the front door.

"I'm fine now," Clare says. "Thank you."

Nate rings the bell.

"Go on," Clare says. "I'm fine."

The light is already on and Paul comes immediately. He opens the door, his face frantic. His expression darkens into a glower as he looks at them, standing on the porch under the light.

"Here's Clare," Nate says. "She has something to tell you."

Clare turns cold. She looks at Nate and he looks at her. It's a hard tenderness in his eyes. Her knees are trembling uncontrollably.

Paul looks at Clare and at Nate. He looks at them looking at each other and then he clenches his mouth and narrows his eyes and brings his right fist squarely into Nate's jaw. Nate's not anticipating it this time and takes the full impact. He makes a sound that reminds Clare wildly of one she's heard from Paul while making love, and then for one long, suspended moment, Clare sees Nate falling, to the side, like a cartwheel spin, leading with his arm, which he's put out to catch himself.

No one speaks. No one moves but Nate, falling until his hand lands solidly against the house.

"Jesus," Paul says, and he takes hold of Nate's other arm and steadies him. "I'm sorry. Shit. Are you all right?"

Nate's rubbing his jaw as he nods his head. "You're wrong about this, though. It's not that."

Clare says to Nate, "Are you sure you're all right?"

He nods his head again and takes a step backward. "I'll be on my way though. Bye, Clare." He reaches for Paul's hand and shakes it. "Paul."

"Wait. You don't have a car," Clare says. "He needs a ride," she says to Paul. "He needs some ice," she says to Jeanine, who's standing now at the open door.

"No, I'm fine," Nate says. "I'll walk. It's not far."

"I'll give you a ride," Clare says.

"No, I'll do it," Paul says.

Jeanine is back with a bag of ice. Nate thanks her and puts it to his jaw. "I'll walk. I'm gone," he says.

"You can ride my bike," Jeanine offers. "I won't be needing it. We can come get it when we get back from our trip." She's already walking out to the driveway. She opens Clare's car and presses the button on the garage door opener. It opens and she wheels her bike out onto the driveway.

Nate shrugs and follows her. "Okay," he says, getting on the bike. The seat's too low for him and his knees angle out awkwardly, but he pedals off that way. When he waves, the bag of ice is in his hand.

They stand on the porch, waving to him as if he's been a guest in their home. They shout goodbye and he turns and says, "Yup. Bye." They stand there until he's out of sight and then they go into the house.

43

"What then?" Paul says before Clare even has the door shut. To Jeanine he says, "Go on to bed."

Jeanine goes. Without a word or even a direct glance, she goes to the stairs.

"What's going on?" Paul says when she's gone. "Where have you been? Do you know what time it is? Why are there letters all over the bedroom? Clare?" He's pacing like a lion, his head forward and heavy like that.

He's worked up again, or still. It may have been just a moment of civilized calm that intervened there on the porch. She looks at him and he, too, has the stubbly chin and the wild hair and Clare wonders if every man on earth looks this way tonight. She hears his questions and it's just too many. She tries to pick an easy one. No, she doesn't know what time it is. She wonders fleetingly if it's time to go to the airport. The other questions are even harder. She certainly doesn't want *What's going on?* She looks at him again. Stubble. Hair. God, she's exhausted.

"You didn't have to hit him," she says.

Now he sounds like a lion, too. Growling. My God. Clare's reminded of the night they had dinner with the dairy company people and Paul was so taken with Melody.

In bed later, he reassured her with a hug and a growl, and then he asked her if she still believed in fidelity.

"I've been looking for you, waiting for you, worrying about you for two hours and you want to talk about *him* now?" Paul says.

There's nothing reassuring about tonight's growling. In fact, for twenty seconds, Clare's afraid. She makes herself move. She walks into the Singing Room and turns out the lamp.

"All right," Paul says. "Let's talk about him then. He seems to be part of the picture. He brought you home. That was big of him."

"It was," Clare says quietly. Paul doesn't hear. She goes over to the fireplace. The clock is there on the mantel where it always is and it looks strange there tonight. The hands are at one-thirty. That looks strange, too. Paul's followed her.

"It's one-thirty," Clare says.

"I know that," Paul says. "I've been supremely conscious of the time tonight. What else did he do? Before he delivered you back to me, I mean. The guy's got balls, I have to say that."

"Nothing," she says. "Nothing," she shouts. "There's been no fucking. Is that what you want to know? He could have and he didn't and he did deliver me back to you and he sure as hell didn't deserve to have the lights punched out of him." Clare takes a breath and drops down on the couch.

Paul stares at her a moment. "Jesus Christ," he mutters to the ceiling. He drops his head and prowls a little more.

"How do I know this is true?" he says then.

"Because I'm telling you."

"Well you sure as hell are going out of your way to defend him. You sure as hell feel something for him."

Clare doesn't look at him. "I can't help that."

Paul turns away from her. "Well that's just great," he says.

Clare says nothing.

"He was here the other night," Paul says then. "When I was in Phoenix, he was here."

Clare looks to the stairs, then at Paul. "Nothing happened then either," she says, and gets up from the couch and walks into the kitchen.

Paul follows her. "Were you at his place tonight?"

"Yes."

"Why?"

"I wanted to talk to him."

"I was waiting for you downtown."

"I'm sorry."

"I worried."

"I'm sorry."

Clare's moving in a pointless pattern around the kitchen. She opens the refrigerator and there's nothing to get out. She turns on the faucet and there's nothing to wash.

"I came home and saw all those letters and you weren't here. I didn't know what you'd done. I was worried nuts, Clare."

"I'm sorry." Her voice is straining.

"Crazy nuts."

She stops her circling and wraps her arms around herself and lets the tears come into her eyes.

"I was afraid you'd gone off and killed yourself or something."

"Well, would you have cried if I had?" The tears turn angry hot and she can't hold them in her eyes. She looks at him and he's staring in disbelief. "You never even cried," she says, her voice pained and weak. Then she shouts it at him: "You never even cried. When Dad came and told us, when they found him, when they brought him to the hospital, when they took his organs, when we buried him. Never once."

She pushes past him and goes into their bedroom. "Didn't you care?" she shouts and then he's there with her in the bedroom. "Didn't you love him?" She picks up one of the letters from the bed and throws it at him. Then a handful. She throws them anywhere and she keeps talking. "Why didn't you put a life preserver on him? You're his father. Why didn't you take care of him?"

She stops then and looks at him and sees him. He's leaned against the edge of the dresser, his legs out and his head down. His hands are over his face and he's completely quiet. She can see herself in the dresser mirror. Her face is white and wet with tears and her hands are full of letters. She lets them drop and sees them flutter in the reflection.

She goes to Paul and takes his hands. He lets her move them from his face. She looks at him. His face is white and wet. He looks like her.

"It wasn't his fault," Clare says. She looks at the letters scattered on the floor. "He thinks I've blamed him all this time. He thinks he's lost me the way we lost Michael." She squeezes Paul's good and gentle hands. "I'm sorry, Paul. I'm sorry for saying those things. I know you loved him." She looks at him and sees the new tears she feels on her own cheeks. "I didn't go to bed with him."

Paul squeezes her hands. He looks at her. "I know," he says.

"I could have put it on him," Clare says. "I was there on the dock, too. It was no more your fault than mine. I should have done it." She sobs and this sound, too, is like something out of their bed. She knows she's made this very sound in pure joy while in Paul's embrace.

Paul opens his arms and takes her. "Oh Clare," he says. That old refrain. He pulls away and holds her arms and looks at her. "Clare, it was an accident. Look at me. An accident. No one's to blame."

She lifts her head, looks at him. She looks into his eyes. "I know, Paul. I know it."

He takes her in his arms. He holds her.

At the open bedroom door there's a soft knock. Jeanine is there and her face is like theirs. She has Paul's eyes and Clare's mouth and she's pale with fatigue or worry.

"I know it's none of my business," she says, her voice small and young. She looks at the letters on the floor and on the bed and then again at her parents.

"Come here, Baby," Clare says. She holds out one arm. Jeanine comes and slides under it.

For a few moments between night and day Clare holds them both. They're her man and her child. They're Paul and Jeanine.

44

As the plane approaches Minneapolis, the day is clear and Clare can look past Jeanine, who has the window seat, and see green. As they descend, it becomes a lush green. The vegetation here has a generosity, an uncontrolled growth that contrasts to the manicured patches of color she's become accustomed to seeing in the desert. It's a place to have been young, a place to have grown up in.

Jeanine is wearing the plastic earphones the flight attendants passed out at the start of the flight. She's plugged them into the armrest between her and Clare and has set the dial to five. She's slept part of the way and when she's been awake, she's been quiet. But when Clare looks at her, she smiles the way she did the morning when she was pouring coffee and sympathy into Clare's cup. The morning Clare let her and Paul believe the lyrics she'd written for the show had been displaced by some mysterious new music.

There have been omissions. There have been some things left unsaid that should have been said. Things that have been said but not heard. Now there's a lot to say and she and Paul have started, in whispers, over the garbled sounds coming from the stereo hook-up in the armrest between them. It feels like speaking a new language or speaking through some strange medium. This is how it would feel to sing underwater.

Then Paul looks at her in a way Clare recognizes is extraordinary. This, Clare thinks, is how a man looks at the woman who is his wife when they've been immersed in a confusion of sounds and touches and then they surface at the same time, together, all their senses intact, for a rare moment of clarity. What you do at that moment is breathe it in deep and try to make it last through the next dive.

❦

The plane lands, they gather their bags and Paul gets the collage, which has been stowed up front. They move along with the other travellers through the skyway. It is humid and hot even in this indoor air. Clare wonders how her parents will look, what they'll say, and whether they'll hug her or wait for her to make the first move.

Clare comes out of the ramp ahead of Paul and Jeanine and sees her father standing alone along the wall. She gets to watch him unobserved for a few moments before he lays eyes on her. He looks older than she expected. The skin on his neck is loose and wrinkled and looks, Clare thinks, like the stretched skin on her belly. He looks confused, as if he's trying to remember where he put his keys or the whole car. Or maybe he's trying to remember her, Clare thinks, when he first looks directly at her and doesn't recognize her immediately. But then he smiles and waves and he looks just as he did when she was seven and he was about to go fishing or when she was twenty-one and about to take his arm and walk up the aisle to marry Paul. It's her father. The same man.

It seems they've been watching each other a long time by the time Clare works through the crowd and they can touch. It's been determined in that steadily shortening gaze that yes, he'll hug her, and yes, she's forgiven him. She tells him with her eyes first and then with her arms around his neck and then right away—it can't wait—with her words in his ear. It takes so few. He hears them and tightens his arms around her. Later they'll talk more. In grieving and in loving, there is always more.

"Where's Mom?" she asks as he reaches next to hug Jeanine.

"My God, she's a woman," he says of Jeanine. "Oh, you know your mother. She wants to have dinner waiting for you when you get there. She's at home."

They've quarreled. Clare knows it instantly and the childlike apprehension in her stomach is familiar as well.

"Hello, Clarence," Paul says, and he gets a hug too.

They move to the luggage carousel, and then to the car, to the highway, to the lake shore. They come around the bend in the road where the lake becomes visible through the trees. There are white caps today and the few fishing boats on the lake are rocking rhythmically. The pines are thick and close and the elms stand along the roadside like survivors, the sticky bands painted around their trunks years ago to protect them from Dutch Elm disease still visible. They pass the neat, compartmented mailboxes and then they arrive at the place where Clare can say to everyone in the car, "Here. Here's the place," and trust that they will each know what she's saying.

❦

The pail of water and towel are still at the door of the cabin for rinsing sand off of feet, despite the fact that, inside, the linoleum is now grayed and pitted. Clare's mother looks remarkably unchanged. Clare is not sure if this is because she still looks young or because she's been old so long already.

Roberta has hugs and words for everyone but Clarence and dinner is in the oven. "Sorry I couldn't meet you at the airport," she says. "Your father was afraid there wouldn't be room for everyone in the car with the luggage."

Paul carries the collage back into the old purple bedroom, which will be theirs while they're here, and hides it in the closet until the anniversary next weekend. Sam and his family are due on Thursday, Roberta says. Bernice may stop out tomorrow.

They take a walk up the road before dinner and Clare shows Jeanine the cabin where she took dance lessons from Mrs. Bonet and then they walk in the other direction to the mailboxes. There's a large gray scar on the big elm tree in front of the Mattinglys' and Roberta explains that it's from when Mr. Mattingly had his heart attack and ran the truck into the tree. Mrs. Mattingly sold the property shortly after that. Claudia moved to Seattle in 1987.

"You never told me any of this," Clare says.

"It's not what I think of on the phone," her mother says.

❧

When it gets dark Clarence has sparklers for Jeanine. He hands one to her and lights it and Jeanine holds it at arm's length and smiles. "Now write your name," Clarence says, waving his own arm in the air. "Like this."

Jeanine indulges him. She pretends she's never had a sparkler in her life, though she's had them every year forever.

Across the lake the first fireworks are shooting into the sky. Clarence goes to put Jeanine's burnt-out sparklers into the water pail by the door. It's something he's always done, to be sure they're out and that no one steps on a hot one with bare feet. Clare begins to tell him it will make her mother mad if he puts them in the pail, but then supposes he already knows it. Her mother will say, Dip them in the lake why don't you? and her father will say, Oh what difference can it make? and they'll be started again.

Clare and Paul and Jeanine walk out onto the dock to watch the sky. The public fireworks display is directly across the lake, but small bursts of light are visible elsewhere along the shoreline. Clare imagines young fathers placing bottle rockets into pipes and lighting them to the delight of their children. She slips off her shoes and sits down on the end of the dock. She leans against one of the tires slung over the dock pipes to protect the boat. The boat, on the lift, is covered with the canvas tarp.

Clare puts her legs down over the edge of the dock and dips her feet into the water. She's been spoiled by Arizona heat or she's just forgotten how cold the lake is, even in summer. Jeanine sits down next to her and unties her shoes. She takes them off and puts her feet into the water. She takes a quick breath. "You swam in this?" she asks.

"We didn't know any better," Clare says.

The sky is partly clouded now, but the stars are starting to come out. The trees at the shore rustle in the slight breeze. Paul crouches down behind Clare and Jeanine and puts an arm over each of their shoulders. Clare feels his knee pressing against her back and turns and brushes her face against his hand dangling over her shoulder.

"There's a pretty one," he says, and they look out over the lake to see a silvery burst of sparkling light. Smaller rockets seem to shoot out of the silver circle and these arch in all directions and drop through the sky like embers.

"They're falling stars," Jeanine says. "Get your jar ready, Mom."

"One of those could have been," Clare says. "How do you know they were all fireworks? There could be a star falling right now behind a cloud where we can't see it."

"Sure," Jeanine says. "Right."

"Listen to your mother," Paul says. "She knows about these things."

"Your grandpa taught your brother to write his name in the air with a sparkler, too," Clare says. "You remember that, Paul."

"It made him mad when it disappeared before he got it all written," Paul says.

"Check your feet now," Clare tells Jeanine.

"My feet?"

"Check and see if they're there."

"Of course they're there."

"Check."

"Mother—"

"Can you see them? Can you feel them?"

"Where else would they be?"

"Check."

Clare feels the water move and knows Jeanine's doing it. Under the surface she's tapping her feet together, checking.

"Still there," Jeanine says.

"Good," Clare says. "That's good."

It's so dark now that she can't see Jeanine's face. She can hear her voice and her breathing and if she were to reach out her hand she would touch some part of her. An arm, a thigh, a strand of her hair. Clare can feel Paul's knee against her back and his arm over her shoulder and thinks it may be his breath on the back of her neck. It's his breath or the breeze. She leans toward him just enough to see if his face is there and she bumps against his chin. It is his breath. He's right there.

Clare looks into the sky again and sees the million stars and then she brings her own feet together. Under the water, she taps them together and they, too, are there.